D0037197

Praise for
A Date with the Other Side

"Do yourself a favor and make A Date with the Other Side."
—Bestselling author Rachel Gibson

"One of the romance writing industry's brightest stars . . . Ms. McCarthy spins a fascinating tale that deftly blends a paranormal story with a blistering romance . . . Funny, charming, and very entertaining, *A Date with the Other Side* is sure to leave you with a pleased smile on your face."
—*Romance Reviews Today*

"If you're looking for a steamy read that will keep you laughing while you turn the pages as quickly as you can, *A Date with the Other Side* is for you. Very highly recommended!"
—*Romance Junkies*

"Fans will appreciate this otherworldly romance and want a sequel."
—*Midwest Book Review*

"Just the right amount of humor interspersed with romance."
—*Love Romances & More*

"Ghostly matchmakers add a fun flair to this warmhearted and delightful tale . . . an amusing and sexy charmer sure to bring a smile to your face." —*Romantic Times*

"Offers readers quite a few chuckles, some face-fanning moments, and one heck of a love story. Surprises await those who expect a 'sophisticated city boy meets country girl' romance. Ms. McCarthy delivers much more." —*A Romance Review*

"Fascinating." —*Huntress Book Reviews*

Praise for Erin McCarthy

"Laugh-out-loud funny!" —Lori Foster

"Sexy, sassy . . . filled with humor." —Rachel Gibson

"Both naughty and nice . . . sure to charm readers." —*Booklist*

"Will have your toes curling and your pulse racing." —*Arabella*

"Erin McCarthy writes this story with emotion and spirit, as well as humor." —*Fallen Angel Reviews*

Heiress
for Hire

Erin McCarthy

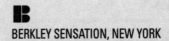

BERKLEY SENSATION, NEW YORK

THE BERKLEY PUBLISHING GROUP
Published by the Penguin Group
Penguin Group (USA) Inc.
375 Hudson Street, New York, New York 10014, USA
Penguin Group (Canada), 90 Eglinton Avenue East, Suite 700, Toronto, Ontario M4P 2Y3, Canada
(a division of Pearson Penguin Canada Inc.)
Penguin Books Ltd., 80 Strand, London WC2R 0RL, England
Penguin Group Ireland, 25 St. Stephen's Green, Dublin 2, Ireland (a division of Penguin Books Ltd.)
Penguin Group (Australia), 250 Camberwell Road, Camberwell, Victoria 3124, Australia
(a division of Pearson Australia Group Pty. Ltd.)
Penguin Books India Pvt. Ltd., 11 Community Centre, Panchsheel Park, New Delhi—110 017, India
Penguin Group (NZ), 67 Apollo Drive, Rosedale, North Shore 0745, Auckland, New Zealand
(a division of Pearson New Zealand Ltd.)
Penguin Books (South Africa) (Pty.) Ltd., 24 Sturdee Avenue, Rosebank, Johannesburg 2196, South Africa

Penguin Books Ltd., Registered Offices: 80 Strand, London WC2R 0RL, England

This is a work of fiction. Names, characters, places, and incidents either are the product of the author's imagination or are used fictitiously, and any resemblance to actual persons, living or dead, business establishments, events, or locales is entirely coincidental. The publisher does not have any control over and does not assume any responsibility for author or third-party websites or their content.

HEIRESS FOR HIRE

A Berkley Sensation Book / published by arrangement with the author

PRINTING HISTORY
Berkley Sensation trade edition / January 2006
Berkley Sensation mass-market edition / July 2007

Copyright © 2006 by Erin McCarthy.
Excerpt from *My Immortal* copyright © 2007 by Erin McCarthy.
Cover art by Pinglet.
Cover design by Rita Frangie.
Interior text design by Kristin del Rosario.

ISBN: 978-0-425-21484-8

BERKLEY® SENSATION
Berkley Sensation Books are published by The Berkley Publishing Group,
a division of Penguin Group (USA) Inc.,
375 Hudson Street, New York, New York 10014.
BERKLEY SENSATION is a trademark of Penguin Group (USA) Inc.
The "B" design is a trademark belonging to Penguin Group (USA) Inc.

PRINTED IN THE UNITED STATES OF AMERICA

10 9 8 7 6 5 4 3 2 1

Heiress for Hire

♡

Chapter 1

There were some things money couldn't buy. For everything else, there was her father.

Since Brett Delmar couldn't—or wouldn't—provide Amanda Delmar with love, affection, or respect, at the very least she figured he should foot the bill for a few of life's necessities. And luxuries.

"Daddy, just two hundred. That's all I need." Amanda checked out her manicure and grimaced. If he could only see how god-awful her nails looked, he would understand that this was an emergency.

"Why not make it two thousand? Why not make it ten thousand?" Her father's sarcasm came crackling through her cell phone.

She decided to ignore it. "That's so sweet of you! And it's not even my birthday."

That wheezing was probably the sound of his blood pressure going up. She felt a momentary twinge of guilt. She didn't want to give him a heart attack. She just wanted a manicure.

"Amanda Margaret."

Ouch. Trotting out the middle name was never a good thing. Amanda set her front porch swing swaying. She ran her fingers idly through the lilac bush that hugged the porch as she rocked back and forth.

She was enjoying her summer in East Bum Fuck, or if you went by what the map said, Cuttersville, Ohio. It was quaint and different and full of fawning men, eager to pay court to the rich girl from Chicago. Visiting the country had been a lark to quell boredom, and following Boston Macnamara to Cuttersville had given her both a destination, and another way to piss her father off. But the town had its drawbacks in that there were actually establishments that only accepted cash, as unbelievable as it seemed. And her father, with his many mountains of money, was back in Illinois, getting cranky about her spending habits.

Which was ironic, considering he had created those spending habits, nurtured them in her. He had praised her beauty and her style as a child and scoffed at her attempts to use her brain. Now he found those very traits he had fostered in her annoying.

All her attempts to please him had failed, and around about her eighteenth birthday she had stopped trying.

"Yes, Daddy?" If he could use sarcasm, surely he would recognize it.

"Have you heard of tough love?"

Amanda stopped playing with the tips of her hair extensions and frowned. Maybe she had been in the country too long, ogling brawny farmers and getting back to nature. "Is that a new designer? Did P. Diddy start a line of street wear? Why haven't I heard of it?"

He snorted. "No, it's not a goddamn clothing line. It's what I'm about to do for your own good, because I love you and you need to get serious, Amanda. You're almost twenty-six goddamn years old. When I was your age, I was making half a million a year already."

Amanda moved her mouth in a silent "blah, blah, blah." She had heard this speech before. Could recite it backward and forward and in French.

"You need to work for your money."

She was. Listening to him blather was hard, painful work, and she had to endure it every time she needed cash. It was as bad as flipping burgers at McDonald's would be, she'd bet.

Maybe it was time to get a job. Not that she was qualified to do anything, given her degree in art appreciation. But it was getting a little old to beg for money all the time, and the childish satisfaction of spending her father's fortune no longer had quite the same charm.

My God, maybe she was actually maturing. There was a scary thought.

Amanda reached down and scooped up Baby, her teacup poodle, and stroked her downy head. She was getting stressed out, and Baby was soothing, her fluffy fur poufing around Amanda's fingers. Baby's devotion was simple and uncomplicated, and Amanda appreciated that.

"So, this time, I'm serious, Amanda, I've had it. I'm instituting tough love. In the end we'll both be happier this way."

Amanda heard herself sigh. She really was getting too old for these circular arguments. There was no fight left in her. That's why she was nesting in the country, to relax. "What are you talking about? What does tough love actually mean?"

"It means I'm cutting you off. No more money."

"What?" The words didn't make sense. They were unintelligible to her. Daddy was money, money was Daddy, and he couldn't possibly mean . . .

"No. More. Money. Ever. That's what I mean. You'll have to fend for yourself from here on out. I know your rent is paid for the duration of the summer, so you'll have plenty of time to look for work. There's the two thousand

I gave you last week. That should hold you over until your first paycheck."

"It's gone already! Baby needed dog food." And she had needed a new handbag, one better equipped to handle the dust of the country.

"What the hell is the dog eating? Beluga? Christ, Amanda, give me a break. That dog is the size of an egg. It probably eats a can of dog food a month."

Amanda felt the beginnings of panic, followed by pure anger. How absolutely like him. He gave, and he taketh away. Her father had a serious power trip going on. He just loved being the one in control, holding the cards, manipulating her life.

Well, she wasn't going to beg. Not this time.

She'd just run to the money machine instead and make a large cash withdrawal on her credit cards. All six of them.

"Well, if you're really serious about this . . ." She paused, giving him time to regain his sanity.

"I am."

"Then I have to go. I have to find a job before I die of starvation and exposure."

Or worse, her cell phone ran out of minutes.

♡

Danny Tucker wiped his forehead on the sleeve of his T-shirt and watched the car pulling in his driveway. Didn't look like anyone he recognized, at least not from first glance at the black Ford pickup. The truck passed the turn-off to Danny's parents' house, the big Victorian farmhouse in the center of their property, and headed back toward the squat brick ranch that belonged to him.

In no big hurry to see who it was, and only mildly interested, Danny stepped over a row of soybeans and started toward the house, slow and steady. That's what he was, slow and steady. That's what his father called him. That's what his first wife, Shelby, had claimed to admire in him.

And Danny was who he was, and there wasn't any sense in trying to change that.

But slow and steady somehow hadn't served him quite the way he'd wanted them to. There were only two things in life Danny had ever wanted—to work this farm and to raise a family.

He had the farm. Pinching a leaf off as he went down the row of lusty green plants, he surveyed his crop and was satisfied. It was a good year, so far. Farmers never counted their crops before the harvest, but so far, so good.

What Danny didn't have was the family. No wife, no kids. An empty house and an even lonelier bed. It was a problem. One he had been aiming to fix when he'd been sideswiped by a strange lust for the new woman in town, Amanda Delmar.

He shook his head, even as his body reacted just to the thought of her tall, thin, sun-kissed body. "You're a damn fool, Tucker," he muttered.

A woman like that wouldn't look twice at a lug like him—and if she did, she'd toddle herself right back out of town on her toothpick heels after she'd tired of him. Wasn't a future with a woman like that.

Rubbing his hands down the front of his jeans, Danny stopped in his drive and watched the pickup crawl to a stop in a cloud of dust. He could see a man and what looked like a little boy in the passenger seat. He was starting to think maybe they were lost.

"Can I help you folks?" he asked, as the man stepped out of a truck that looked like it had just slid off the assembly line, shiny and dent-free under the layer of farm dust that had just coated it. The tires were three sizes too small for the height of the truck, which must have jarred the guy's teeth coming up Danny's dirt driveway.

The man himself was tall and lanky, wearing low-slung nylon cargo pants and a basketball jersey, his thick, gold chain necklace flashing in the sun. Danny wasn't overly impressed with his done-up car or his abundant jewelry. There was something about a man who primped like a girl that sat wrong with Danny. But he would be friendly, a nice guy, until given a reason not to be.

"You Danny Tucker?"

"Yeah." Danny's shoulders went up at the man's belligerent tone. "Do I know you?"

The guy snorted. "No. But you knew Nina Schwartz, didn't you?" He turned and called over his shoulder, "Get out of the truck!"

Nina Schwartz? Danny didn't know a Nina. It was a small town, and he didn't leave Cuttersville too often.

Slowly, the passenger door creaked open and two small gym shoes hit the dirt. A solemn set of eyes, set in a thin face half covered by a baseball hat, peered around the door at him. It was a kid. Just a little kid, no more than eight or nine years old.

"I don't know any Nina Schwartz."

"Maybe she never told you her name, but you knew her alright. About nine years ago, I imagine. When was you born, Piper? I can't remember exactly."

"April 23," the child said with a soft, frightened voice.

Big brown eyes locked with his before skittering away and Danny had a suddenly horrible feeling that this man was trying to tell him something he didn't think he wanted to hear.

"So what was you doing in July nine summers ago, Danny Tucker? You meet a girl from Xenia and get it on?"

Nine years ago. That had been the summer between his junior and senior year in high school. The summer he and his longtime sweetheart, Shelby, had broken up over a misunderstanding about sex. He had wanted it; she hadn't. So when he'd been footloose, fancy-free, and more than a bit heartbroken, he'd gone to the county fair.

And met a girl named Nina from Xenia, who had been a friendly sort. Friendly enough that she had suggested they go for a drive, which had resulted in them both naked and him losing his virginity.

Oh, shit.

"I can see from the look on your face that your memory's coming back." The guy reached into his pocket. "She put you on the birth certificate."

Danny cleared his throat and tried not to panic. He glanced at the kid, who was making circles in the dirt with his toe. This could not be his child. It just couldn't be, because this kid was half grown and, and . . .

He took the piece of paper. The words blurred together, but he managed to make out the vitals. Mother: Nina Schwartz, age 16.

Christ almighty, she had told him she was eighteen. He'd knocked up a kid, nothing more than a kid.

Of course, that kid had shown him a whole range of sexual tricks he'd never even dreamed of, but that was beside the damn point.

Father: Daniel Tucker, age 17.

A sticky note was attached to the front of the birth certificate. Danny Tucker, 1893 Mill Road, Cuttersville. There was a heart drawn around his name.

Oh, boy.

"Why didn't she ever tell me if she thought I was the father?"

"She told her boyfriend it was his, and they got married. But Nina wasn't all that bright, and she put your name on the birth certificate. He found it a couple of years later and walked out."

"Who are you then?"

"I'm Nina's third husband, Mark Johnson. She's dead now. Nina got a bit too attached to her happy pills and took one too many. We had some good times, and I was torn up when she died, but that doesn't mean I'm willing to keep her brat."

Danny watched in shock as Mark reached into the truck

and pulled out a battered suitcase, then a box heaped with dingy stuffed animals and a faded yellow blanket. He carelessly dumped them on the driveway.

"Here's all her stuff."

"Her stuff?" Danny looked dumbly at the box, the birth certificate still clutched in his hand.

"Yeah. Piper's shit. Your daughter. I can't keep her anymore. The kid always did creep me out with her big eyes and her imaginary friends."

Mark Johnson climbed into his truck and gave him a wave.

Then he pulled out and started down the drive with more speed than was strictly wise on a dirt road. He'd tear up his shocks doing that.

Danny looked at the kid he'd thought was a boy. The kid who was supposedly his kid.

And decided it wasn't wise to wish for things. Sometimes they arrived when you least expected it, in different packaging than you'd planned.

He'd just gotten his family in the form of one very skinny, silent, eight-year-old girl.

Whose mother had overdosed and whose stepfather was a selfish asshole.

Oh, boy.

Chapter 2

 $\mathcal{D}$ anny took a deep breath and looked down at the kid. Piper. His kid. Daughter. *Damn.*

"Hey," he said, crouching down into a squat so he could get a better look at her. "So your name's Piper, huh? Is that a nickname?"

She shook her head, the bill of her Cincinnati Reds baseball cap covering her face. The hat looked filthy, old, the bill cracked in the middle and an oily line of dirt circling the rim. Her shoulders were dusty, her white tank top thin from too many washings and faded into a dingy gray. The denim shorts that hugged her tiny waist were too small for her, which was amazing considering a dandelion fluff probably weighed more than she did. He was guessing those shorts were meant for a toddler, not an eight-year-old girl, and the sight of it made his heart clench and his gut churn.

No one had been taking care of this child in a long time. "So, okay, Piper's your real name. Got a middle name? A last name?"

A long, slim finger stretched out and pointed to the birth certificate. Right. Her name must be on it. He studied it. "Piper Danielle Schwartz. Now that's a fine name. Got style. Says you're coming into a room."

She shrugged her shoulder.

Okay. So this wasn't going to be easy. "My name is Danny Tucker."

Nothing but a nod.

He spoke in what he hoped was a gentle voice. "Can your take off your hat, Piper? I'd just like to see you."

A violent shake left and right. Her hands gripped the hat on her head, holding it in place.

"Alright, that's fine. You don't want to take it off. But can we just twist it a little to the side so I can take a gander at you? I never knew I had a daughter, and I'm pretty excited about it." Danny couldn't stop himself from touching one of her tiny hands, stroking it just a little. He could hear her quick breathing, feel the tension in her body. "I'm probably going to get on your nerves over the next couple weeks, because I'm going to be staring at you all the time, thinking how lucky I am you came along.

"I'm going to twist your hat, just a little now." Heart pounding, he turned the cap until the bill hung over her ear and her face was clear for him to see in the burning afternoon sun.

Piper had a long, angular face, a ruddy complexion, and brown eyes that were the exact shade of hot chocolate. Just like his. He felt punched in the gut, kicked in the nuts, clawed in the eyes. Jesus Christ, she looked just like him. There was no doubt in his mind this was his kid.

And he'd never known a thing about her. All these goddamn years, when he could have put her in nicer clothes, given her the love she so clearly wasn't getting, he hadn't even known she existed.

"Well, aren't you a pretty little thing," he whispered, because it was true. She was dirty and thin enough to cause concern, with big limpid eyes that knew too much, feared everything. Her hair seemed to have been cut short like a boy's, none of it showing beyond her hat. But she had great bone structure, long eyelashes, and a plucky kind of backbone that had her shaking her head immediately.

"I'm not pretty." The words were soft but confident.

"Says who?"

"Mark."

"Well, what does he know? He doesn't look all that bright to me." And it was a good thing he'd left when he did, or Danny would have been hard-pressed to keep his fist out of Mark's face.

"He's a butt head," Piper said.

Danny laughed, pleased to see his daughter was a good judge of character. "I think you're one hundred percent correct. If ever I saw a butt head, Mark is it."

He stood up, put his hand on her shoulder. Slow and steady. That's what he needed now. "You hungry?"

She shrugged.

"Well, I am. Working in the fields all day makes a man hungry as a bear. I'm not much of a cook, but if we're lucky, my mom has fried up some chicken and baked some biscuits." He pointed to the farmhouse across the field. "That's where my mom and dad live. Your grandma and grandpa."

She stiffened beneath his fingers.

"But first we'll take your stuff into my house and let you pick a bedroom. I got two spare ones you can choose from. You like looking at the front of the yard or the back?"

"Don't matter. I can sleep on the couch."

Danny had to uncurl his fist from his side. There wasn't a damn thing he could do about the past. He had Piper now. All he could do was try and make it right from here on out. "Nah. Since you're going to be living with me forever, you got to have your own room. A girl needs her space, a place to get away from her old man."

"Forever?" Piper said, her small voice sounding frightened and insecure.

"Yep. See this land, Piper? See all these soybean plants growing as far as you can see?" Danny pointed with his hand over all the land that was his, his parents', and he felt the familiar comfort, the pride, the joy that came from knowing this was Tucker land. Always had been, always would be. "This here farm belongs to me and my parents, and my dad's parents before, on back more than a hundred years. Tuckers own this land, and we're the kind of folks who stick. When we say forever, we mean forever. And nothing, not drought or bugs or floods, can make us leave. You see what I'm saying?"

She shook her head, stumbling a little over the rough gravel as they walked to the house.

"I mean that forever is until the end of time." He took her chin, tilted her head toward him. "If I'd a known about you, I'd a come for you. And now that I've got you, I'm keeping you."

It was as simple as that, even if it made his palms sweat and his heart race.

♡

INSUFFICIENT FUNDS.

Amanda punched the screen of the ATM in frustration as the message mocked her. The stupid thing was broken, obviously. It claimed insufficient funds on all six of her credit cards, which was absolutely impossible. She had thousands and thousands of dollars available for cash withdrawal on these cards.

Yet this was the third machine to tell her she didn't, and she was pretty damn sure it was the last ATM in Cuttersville.

Her father had instituted his little plan of tough love, no money ever, before he'd even talked to her. He had premeditated her pennilessness. If she wasn't the victim, she might actually appreciate his cunning.

As it was, she just wanted to scream like a bad actress being slashed by a killer.

Pulling her rental car into a parking spot, she dug her Coach wallet out of her brand-new handbag. Coach was really much more appropriate for Cuttersville than her Hermès bag. It could withstand the dust and the bacon grease that had created a permanent sheen on the seats at the Busy Bee Diner. And if it got trashed, she was only out five hundred bucks instead of five thousand.

It had made perfect sense. Yesterday. Now she wished she had the five hundred bucks so she could buy a plane ticket back to Chicago where she knew people, had friends she could beg for a place to stay and contacts to get a decent job. Here in Cuttersville, she had a cottage for another six weeks that the locals claimed was haunted and a multitude of minor acquaintances.

Including the change in her wallet, she had exactly fifty-seven dollars and twelve cents. She was going to die.

Tapping her fingernail on her lip, she assessed her options. She could hitchhike back to Chicago, with the likelihood of being murdered along the way about ninety-seven percent. She could call her mother, but she was in Europe at some spa Amanda couldn't remember the name of, having miraculous treatments designed to restore elasticity to her aging skin. There was her cousin Stuart in New York, but he was as dependent on her father's money as she was. If he helped her, it was likely he'd get cut off too.

She could call a friend and ask to borrow money, which would be humiliating in the extreme and a last resort.

Or she could get a job in Cuttersville and earn the money to get back to Chicago.

Not that she had any skills, so to speak, but she was intelligent. She could learn on the job. And Boston Macnamara was almost like a friend and understood how difficult her father could be since he worked for him.

Boston could get her hired at Samson Plastics, the factory that fueled Cuttersville's economy and just happened to be owned by her father. It would burn ol' Daddy Delmar's butt if she got hired on at Samson.

Mentally shifting through her wardrobe to see if she'd brought any cute little suits with short skirts, Amanda pictured having her own little office, a phone with a cordless headset, and a personal secretary to fetch her coffee. Sounded like the perfect job for her.

♡

"What do you mean you can't hire me?" Amanda lay on the ugly chintz couch in Shelby and Boston's living room and rubbed her forehead. Her head hurt. Her feet hurt. And she was hungry. Baby was lying in a ball on her stomach, looking as forlorn as she felt.

Boston put his hands into the pockets of his immaculate black pants. He looked nearly as out of place in Cuttersville as she did. But somehow, he had fallen in love with a local girl and was staying permanently. In this fussy Victorian house that was the showpiece on the Haunted Cuttersville Tour.

Amanda wished one of those alleged ghosts would reach out and slap him right now.

"I'm not in HR, Amanda. I don't do the hiring."

"So? You're the freaking VP. Can't you tell HR to hire me?" She instantly detested the desperate tint to her voice. She knew she wasn't pathetic enough to beg, she just knew it, but she'd never been in this position before. She felt . . . unsure of herself, and she didn't like it.

Shelby, Boston's new wife, came into the room with a glass of lemonade. "She's our friend, Boston. Surely there's something you can do for her." She held the glass out to Amanda. "You look peaked. Have a drink."

Great. She was penniless and she looked peaked. "Listen to your wife, Boston, she's a wise woman." Amanda didn't bother to sit up but sipped the lemonade sideways and then set the glass on the floor. Baby gave a yip, so Amanda put her down on the floor and watched her rest her button size front paws on the top of the glass and stick her nose down into the lemonade. She gave a tentative lick then jerked back in surprise at the tartness. It was cute enough to almost make Amanda feel better. Almost.

"I would hire you, Amanda, but I really can't. It's like this. Say I work at McDonald's."

Amanda wasn't sure whose snort was louder, hers or Shelby's. They exchanged amused glances.

Shelby was not exactly the match Amanda would have chosen for Boston. His brand-new wife had never left Cuttersville, had enough hair on her head for six people, and thought dressing up was wearing something knit. But Shelby was an honest, down-to-earth woman, and one of the most truly decent people Amanda had ever met—not that that was saying much. Good people were harder to come by than a funny sitcom.

But the relationship between Boston and Shelby seemed to work. Well. They seemed to balance each other out and had a love so strong it was palpable in the room whenever they were together. Generally speaking, it made Amanda equal parts jealous and nauseous.

"Okay, you work at McDonald's," Amanda said. "I'll suspend all reality for a minute and accept that you would ever do that."

Boston held out his hand and pointed to the right. "And I work the drive-thru window."

Shelby grinned. "Do you wear one of those hats? You know, with the visors?"

He just stared at her until she wiped the smile off her face. Or hid it behind her hand, really. "Sorry, go ahead."

"Thank you. So I work the drive-thru, and that's all I do." He pointed to the left. "Then there are cashiers and burger flippers and a fry girl. So say a friend of mine comes to the counter. I can't leave the drive-thru to go flip her a special request burger just because she's my friend. We all have a certain job to do, and mine is the drive-thru."

Amanda was temporarily amused out of her panic. Crossing her legs and smoothing her Ralph Lauren tennis skirt, she raised her eyebrows. "What the hell are you talking about? Am I supposed to be a fry girl or a cashier or what? You've completely lost me."

"I'm saying I can't hire you. That's not my job."

She was saved from voicing something she would probably regret by the front door being thrown open.

"Shel, honey? Shelby?"

Amanda knew that voice. It belonged to the big, brawny farmer, Danny Tucker, who looked like he could take a woman for a really wild ride on his tractor. She had tossed some light flirtation his way, only to have him smile politely and not take the hint. It had stung a bit to have him reject her, but she wouldn't admit that for all the Harry Winston diamonds on Oscar night.

"Shelby, I thought you were going to talk to him about that." Boston's voice was low, urgent. "He is your ex-husband. E-X. That means he shouldn't be just walking into our house without knocking, and he shouldn't be calling you 'honey.' "

The jealousy from Boston was kind of cute. Definitely amusing. Amanda looked to Shelby for her reaction.

"Ex is right, so stop making a mountain out of a molehill." She rolled her eyes at her husband and called, "We're in the parlor, Danny!"

When Boston would have protested further, she slid her hand across his chest. "Who am I in bed with every night, hmm? Who am I so in love with I want to be naked all the time?"

Hands began to roam and a really loud, wet kiss commenced.

"Third party here," Amanda called, hoping to stave off a make-out session. She was already hungry and flat busted broke. She didn't need to be reminded that it had been many, many long and lonely months since she'd had an orgasm. With a man present, anyway. "You're corrupting my innocent dog."

"Your dog just knocked a glass of lemonade over onto my floor," Boston said, jerking his mouth off Shelby's and looking around wildly, like a towel might materialize out of nowhere. "Shel, use your T-shirt to clean it up. The wood will be ruined."

"My T-shirt? Use your shirt!" But Shelby headed toward the kitchen.

Amanda forced herself to sit up. There was a mess of spreading liquid puddling on the wood floor with her dog plopped butt-down in the middle of it. "Baby! Sorry, Boston, I didn't even know she was strong enough to knock that over. But you know, it was probably the shock of seeing you two groping each other. I'm single, and Baby isn't used to depravity. Except when I have on Bravo. It probably scared her and she jumped."

Pushing her poodle out of the wet spot, Amanda winced. "Look at your fur . . . you have to realize we're poor now, Baby. I can't pay the groomer to shampoo you."

"You're poor?" Danny Tucker asked in disbelief.

Amanda looked up and saw the farmer standing in the doorway to Shelby and Boston's minute floral parlor. He filled the whole door frame with muscular man. Completely filled it, entirely from one side to the other, and Amanda felt a tingling in her breasts that was not the aftereffects of surgery. At twenty-one she had gotten breast implants as a college graduation present to herself. At twenty-five, she'd gotten them removed, having decided that breasts didn't make the woman.

Clothes did.

And she liked her body to be completely her own, with no embellishments, although unfortunately right now her au naturel body was choosing to be sexually stimulated by the mere sight of Danny Tucker standing in a doorway.

She did not understand her attraction to him. She'd never been one for the brawny type—the outdoors, work-with-his-hands manly man. To her, they had muscles—sure, that was good—but manual laborers were also just sweaty and dirty, something that so did not appeal to her. Yet Danny Tucker brought out primal female urges in her—in what she had determined was the instinctive need to mate with the strongest in the herd.

It was sociological, really, that was all. Evolution at its best, and had nothing whatsoever to do with her actually liking a small-town farmer. Because that would be ludi-crous for any number of reasons, starting with dirt and ending with bugs. She wasn't fond of either one, so she couldn't actually like Danny Tucker.

Yet after her last relationship, which had been akin to swimming in moral sewage, Danny Tucker was really appealing.

"Yes, I'm poor. I've been cut off. Stranded. Abandoned." She was about to wax enthusiastic on the cruelty of fathers rearing socialite daughters only to abandon them to the tender mercies of poverty when she realized there was a child standing behind Danny.

So did Shelby, who dropped the towel in her hand on top of the lemonade puddle, sending Baby scurrying out of the way.

"Who's your friend, Danny?" Shelby asked.

Amanda mopped at the floor while Baby tried to take in a few last frantic licks of the sweet liquid.

"This is Piper." Danny's hand went on the kid's shoul-der. "She's my daughter."

Amanda hadn't seen that one coming. She let go of the towel and sat up, taking a closer look at the kid, astonished. Danny Tucker just didn't seem like the kind to have a child nobody knew about.

But given the fact that a Mini Cooper could drive into Shelby's gaping mouth with no trouble whatsoever, no one knew about this one.

"Excuse me?" Shelby asked, her voice tight.

Boston shot her a nervous look.

The little girl, who was scruffy at best, dirty at worst, took a tentative step forward, her eyes on Amanda's dog.

Picking up Baby and grimacing at the stickiness of her coat, Amanda held her out. "Did you want to see her? She's a teacup poodle, and two pounds of terror."

The little girl glanced up at Danny reluctantly, then over to the dog with longing. She shook her head.

"Go on," Danny told her. "It's alright. She's a cute little puppy, isn't she?" He gave the girl a nudge, and she took two steps, dragging her feet.

Amanda heard the gentleness in his voice, but she also saw the pain on his face. Saw the way his hand shook just a little. It did something to her chest, made it tighten, made her feel an uncomfortable sort of something for him that was completely unrelated to sexual attraction.

She smiled at the girl but listened to Danny murmur to Shelby, "I didn't know anything about her. Her stepfather just dumped her on my doorstep."

Oh, wow, that was rough. Amanda could say a lot of things about her father, but he'd never been out and out cruel. Neglectful, yes. Judgmental, yes. Incapable of being pleased, oh yeah. But never cruel. It made her realize that in the grand scheme of things, she didn't have a whole lot to complain about.

Danny's words had Amanda's smile going brighter, as she held out her dog for the little girl, hoping to distract her. Not that she knew a damn thing about kids, but everyone liked puppies, and God, she wanted this kid to feel better. She knew the pain of rejection. This kid's must be a thousand times worse. "Her name is Baby. What's your name again?"

"Piper." The voice was quiet, wavering. Her hand came out and tentatively touched the top of Baby's head before she jerked it back.

"Who's her mother?" Shelby asked in a low voice, and Amanda couldn't mistake the jealousy there in her voice. Hell, who could blame her? She realized Shelby must have been married to Danny at the time of Piper's conception.

Amanda would have thought that he was better than that, Danny Tucker, and her own naivete made her want to laugh. God, how stupid could she be? When would she ever learn that men just did what they wanted, when they wanted. Coming to the country in a quest for a better male specimen was doomed to failure.

Not that she had done that. Please. But if she had been hoping that somehow the men of Cuttersville were truer, better, more honest, then clearly she would have been wrong. Men were all alike. Different dick, but still the same prick.

"She likes it when you scratch behind her ears," she told Piper, disgruntled at her disappointment that Danny was just another ordinary, selfish man like all the ones she had met before. He could hide it behind a smile and a polite good ol' boy charm, but if he had cheated on his wife, he was a jerk, plain and simple. She should be glad he hadn't responded to her flirting.

Danny's voice was low, so Amanda had to strain to hear him. "Uh, Nina Schwartz, a girl from Xenia I met at the county fair. It was just that one time, Shel, and it was that summer we were split up, remember? That summer you dated Eric White, the football player."

Amanda watched Shelby pull a face. "Eric was an idiot."

"So was I apparently." Danny paced back and forth. "The stepdad says Nina died. She never told me there was a baby, Shel, not even a hint. She never even asked for my phone number or to see me again." His voice rose. "How was I supposed to know?"

And how was Amanda supposed to stay irritated with him when he went and showed he wasn't a complete and total asshole? And why did his distress and confusion make her feel so flipping happy?

Because she wanted to believe Danny Tucker to be the nice guy she'd thought him to be. She wanted to shed some of the cynicism that coated her like a spray-on tan.

Which meant it was time for a mental eye roll. *Mea culpa*, she was becoming an Oprah Book Club Pick. Maudlin, yet hopeful.

Poverty was making her insane, and it had only been four hours.

Shelby put her finger to her lip. "Shh, keep it down." Her head jerked toward Piper.

Amanda couldn't hear their words after that, but she saw Shelby reach out and take Danny's hand and squeeze it. Saw Boston huddle together with the two of them, Danny casting worried glances at Piper. His daughter.

Piper was petting Baby's head, the kid's tongue pushed out between her lips in concentration. Amanda took Piper's arm and rested it under Baby. "Here, you hold her for me."

Piper's mouth went wide, and she tensed up. "What if I drop her?"

"I've dropped her before, and she always lands on her feet. No biggie. But you look reliable."

The little girl bit her lip, anxious, undecided. Amanda moved her hand back so Piper was holding Baby on her own.

Piper sucked in her breath, but a slight smile tipped up the corner of her mouth. Amanda tried not to breathe at all. The kid smelled. *Oy vey.* Taking minute drags of oxygen through her lips, Amanda concentrated on preventing air from going up her nostrils. Piper needed a bath. A rank odor was floating off of her, reminding Amanda of when her father had inadvertently kicked a peeled banana under his desk then headed to New York for a week. When he'd returned, his whole home office had reeked, the sweet, sickly, putrid stench wafting into the hallway for two days until he'd found the source.

Piper smelled a little like rotten banana.

She figured it must take a rather long time for a child to ripen to that extent, which meant Piper hadn't bathed in God knew when.

"She likes you," Amanda said, a funny lump lodging in her throat, as Baby snuggled into the crook of Piper's arm. "See? She's lying down for a nap."

"She's so soft." And Piper gave a beatific, heartfelt sigh.

And Amanda found herself wanting to stroke Piper's arm just like the little girl was petting Baby.

Chapter 3

*D*anny was feeling a little like he had when his cousin Jimmy had run over his foot with a tractor. Stunned, panicked, and just about blind with pain.

"So what are you going to do with her?" Shelby asked.

Rubbing his temples, Danny shrugged. "I'm keeping her. Her mother is dead, her stepfather's an idiot, and given the looks of her clothes, no one else gives a care about her."

"How do you know she's really your kid?" Boston asked, darting a glance over at Piper.

His daughter was petting Amanda's goofy little dog, a rapturous expression of terror and joy on her face. "The timing is right. And she looks like me."

"She's got your eyes," Shelby said, her voice sounding amazed. "And look at the way she tilts her head. That's just the way you do it."

It was pretty damn amazing. And Danny was finding that he liked it, once he mucked through the fear and the panic and the guilt that Piper had been around for eight years and he'd never once set eyes on her.

But he wouldn't have hurt Shelby for the world, and she was looking a bit like she'd taken a punch to the gut. "Shel . . . I'm sorry. I didn't know, please believe that."

It wasn't just about the fact that he'd been intimate with another girl when he and Shelby had been taking a break that summer; it was that not so long after, Shelby had given in to his increasing pushy demands for sex. And wound up pregnant. They'd gotten married, only she had suffered a miscarriage.

So while Piper was standing there petting Baby, Danny was damn sure it was causing Shelby to remember their child who would have been seven years old already.

"Hey." Shelby took his hand, squeezed it. "It's alright, Danny. Water under the bridge, and neither one of us did anything wrong. It just turned out the way it turned out. And now I've got Boston." Her husband put an arm around her waist, and she leaned into him. "And you've got Piper."

That relieved him. He cared a great deal about Shelby and wouldn't want any rift in their relationship.

"Even if I did a DNA test, even if it was negative, I can't give her back. She's mine now." There was no way he could close his eyes to Piper's need, her vulnerability. And deep in his gut, he was certain that any paternity test would only verify what he already knew. This was his daughter.

"I wouldn't expect that you would, Danny Tucker." Shelby smiled at him. "So what now?"

Now he needed some help. His mother wasn't home, and he'd only spoken to his father on the phone, who in spite of the shock of learning he had a grandchild, had been very supportive and reassuring. But his father didn't know any more about taking care of a little girl than he did, and Danny was hoping Shelby could give him her female opinion.

"I need you to go shopping with me. She needs a bath."

He kept his voice low so he wouldn't hurt her feelings. "But I couldn't bring myself to get her all clean, only to stick her back in those nasty clothes. So I figured we should go shopping first."

"Shopping?" Amanda Delmar straightened up, her perfect chin jutting out just a little as she honed in on what Danny figured was her favorite word. She could probably hear it even if she were sitting in a soundproof booth.

"If someone is going shopping, I want to go too."

Just run a pitchfork through him. There was no way in hell he wanted to go shopping with Miss Madison Avenue. She was extravagant, impractical, and worst of all, sexy as hell. He didn't need her distracting him right now with that Barbie-doll-size skirt she was wearing.

So he ignored her.

"I don't know anything about clothes for kids, especially little girls, so I really need your help, Shel." Danny subtly turned his back toward Amanda so she wouldn't hear what he was saying.

But Shelby was already shaking her head. "Sorry, Danny, I can't tonight. I have a ghost tour I'm running at seven o'clock. Whole busload of tourists want the 'real' story of Red-Eyed Rachel and her attack on Boston. I can go tomorrow if you want. Or I'm sure your mom would go with you."

"I'll go," Amanda called from the couch ten feet away. "I'm an expert at shopping."

He'd just bet she was. Danny sighed. "Not this kind of shopping, Amanda, trust me. I guess I'll just go by myself. I forgot my mom is out of town. She went on a tour of the Longaberger basket factory today in Newark. She won't be back until tomorrow."

He was about to call to Piper to come along, when Amanda stood up and took a step in his direction. Danny froze. Damn, she did it to him every time. She laid one look on him, and he was like a drooling dog. Half the time he felt like turning tail and running away to save his ass, the other half he wanted to just dig his fingers into her platinum blond hair and ram his tongue down her throat.

Neither seemed like a good plan with his ex-wife and his daughter looking on, so he stood his ground.

Amanda flipped her hair over her shoulder and stuck a hand on her naked hip. Her clothes always looked like she'd shrunk them in the dryer on high heat. Her skimpy skirt only covered enough to keep her PG-13, and her top was like a blue rubber band stretched across her firm breasts.

"I'm an expert at *all* shopping. Any kind. Day, night, clothes, furniture, art, anything with any sort of fabric that might go on your body or in your house belongs to me. I don't know about tractors, or crops, or why farmers always seem to have a plug of tobacco stuck in their cheek, but I know shopping."

She almost sounded insulted, and it suddenly amused him. So Amanda knew Chicago shopping. He'd bet the farm she'd never set foot in a Wally's World. "Ever been to Wal-Mart?"

"Nooo," she said carefully, a white-tipped fingernail running over her bottom lip, licking at the control he kept over his libido. "But I know what it is and you can buy clothes there. So we're all set. One complete wardrobe for a cute eight-year-old girl coming up. Break out your credit card—this will be fun."

Danny didn't move, hoping someone would save him. He darted a pleading glance at Shelby, but she just shrugged.

Amanda sailed out of the parlor on her skyscraper shoes. "Come on, Tucker. These things take time, and you're burning daylight. Bring my handbag, please. Piper has the dog."

Shelby grinned. Boston smirked. Danny felt complete and utter terror. Amanda Delmar in a discount store wasn't going to be pretty.

But like an idiot, and left with no choice if he didn't want to be completely rude, he picked up her gigantic straw purse. He gripped the pink leather handle while Shelby busted out with a laugh.

"If only I knew where the camera was. Dang, that's too funny seeing you carry that."

He knew his damn face was red, he could feel it. "Boston, control your wife before I smack her with this ugly straw basket from . . ." Danny caught himself before he swore in front of Piper. Couldn't be just blurting things out anymore. He had a daughter to raise proper.

One who'd seen God only knew what. Worried he might have scared her with his teasing Shelby, he glanced at Piper. She was still holding the dog, but she had leaned around the side of the coffee table, peering behind the lamp with the colored glass shade. It didn't seem like she'd heard their conversation, all her concentration focused toward the back wall by the fireplace.

"What's the matter, Piper? You see something?"

Her head jerked back and forth, but her eyes stayed trained on the corner.

"You sure?" He didn't see anything, but she was staring so intently, he walked in that direction.

One of her soft, cool hands gripped his arm, halting his progress. "No."

Danny looked down at her. The grimy baseball hat prevented a clear view of her face, but she shivered slightly, her one hand grip on the poodle tightening. "You can tell me if something's wrong, you know."

Not that he knew how to fix it. Or how to read Piper's expressions and emotions. They were total strangers to each other, with eight years to make up for. But he already felt protective of her. He felt love, brand new and fledgling, like a spark on kindling.

She just nodded and turned toward the door, her willowy shoulders straightening. "Are we bringing the dog?"

He didn't want to, but he didn't think Amanda would give him much choice. "Yeah. Let's go before Amanda starts shopping without us. You'll end up with nothing but high heels."

Guiding Piper with a hand on her back, he headed for the door. "Thanks, Shel. Boston. I'll talk to you soon."

"We'll help any way we can, Danny."

That the words came from Boston meant a hell of a lot to Danny. "Thanks."

"Nice meeting you, Piper," Shelby said.

That brought his daughter up short. She looked up at him, her eyes worried. Danny sensed her confusion, that she didn't know what to say. "Nice to meet you, too," he whispered to her, giving her a wink.

The words came out on a painful whisper, but she said them, her little chin coming up with gutsy determination.

Danny gripped her shoulder and felt the damnedest thing. Pride.

Then the yipping dog wiggled, upsetting Piper's hold. He caught Baby in a quick save before there was a poodle pancake on Shelby's floor.

Baby scratched his wrist with her tiny claws, searching for a hold. He grimaced as his broken flesh stung a little.

Piper sighed in relief.

And Danny realized he was carrying both Amanda Delmar's overpriced purse and her damn dog like an errand boy.

♡

Danny winced as they went through the automatic doors at Wal-Mart. Two feet in the store and Amanda was already attracting attention.

"Hello, welcome to Wal-Mart."

Amanda lifted up her pink sunglasses to gape at the old guy in the requisite blue vest. "Ohmigod, it's just like the commercial. If a smiling yellow dot bounces toward me, I'm going to freak out."

Good thing she'd kept her voice down. It wasn't like twenty people had just turned and stared at her, slack-jawed. Danny pulled off his hat, scratched his head, and tried not to turn tail and run. He plunked his hat back down and grabbed a shopping cart, determined to get this over with. "Freak out after we're done."

"Miss." A store manager, tugging on the collar of his button-up shirt, cleared his throat. "You can't bring your dog in here."

Geez almighty, she'd brought the poodle, even after he'd told her to leave it in the car. Baby's tiny tongue hung out over the strap on Amanda's purse as she panted enthusiastically. Danny wasn't sure which irritated him more, Amanda's disobedience, or the way Piper edged herself closer to Amanda's leg.

Her long and lean, bronze and beautiful leg.

This was a huge mistake.

"Oh, it's okay. Baby is a working dog." And Amanda strode forward, stopping only briefly to touch a striped women's shirt on display. Her lip curled in disdain.

Danny pushed the cart behind her, amazed at her nerve. "A working dog?" he asked, when she paused to read the department signs hanging from the ceiling. "What could that dog do? Guide blind mice?"

Piper laughed, a quick giggle before she clapped her hand over her mouth.

Danny grinned, pleased he had made her laugh.

Amanda didn't look amused. She sniffed. "Farmer Funny. How quaint."

They locked gazes. While her expression was aloof, Danny saw something in those green eyes that gave him pause. If he didn't know better, he'd think that was interest there. Attraction. Lust.

But he did know better, and he wasn't falling for the trick his body was playing on him. There was nothing good that could come out of dallying with Amanda Delmar, and that was even more obvious now that he had a child to look out for.

He broke eye contact and pointed behind her. "Girl's department. Right there."

♡

Danny Tucker liposuctioned the fun right out of shopping. He had to be so damn practical.

"Where is an eight-year-old girl going to wear high heels on a farm?" he asked calmly when she showed him an adorable pair of hot pink kitten heels that had an absolutely heart-stopping price tag of only twelve ninety-nine.

"Who cares? For twelve ninety-nine she could wear them once in the house and it would still be a bargain."

Danny shook his head. "Put those back."

She rolled her eyes and slapped them on the shelf, disgruntled. That was the fourth pair of shoes he had vetoed since they had measured Piper's foot with the metal thingy.

He picked up a pair of gym shoes and held them out to her. "What about these?"

"Perfect, if you like ugly and have absolutely no sense of style whatsoever." Amanda pushed them away from her, afraid their hideousness might contaminate her airspace. "They're white and clunky and generic. Eeww."

Piper sat on the floor, letting Baby run around her lap. She looked only mildly interested in their conversation, which was unfathomable to Amanda. Here they were deciding her entire fashion future, and Piper would rather pet the dog.

"Okay, so white and clunky is out. You pick something cute then, since I'll admit I don't know anything about cute. But just nothing with a heel, alright?"

He *didn't* know anything about cute. He had no idea how freaking cute he was himself. Amanda turned away from him to study the sneaker section. It was starting to annoy her that she was attracted to him. Here they were shopping, which should be taking all her concentration, and she was doing the nipple-tingle thing again.

Maybe it was his modesty that she found so intriguing. Or the way he never lost his cool. Steady as a rock. A very big, buff rock.

Tingle. There it was again. Damn.

Amanda snagged a lavender pair of shoes off the rack. "These aren't bad. A little rubbery for my taste, and the stitching looks uneven, but what can you expect for fifteen bucks? Children in third-world countries can't be expected to sew our cheap shoes straight."

Danny inspected the shoes. "These are fine. Flat sole."

Amanda held them out for Piper. "What about these shoes, Piper? Like them?"

The little girl's eyes widened with naked pleasure. She swallowed hard. "How much do they cost?"

"Fifteen dollars."

Piper's shoulders sagged. "Those are too much money. I don't really need new shoes, these still fit."

And could be condemned by the health department. Amanda didn't even want to consider what vermin had crawled over those grubby shoes Piper was wearing. Plus there was a hole gaping at the toes of the left one.

Danny looked horrified. His jaw locked and his eyes were dark, though he kept his voice even, gentle. "I want to get you new shoes, Piper." He squatted down next to her. "See, I didn't get to buy you shoes for eight whole years, and I've got some time to make up for. It would make me feel better if you let me buy you these."

Amanda didn't see how Piper could resist that kind of earnest plea. Hell, after that speech, she'd let Danny buy her shoes if he wanted.

Piper nodded.

He reached for her hand, and she took it, letting him pull her to her feet. "Let's go get some shorts and T-shirts."

T-shirts. How exciting. He really wasn't getting into the spirit of this. Amanda took the cart and started to push it along behind them, slowing down as she passed the flip-flops. She grabbed a white pair in Piper's size. Then a red pair. And the pink kitten heels.

Piper spotted them in the cart the minute Danny started wandering through the clothing racks, looking at shorts. Her eyes widened, and she glanced at Danny's back.

"It's okay," Amanda reassured her. "You need flip-flops for the pool."

Not that she was sure a pool even existed in Cuttersville, but it was summer. Gym shoes made your toes sweat and shrivel into little white sausage links. Every girl needed flip-flops, and they were only three bucks a pair. She couldn't get a cup of coffee for three bucks in Chicago.

If the kid bit her lip anymore, she was going to do permanent damage. And then how would her lip gloss look? Amanda gave her a reassuring smile. "Trust me, Piper. Auntie Amanda is going to hook you up."

Piper cocked her head. "You're my . . . dad's sister?"

God forbid. That would make her a farmer's daughter, and that would mean she couldn't be staring at Danny Tucker's butt right now. Which she was. His butt was nice and tight in those well-worn jeans.

"You do kind of look alike," Piper added.

That made Amanda laugh. "We both have blond hair, don't we?" She just had a hell of a lot more, not that all of it was real. She had chin-length hair, but her extensions went down to the middle of her back. Other than the hair color, though, she didn't see the resemblance.

"But no, I'm not your dad's sister. We're just like friends." Sort of. Not really. "When I came here to Cuttersville, the only person I knew was Boston, Shelby's husband. And Shelby is your dad's ex-wife. So that's how I know Danny." And that sounded really complicated to be explaining to an eight-year-old.

But Piper nodded. "My mom had two ex-husbands, and Mark had an ex-wife. Is Shelby a greedy bitch? That's what Mark said all ex-wives are."

Okay, then. Amanda covered her mouth so it wouldn't free-fall open. "Ummm . . ." There probably wasn't any good answer to that, so she improvised. "Not all ex-wives are . . . what Mark said. Just like not all people are mean or short or have blue eyes. Shelby's a nice person, and she and Danny are still really good friends."

Piper's mouth pursed. "Oh. So do you live with my dad?"

Hel-lo. "Uh, we're kind of brand-new friends." As opposed to live-together-sleep-in-the-same-bed friends. Amanda grabbed a cute little red sundress. "What do you think of this dress?" When in doubt, change the subject.

"That's nice," Piper said with the enthusiasm Amanda's father showed for the opera.

"Okay, maybe not." Amanda stuck it back. "I bet you look great in blue." She fingered a blue-striped skirt and tank top. "What about this one?"

"I guess. Sure." Piper kicked at the carpet on the floor and stuck her hands in her pockets. "Anita doesn't really like it, though."

"Who's Anita?" And why was Amanda supposed to give a crap what she thought?

"She's my friend." Piper pointed to the empty spot right next to her.

Ah. The imaginary friend thing. That didn't bother Amanda, except Anita had no taste. She vetoed the next three dresses Amanda held up.

"Does Anita like this one?" Amanda grabbed at a pink terry dress with spaghetti straps.

"Uhhh . . ."

Danny walked over with three pairs of denim shorts and three T-shirts. One red, one blue, and one white with a rainbow on it. "How about these?"

Piper's face lit up. "I like those." Her finger reached out and traced the rainbow.

Like father, like daughter apparently. The kid liked the most basic, boring outfit in the whole store. Amanda glared at Danny.

He shrugged. "What? They're good farm clothes. Running around, getting dirty. That's what kids do."

Amanda didn't remember ever getting dirty as a child. She had always been pretty certain it was against the law. "She'll need at least ten outfits to start out with, if you don't want to do laundry every day. Jeans and a sweater for cooler nights. And she has to have some kind of dress or capri pants for eating out in restaurants, going to weddings, vacations, that sort of thing."

Danny lifted his hat off his head. "Well, I don't really do any of those things."

"You don't ever eat in restaurants?" This town wasn't exactly a happening mecca of gourmet cuisine, but everyone had to eat out once in a while. Didn't they?

"Just the Busy Bee. And no one needs a dress to eat there."

That was true. "Just buy a dress," she said in irritation. Who was the shopping expert here? "You never know when she'll need one. And she'll need three bathing suits, four or five nightgowns—bare minimum—panties, a belt, and jewelry."

"*Jewelry?* Why?"

Why not was the better question. "Because every woman needs some bling."

Danny figured Amanda had enough bling to count for all of Cuttersville. Besides, Piper didn't look like a bling-bling kind of kid. She was recoiling in horror at the silver chain belt Amanda was dangling in front of her.

They'd be lucky if they got that grubby hat off her head. They weren't going to succeed in making her over into a mini-Amanda. He was starting to think it had been premature to panic and request help. He could have handled this whole shopping thing himself. Kids weren't all that different from adults. They needed functional clothes, in all the same number that he had.

Not high heels, a whole stack of dresses, and diamonds.

"We'll save the bling for another day. Right now we just need the basics."

Amanda sighed, but she popped her dog back into her purse. "I need two hands, or we'll be here all night."

The thought gave him indigestion. The Cuttersville Wal-Mart wasn't open twenty-four hours, but it was still almost two hours until the ten P.M. closing time.

"Okay, just the basics." Then she was off and running, slapping together shorts and shirts in a dizzying variety of colors and styles, holding them up to Piper before flinging them in the shopping cart. No fewer than six packs of underwear were tossed on top, from the princess pair, to a floral pack, to a matching purple undershirt and panties set.

Amanda was heading toward the nightgowns when she was sidetracked by the umbrella rack. "Oooh, Hello Kitty. *Trés adorable*." And she popped open the umbrella right in the middle of Wal-Mart.

"I don't really think Piper needs an umbrella. That's what a hood is for."

"It's not for her. It's for me."

Of course. He should have known that. Not.

Now she was loading stationery and pens into the cart. She pulled them from a strategically placed display designed to suck in young girls while they were shopping for socks. Or twenty-five-year-old heiresses.

"Look, it's little tiny envelopes and tape with Kitty on it, and Post-it notes. This is too cute."

He looked at Piper and rolled his eyes. She giggled.

Amanda twirled the open umbrella on her shoulder and struck a pose. "Is it me?"

Her leg was bent, her hip out, lips open in a pouty smile,

hair trailing down her chest. All that bronze and bare skin taunted him, teased him. That skirt was so short, he could slip his hand under it and be right there. The thought made his mouth go dry. He was getting used to feeling a kick of lust whenever she was around, but that didn't make it any less uncomfortable.

And now he had a kid. It would just be *wrong* to get a boner with his daughter standing next to him. Fortunately, he was old enough and celibate enough to have a great deal of control over himself. Which he suspected he was going to need while Amanda was in town.

"Oh yeah, it's you."

She gave him a saucy smile. "I thought so." The nylon collapsed and she twirled the tie around the umbrella and snapped it shut. Swinging it with one finger, she pointed the tip toward a rack with nightgowns. "Oooh, that one. The hot pink. Grab one of those, Danny."

"It's awfully shiny-looking." It looked more appropriate for a disco then for a kid climbing into bed.

"It's a satin peignoir set. Too cute. Look, it's shorts, a shirt, and a robe. I bet there's slippers somewhere around here."

"It's kind of over the top. When I was a kid I used to just sleep in cotton shorts."

"And you were a boy."

She had him there.

Amanda started pawing through the racks, ripping the labels back to check for sizes. Piper had crawled under a rack and was whispering to herself, fingering the bottom of a row of denim skirts. Danny stood there feeling very conspicuous. That whole umbrella twirling bit had drawn some attention to them. A woman in her late twenties with a baby on her hip was staring in their direction. Or more accurately, she was staring at Amanda.

This woman looked like what he was used to. Just an average, everyday female, wearing denim shorts and a bulky T-shirt with a mysterious brown stain on the shoulder where the baby was gripping. Her hair was brown—just plain, regular, everyday brown—like the color of dirt and bears and wood. It was pulled back in a ponytail.

No miniskirt. No done up fingernails. No long legs.

The woman glanced over at him, and he realized with horror that he knew her. Even worse, she knew his mother. "Hi, Janice."

"Hey there, Danny." Curious, gossip-hungry eyes locked on his. "Haven't seen you around lately. You been busy?"

With zero subtlety, she looked first at Amanda, then at the overburdened shopping cart.

"You know how it is. Busy time of the year watering crops and spraying."

Janice went to church with his mother. Janice's father went to the same lodge as his. Janice herself had once shown him her breasts in the eighth grade, such as they were at the time. An aggressive girl, she'd been one of the first to get married after high school, just beating him and Shelby to the altar by one week. Only her marriage was eight years strong and had produced three kids, a backyard full of plastic toys, and about fifty extra pounds on Janice in various spots.

Normal stuff. The way life was supposed to go. The way he'd always pictured his going.

He'd been in for a hell of a surprise.

"Aren't you going to introduce us?"

He'd been hoping to avoid it, actually. "Uh, sure, this is Amanda Delmar, a friend of Boston Macnamara's from Chicago. Amanda this is Janice Kirkwood, and her little boy." Whose name he couldn't remember, but the kid was a baby, so it didn't count. Names only started to matter when kids could talk.

"It's a pleasure to meet you." Janice smiled at Amanda, but it was tight and fake. "I've heard you were spending the summer here, but I had no idea you were dating Danny.

Seems to me you were seen running around with Howie and Stan. How many men does one woman need?"

Oh, Lord. Danny hated getting sucked into these female face-offs. He never understood what they were about, but he knew tension. And Janice was oozing it.

"Howie and Stan are nice guys," Amanda said, waving her hand in the air casually and hooking the pajamas on the side of the cart.

Danny could have kissed her for not responding to Janice's verbal drawn sword. Well, actually he could have kissed her for a lot of reasons, including wearing that short skirt, but that was beside the point.

"But I wasn't dating them. And I'm more like Danny's personal shopper."

"He can't dress himself?" Janice snickered.

"Oh, he can dress himself." Amanda glanced over at him, and he swore she zeroed in right on his crotch.

He wondered what she thought of it.

"And *un*dress himself, just fine." Amanda leaned on the rack. "But I'm helping him shop for his daughter."

"Daughter?" Janice's eyebrows disappeared under her bangs. "What daughter?"

"The one he didn't know he had, who is eight years old and has come to live with him. But don't worry, conception occurred when he and Shelby were broken up the summer between junior and senior year and he met a girl at the fair."

Well, how nice of her to clear that up in case anyone was wondering. Like it was anyone's goddamn business but his. Danny was blushing. He could feel it, damn, right on each cheek, burning heat.

"But we have to go now. Nice meeting you." Amanda nudged his arm and started walking away. She ducked down once to call to Piper, who scrambled out from under the clothes rack. "Grab the cart, Danny."

In a minute, they had left slack-jawed Janice behind in girls and were heading toward personal hygiene.

He recovered enough to realize that he was trailing Amanda again. "You know, I'd prefer if you didn't just blurt out my business in the Cuttersville Wal-Mart." He was an easygoing kind of guy, but some things he just couldn't brush off.

Telling Janice Kirkwood about his teen sex life was one of them.

His boots squeaked on the white polished floor as he gripped the cart, moving it down aisle seven—toothbrushes and toothpaste.

Amanda started inspecting the brands, asking Piper if she preferred gel or paste. Piper shrugged.

He didn't give a crap either. He wanted to know who the hell she thought she was telling Janice his business.

"Gel." Amanda tossed a box toward the cart, not bothering to make sure it landed in its destination. "Don't worry about it, Danny. In one sentence I took care of any future gossip that might get started. Janice will tell everyone about Piper and the circumstances, and you won't find yourself answering the same nosy questions over and over again."

Danny wanted to blast her. Wanted to give her a good talking to about butting out, but the truth was, he didn't have the personality to blast anyone. And she was right on top of it all. The last thing he felt like doing was getting pestered with questions by every housewife in Cuttersville every time he left the farm for the next year.

"Well, I suppose you could be right."

Amanda held a toothbrush to her chest and staggered back dramatically. "You admit that I'm right? Wow, this is a beautiful moment."

He grinned. "I'm a big enough man to admit when someone else is right. You're a smart woman, Amanda, under all that hair."

Amanda figured there was a compliment somewhere in there. It was just hidden under the rudeness. "Thanks. But you'd better hold back with the gushing, or I'll get an ego."

"I do believe you're being sarcastic with me." Danny pushed the cart, then climbed onto the back and rode with it down the aisle, hunkered over the pile of clothes.

"I do believe I am, Farmer Tucker." Amanda got out of the way as he sailed past, looking a little precarious perched on the metal rungs. He was a little large to be hanging on the cart like that. "And be careful, you look like you're going to . . ."

Danny lost control and hit the wall of contact lens solution.

"Crash." She looked at Piper, who made a little sound of distress. "Boys," Amanda said in exaggerated disgust. "Always fooling around."

Though he looked like a wall of bricks could fall on him and he wouldn't break a nail, Amanda still asked, "Are you okay?"

"Fine." He pulled the cart back and picked up the one container that had fallen. He turned to Piper, his face a mask of faux contrition. "I guess I shouldn't have been doing that."

She shook her head, but she had a shy smile on her face.

Amanda went around the front of the cart and climbed onto the bottom rungs, facing out. She gripped the basket of the cart and leaned back for stability. "This way is probably safer. Someone to steer and someone to hold on."

It was murder on her spine, but it had the potential to be amusing. They all needed a laugh, she figured. "Get in the basket with the clothes, Piper."

The little girl's eyes went wide, but she didn't protest when Danny lifted her up and tossed her on the towering pile. Piper's legs were a little long and dangled over the side, but she lay on her back, pajamas rising on either side of her face, plastic hangers above her head. That worry, that fear that seemed to have permanently taken up residence in Piper's eyes, made Amanda feel reckless, determined to draw a laugh out of her.

No child should have that much heaviness on her heart, not when her whole future lay in front of her. Not when she had a father like Danny Tucker, and a cart full of new clothes. But as Amanda knew only too well, you couldn't just shake the past off that easily, and you couldn't fix the scars it left on you. And Piper must have a lot of scars.

"Where to, girls?" Danny pulled the cart back and made adjustments to the wheel position.

"To shampoo and bubble bath. Then on to toys." Amanda peeked back over her shoulder to make sure Baby was still tucked in her handbag in the front seat. Her dog was really good about staying put, but she didn't want her deciding to leap to freedom off a moving shopping cart. But Baby looked complacent, everything but her head in the handbag.

"Okay, we're ready."

One big push from Danny and they were flying down the aisle, cool air rushing past Amanda's face and sending her hair back off her shoulders. It was a straight shot past toothbrushes, and there was enough speed to make her feel an excited little rush of dizziness. "Turn left!"

They careened into the center aisle on two wheels, slapping the inch back to the ground with a metallic squeak. "Faster," Amanda demanded, catching a glimpse of pleasure on Piper's sunburned face. She made a mental note to grab sunscreen. Sun damage caused premature aging. Piper was breeding a colony of future crow's-feet by burning her skin. Not to mention that whole cancer thing.

"Let me grab the shampoo." It was on the end of the aisle coming up at three o'clock, and Amanda stretched out her hand.

But Danny had followed her directive, and they were going NASCAR speed. Her knuckle rapped a shampoo bottle, but she couldn't get a grip. The strawberry-scented shampoo bottle went flying in the direction of first-aid products and clipped a man in the back of the leg.

"Oops. Sorry."

Danny put on the brakes, using those massive farmer arms to drag the cart to a stop. Much faster than Amanda could have ever predicted. She went flying off the end, losing a stiletto and crashing into the display shelf, bottles tumbling down around her. She protected her nails and her hair, the most expensive things to replace, and looked up when the falling stopped. That had been kind of fun sailing through the air.

Which proved she'd been rusticating too long.

"Cool. I've got the bubble bath, Piper." She grabbed a bottle of Disney's princess bubbles and hopped toward the cart. "Where's my shoe?"

The man she'd nailed with the shampoo was holding it out toward her.

"Thanks." She took it and slipped it on her foot, bouncing up and down to adjust it as she tried not to grimace. She really wished he hadn't actually touched it. While he looked like a perfectly normal middle-age man with male pattern baldness and a growing gut, she didn't want his thick fingers in her shoes. She had a thing about feet. If a man was going to be touching hers, that wasn't all he was going to be touching. She didn't take feet lightly.

"You two need to calm down and use these carts correctly. This is a family store. We can't have you running around crashing into things. Someone might get hurt."

Amanda focused on the little nametag pinned to his blue shirt. "Sorry, Jeffrey. It was just an accident."

Jeffrey didn't look appeased. He gave her a stern finger shake. "Do it again, and we'll have to ask you to leave."

Was he serious? "I can get kicked out of Wal-Mart for exceeding the cart speed limit?"

Danny cleared his throat. "Uh, Amanda, let's just finish our shopping."

"Absolutely, we can escort you to the exit. We want our shoppers to feel safe here."

Her shirt had ridden up to her breasts, and Amanda yanked it back down toward her belly button. "Alright, sorry. We'll just be on our way."

"Is that a dog?" Jeffrey asked, looking outraged as he peered around her.

"No." Baby was so much more than a dog. She was friend, confidante, purebred poodle . . .

Amanda turned around and shot Danny a look. "Back up," she hissed.

Danny whipped the cart out of the aisle, and they walked off at a fast, though sedate, clip.

"Well, life lesson here."

"What's that?" Danny didn't look annoyed with her. In fact, he was struggling not to grin.

"Don't ride the carts in Wal-Mart, of course." She tossed her hair back. "Though it would have been kind of fun to tell people that. 'I got kicked out of Wal-Mart on my summer vacation.' By Amanda Delmar."

"Are you in school still?" Piper looked horrified by the thought.

"No. I got a bachelor's degree in Art Appreciation from the University of Chicago, with a focus on the Old Masters."

"Oh," said Piper.

"Wow," said Danny. "That sounds impressive."

"Impressive, but utterly useless." Though she had to admit it wasn't really her degree that was useless. It was more like she had never actively pursued a usefulness for it.

"Couldn't you work in a museum or something?"

Farmers just thought they knew everything. "But then I would be spending all those hours locked away with canvas and oils. It would really cut into my shopping time."

It was a typical Amanda answer. The type that made most people laugh. The answer that would have her father gnashing his teeth together.

But Danny tilted his head and stared at her, his eyes too

knowing, too probing. Like he could see the lie. Like he understood. They had reached the toy department, and she didn't wait to hear what he might have to say. Whatever it was, she was sure she didn't want to hear it, and she didn't want him to look too closely at her. He might be shocked at what he found.

"How much does this shampoo cost anyway? The bottle is huge." She stuck it under the price scanner at the end of the aisle and watched the price pop up on the screen. "Whoa, is this thing accurate? It says the shampoo is only ninety-nine cents."

An eyedropper of Amanda's shampoo cost more than that.

"That sounds about right to me."

"Are you serious?" Amanda stared at the bottle in her hand. "This thing's huge! That's like a penny a shampoo! Does the president know about this? No wonder the economy sucks; they're giving stuff away for peanuts at Wal-Mart."

Danny cocked his head. "Well, how much does your shampoo cost?"

"I think about forty bucks. I'm not really sure." Drawn by the lure of hot pink, she headed down the Barbie aisle. "Look at this! It's Barbie and Ken as *Star Trek* characters. That's hilarious."

She tossed it in the cart, annoyed that Danny had flustered her without really saying a word. He just looked at her, with those steady, logical eyes, and she felt like he saw through the Amanda facade.

"I'm not buying that for Piper—it's goofy-looking."

"It's for me. Piper can pick out her own. Look, Barbie has fishnet stockings and one of those little communicator things."

"Get this one instead." Danny held up a Barbie with long straight blond hair, a red miniskirt, and a faux Burberry handbag with a little dog sticking out of it.

"Who is she supposed to be?" This one just looked like an everyday kind of doll to Amanda.

"I think this is Heiress Barbie. She looks just like you." Danny grinned as he lifted Piper down out of the cart.

The kid went down on the ground and started peering at the Equestrian dolls.

"Here, let me see her," Amanda said, holding out her hand.

Danny gave her the box.

She whacked him on the arm with it. "Watch your tongue. Her bag is *fake*. I would never carry fake."

Danny laughed. He threw his arm around her shoulder and gave her a shake that nearly sent her sailing off her shoes. "Honey, you're a one-of-a-kind, that's for sure. Just plain original."

Growing up an only child, Amanda had never experienced roughhousing with siblings. Nor had she ever been with a lover whose moves weren't calculated, skilled. Danny's touch was just friendly, casual. Nice. It actually felt nice in a strange, aw-shucks kind of way.

She added Knock-Off Barbie to the cart. "I think I'll get her just to feel superior."

"How you going to pay for that? I thought you were out of money." Danny's smile faded into concern. "Maybe you should be saving your cash for food."

Oh my God. He was right. She had forgotten she was poor. She was so used to spending money like there was a steady supply of it that it had never occurred to her that she couldn't have whatever she wanted in this store. Fifty-seven dollars was the sum total in her wallet and all that stood between her and starvation.

And while staying thin was a priority in her life, she had to eat *something*.

There was no money for a Barbie, *Star Trek* or otherwise. Or an umbrella and little Hello Kitty Post-it notes.

Giving a laugh that she hoped sounded more genuine

than it felt, she put the doll back on the shelf. "You're right. I completely forgot that I'm destitute." And that she was a little bit scared. Who was Amanda Delmar without her trust fund?

"What's *destitute* mean?" Piper asked, looking up from the Breyer pony she was studying.

"It means I don't have any money."

"I don't have any money either," Piper said with a shrug.

This laugh was more genuine. "Then I guess we'll be destitute together."

"Well, I'm not destitute," Danny said. "It would give me a great deal of pleasure to buy you both a Barbie."

"Why?" Amanda asked in suspicion. She hadn't even flirted with him. Not much anyway. And he wasn't hinting that he could think of a lot of ways she could pleasure him in return. That was the way it usually went. Men spent money; men wanted something—sex, power, her inheritance. They always wanted something.

It was why her favorite T-shirt read I THINK, THEREFORE I'M SINGLE.

He shrugged, studying her a little too carefully. "I just want to, that's all. Do I have to have a reason to want to buy you a Barbie?"

If she were any judge of character—which was questionable, given Logan—Danny had no ulterior motive. He was just being nice.

Danny Tucker didn't fit into her understanding of men. He was an anomaly. A big one. In boots and a baseball hat.

"You don't have to do that, Danny. It's a waste of money to buy me a doll." For the first time, maybe she could understand that. Money could be spent wisely on necessities, or frivolously. A Barbie for a twenty-five-year-old woman with no income was beyond frivolous. It was a cry for counseling.

"Which would you rather have—the umbrella or the Barbie? Because I'm buying one or the other." Danny leaned on the handle of the cart, his green T-shirt pulling forward at the neck. "Think of it as a gift for being my personal shopper."

"But you don't need a personal shopper," she whispered, feeling raw and vulnerable in a way that she just detested. "You can dress yourself."

He nodded, slow and sure. "And undress myself." He grabbed the Barbie box she had returned to the shelf and added it to the cart.

"I don't know what to say." He was making her extremely uncomfortable.

"Seems to me you ought to just say thank you and be done with it." He cocked a grin and winked.

Smart-ass, she mouthed to him so Piper couldn't see.

But when he laughed, she said, "Thank you."

And popped her umbrella back open and strolled up the aisle.

Chapter 4

Willie Tucker was licking the salt off a margarita when her cell phone rang. She and the women in the
church traveler's group were having a nice, late dinner at
the local Mexican restaurant after a day touring the basket
factory. She should have turned off her phone when she
came into the restaurant. It always drove her bonkers when
people were chatting on those things while they were sitting with other people.

Besides, no one would be calling her but her husband,
Daniel. Or Danny, though that would be rarer still. And
only because of an emergency.

Damn. She dug out her phone, hoping if someone had
died it was her brother Bart. Never could stand Bart.

Caller ID showed it was Daniel, alright. "Excuse me,
ladies, it's my husband, and I'm afraid it might be something important."

"Unlike when my husband calls," Karen Ditko laughed.

"I set foot out of the house, and suddenly he's helpless as a baby."

Daniel wasn't like that. They'd been working the farm together for thirty years and didn't run to each other for foolishness. Her heart picked up its pace.

"Hello?"

"Hey. You busy?"

"I'm having dinner with the girls. Anything wrong?"

Daniel paused, and Willie gripped the edge of the table.

"It's nothing. I just thought maybe tomorrow you might want to skip the afternoon shopping and come on home early. Something's popped up with Danny."

"Why?" Her fear turned to annoyance. Daniel wasn't usually cryptic. "What's the matter with Danny? He sick?"

Not that she could imagine Danny getting sick or laid up. He was as healthy as their soybean crop this year. He was a good boy, too, but she knew he was getting a little restless lately. Lonely. She hoped he hadn't done anything stupid. Like get involved with that blond piece of work who'd blown into town with Boston Macnamara.

Willie wasn't blind. She could see that those long legs had drawn Danny's attention. Danny and every other man in town under the age of ninety.

"Not exactly. He just has some news."

Why the hell was her husband being so guarded? Danny was either dying or his house had burned to the ground. It had to be a disaster, plain and simple, for Daniel to sound like he did. Like he'd been kicked in the family jewels. "What news?"

"I think this is the kind of news that Danny needs to tell you himself."

Oh, God, Danny had run off to Vegas with the blonde. "Daniel, I think you've lost your mind. You cannot call me and tell me Danny has news and expect me to wait until tomorrow afternoon to find out what it is. Tell me. Now."

She took a fortifying sip of margarita, bracing herself for the fact that her child might be dying. God, she couldn't lose her son. He hadn't even given her grandbabies yet, for crying out loud. Didn't that rate special consideration?

That was the problem with only having one son—you decreased your odds of grandchildren. Since Shelby and Danny had split, Willie had lived in constant fear that he would never find another woman to settle down with and fill up the yard with kids.

Not that she wanted him to marry the wrong woman. Like what's-her-name with the high heels. Willie wanted him to be happy. While procreating.

But she reassured herself that if Danny were dying, Daniel would be more upset than he sounded.

"First, do you know where we put the phone number for that lawyer we used to make our wills? Danny came around tonight saying he'd gotten a bit of a surprise."

"Lawyer? What the hell does he need a lawyer for?" Willie met the shocked gazes of her three friends and felt panic swelling up in her.

"I'm getting to that part."

"Well, speed it up." Daniel took things easy, calmly, thought them through. Willie wished for once he could just spit it out. If her son had committed murder and was facing the electric chair, she needed to know.

"Turns out when he was in high school Danny met a girl at the county fair and uhhh, well, was intimate with her."

It wasn't murder, but did she need to hear these things? Willie was going to need another margarita at this rate. "And?"

"She got pregnant. But she never told Danny. Tonight the gal's husband dropped by with Danny's daughter. She's eight years old, and the stepfather doesn't want her anymore."

"A daughter?" She was drunk. That had to be the only explanation for this. Maybe the booze had gone to her head and she was really in bed sleeping it off, dreaming this. "Are you serious?"

"Dead serious. And I want to talk to that lawyer. As far as I'm concerned, we need to establish who has custody of this child. Danny says she's underweight and dirty, Wil. They haven't been taking care of her."

Everything tilted and shifted, and the only thing that mattered now was that she had a granddaughter. Who needed her. Willie scrambled for her purse. "I'm leaving. I'll be home in an hour and a half."

"Wilhemina . . ."

She hung up on Daniel and looked at Trudy, Karen, and Dawn. "I have a grandbaby."

Dawn looked at her in astonishment. "Didn't you know that? Erica Kirkwood called me twenty minutes ago and left a voice mail. Turns out Janice ran into Danny shopping with the little girl at Wal-Mart. Everybody knows by now."

♡

Danny's truck was crammed full with plastic bags, and his credit card had suffered the largest hit since he'd gotten the account six years ago. He wouldn't be surprised if Visa called him inquiring about unusual activity on his card. But it wasn't enough. It didn't feel like enough to make up for eight years of not knowing about Piper.

She was tucked into the truck beside him, her knobby knees crammed against the gearshift. He knew he shouldn't expect otherwise, but she was so quiet all the time. It was hard to know what to say to her.

Despite nearly getting tossed out of Wal-Mart on their ears, he could admit he was glad after all that Amanda had gone shopping with them. At least she filled the silence and gave him someone to bounce his thoughts off of. He wasn't used to having to make decisions about someone else, and it was reassuring to have Amanda back him up.

Or more like disagree with him, which allowed him to argue why his choice made more sense.

They were pulling in Amanda's drive to drop her off, the new bike he'd gotten Piper scraping across the truck bed. Piper hadn't wanted a bike—said she couldn't ride two-wheel—but he hadn't been able to resist. A bike on a farm was a good way to tool around and explore. He'd spent hours racing his BMX around when he was her age.

Maybe it was overcompensation. He was trying to make up for lost time. Fix everything that he had missed. Everything that Piper hadn't had.

But he didn't know what else to do.

SpongeBob SquarePants Band-Aids couldn't take away the past, but it was a start for the future.

"This your house?" Piper asked Amanda, peering through the dark at Amanda's little gray rental.

"Well, I don't own it. I'm just renting it for the summer."

Until she went back to Chicago. Danny couldn't forget that. Didn't matter that she had been amusing in the store, that he enjoyed her quirky company, and that sometimes he thought he saw beneath the chemical-processed cover and glimpsed the lonely woman beneath.

"It's pretty."

"They say it's haunted, but I haven't encountered one ghost. It's been an incredible letdown."

Danny had never seen any ghosts either, but enough folks around town had claimed to, so he was inclined to believe the stories. But he was glad that no disembodied entities had any interest in his house. He'd prefer to stay disembody-less.

Amanda opened the door. "Thanks for letting me hang with you, Piper. I'll see you soon."

"I'll walk you to the door." Danny opened his own door. "Stay in the truck, Piper. I'll be right back."

The panic that flitted across his daughter's face made him curse silently. "Or why don't you walk up with me? We can make sure Amanda gets in safe and sound."

He didn't want Piper to think for one second that he would abandon her. It was going to take time before she learned to trust that this was permanent. Before she learned to trust him.

Piper was so relieved she scrambled right out, even letting him take her hand, which up to now she had shied away from. Danny walked over the gravel driveway, his throat tight at the feeling of his daughter's small, cool hand in his. She seemed so tiny, so fragile next to him. Damn, he didn't want to screw this up and break her. Piper already had chips and cracks all over; he didn't want to be the one to shatter her.

It was a hell of a responsibility.

Amanda was fishing her keys out of her big purse, the plastic Wal-Mart bag with the Barbie in it hung over the opposite wrist. She had set Baby down on the porch, and the dog raced past the wicker chair, squatted, and did her business.

"Why is the dog wearing a shirt?" Every time he looked at that poodle, something seemed off to him. Now he realized it was because the dog was wearing a tiny peach-colored T-shirt. "It's summer."

"It's not for warmth. It's a logo T-shirt." She smiled. "It says NO ONE PUTS BABY IN A CORNER."

All those letters had fit across that itty bitty chest? "What's that supposed to mean?"

"Ah! You don't remember that from *Dirty Dancing*?" She looked astonished. "That's like a classic line."

"I never saw it." He vaguely had the notion it involved gay men, but he could be wrong about that.

"Some day I'll rent it, and we can watch it together. But right now I don't have three bucks for a video, which is a shame, because it's a perfect cheese-ball movie."

"Is your dad really going to stick to his no-money policy?" The whole idea of just cutting off his kid without a dime bothered Danny, but then he figured there was a whole lot to Amanda's relationship with her father he didn't know about.

"I guess. He's never done this before, but he sounded determined. And he is a businessman, first and foremost. I think he's decided I'm a bad investment. Not enough return on his capital."

Amanda's back was to him as she opened her front door, but Danny could hear the tinge of bitterness in her voice.

"If you need anything, Amanda, you can call on me. I'll help you out any way I can."

Her flaxen hair shone in the moonlight. Her porch light was blown, but the night was light enough that he could see the smile that played around her lips as she stared at him over her bare shoulder.

"You know, Danny Tucker, you really are a nice guy," she whispered. "Not many people would feel sorry for the poor rich girl."

Piper was still clutching him, leaning into his hip, so he couldn't say what he really wanted to. Which was that the last thing in the world he felt was pity. That he felt a deep, gut-wrenching, ball-busting attraction to her that had him antsy during the day and downright agonized at night.

So he just shook his head. "What I'm feeling for you isn't pity."

Her mouth slid open, her tongue moistening that plump bottom lip. "Go home, Danny, before I say something that embarrasses me tomorrow."

He knew that there could never be anything between them. Certainly not a relationship. Definitely not an affair. He wasn't looking for immediate gratification—he wanted the long haul. So he couldn't even indulge in a kiss. Because one kiss would lead him to want that gratification, and they just couldn't go there.

So he just brushed his knuckles across her arm. "Friends don't need to be embarrassed around each other, ever."

Amanda studied him for a second, then smiled. "Maybe

not in your world." She clapped her hand to her thigh. "Baby, come here, sweetie."

The dog came scurrying over, a blur of white fur. Amanda picked her up and pushed open the front door.

"Good night, Danny. Good night, Piper."

"Good night." When the door shut, Danny looked down at Piper. Unable to resist, he lifted her up into his arms until she was face-to-face with him. She looked startled but rested comfortably against him.

"Come on, baby girl. Let's go home."

Amanda put Baby down on the wood floor in the foyer and tossed her handbag on the fussy little Victorian table standing next to the stairs. The table even had a little lace doily on it, and it wasn't Amanda's style at all. But she liked this house, despite feeling like she had to duck to get through the door frames. The ceilings were only seven feet high.

Clearly in the nineteenth century, women weren't six feet tall in stilettos.

The entire house seemed to have been built on a miniature scale. Rooms were tight, hallways narrow, the tub wedged under a gable so that the one time she'd tried to use it she'd had to limbo to climb in. Then when she'd settled in the water, her knees had scraped the ceiling.

She'd stuck to showers since then.

"What am I doing here, Baby?" she asked, turning on the lamp in the parlor. She had come to Cuttersville on a lark, bored out of her mind in Chicago. The usual parties and clubs had only emphasized to her how sterile and artificial her life was, how she had many acquaintances and party pals, but very few real friends.

Seeing her ex-boyfriend Logan one night, a barely legal skinny blonde on his lap, sucking back mojitos, had done her in. He was an ugly, painful reminder that she was needy, that she craved love and affection just like a dog did. That no matter how much she said it didn't matter, she still wanted her father's approval. She still wanted him to admit, just once, that he was pleased to have her as a daughter, even though she hadn't been born with a penis.

Kiss, kiss, hug, hug, she had worked that club, letting Logan know she didn't care, it didn't matter, she was Amanda Margaret Delmar, heir to the Samson Plastics conglomerate and she was untouchable. As cool as the diamonds in her earlobes.

And the next morning, she had packed six suitcases, hopped a plane to the middle of fucking nowhere, and had rented herself this little gray house. Boston had told her the landlady had fleeced her on the rent, but she hadn't cared. What did it matter when the money was never-ending? Boston had already been dating Shelby, but just the fact that she was in Cuttersville had irritated her father and left him pondering her next move. He seemed to think she was Napoleon in heels, planning her next capture of an unsuspecting, underarmed, rich man.

So here she was, with a dog and low ceilings.

"Let's see what we have in the kitchen, Baby." She had gone to the grocery store when she had first moved in and bought several boxes of cereal, margarita mix, and tuna packets. Maybe inspiration would hit while she was nibbling Shredded Wheat.

It didn't. And the cereal was stale.

Picking shreds back off her tongue, she got a glass out of the cabinet and turned the tap to cold. She hoped she could drink the water here straight out of the tap, because she didn't have a whole lot of options. San Pellegrino wasn't going to magically appear in her fridge.

First on the agenda was going back to the store and buying food to tide her over. Easy enough. She could grocery shop, had done it before. You just picked things out, put them in the cart, tossed them on the belt, and paid. No problem. She was so damn self-sufficient.

Then she had to find a job.

That one was a little trickier. Because she had no clue how to find a job.

People applied for jobs. They sent out résumés. They surfed job boards for positions. She knew all that. But how they applied, where they got résumés, what jobs they were qualified for—she had no clue. Her father had always smoothed the way for her with everything.

"Baby, this is damn depressing." She sipped her water, picked at her cereal straight out of the box, and looked down at her dog. "Maybe we should go home."

If she called a friend, she could bum the money. It wasn't something she would be proud of, but it seemed like the smartest course of action available to her at the moment. Maybe with some begging she could ask her landlady, Mrs. Stritmeyer, to refund her August rent. Mrs. S was Shelby's grandmother, and Shelby had offered to help. With that thousand bucks, she could get back home and work something out.

But the problem with that was, she had no idea what she would do in Chicago either, or if her father would even let her use her apartment, since he paid the rent every month. Returning to the city wouldn't magically solve her problems anyway, and if she had to be poor, she'd rather do it in Cuttersville, where no one gave a crap. Back home, some people in her circle would give their left fake breast to see her impoverished.

Her cell phone rang, and she dug it out, resigned and wishing for German chocolate cake. "What?"

"Hey, bitch, what's up?" Her friend Yvonne's voice came blaring over the phone, the background crowded with reggae music.

"Just the same old." Getting disinherited and venturing into Wal-Mart for the first time. Everyday B.S. "Where are you?"

"The Caribbean. Can you hear the music? These guys

are so lame, but they're like the hottest thing in town, so of course, we had to be here. You have to get your ass down here. Sierra thinks she saw Orlando Bloom at the pool."

Amanda waited to feel her panties heat up at the thought of Orlando in swim trunks, but for some odd reason it didn't happen. "Sorry, Yvonne, but I think I'm staying here for awhile. There's some hot action I want to see through." If gym-shoe shopping for eight-year-old girls and beginning the great job hunt from hell could be classified as hot.

"Oooh, who is he? Tell all or I'll hate you forever."

A sort of nasty pit assembled in Amanda's stomach, and it wasn't the fact that she had nothing but bits of cardboard masquerading as cereal resting in it. The truth was that Yvonne, who she had always considered one of her closest friends, was not someone she could share her secrets with. She couldn't tell Yvonne that she was out of money. Or ask for advice in gaining an income. Nor could she tell her about this perfectly nice farmer with thick arms who sometimes seemed like he'd walked off the set of *Leave It to Beaver*.

And that she was attracted to that. To him.

Yvonne wasn't her friend. She was a party pal, who would laugh her Pilates ass off if Amanda got sentimental.

"Sorry," Amanda said in a light airy tone that was so phony she made herself want to gag. "I'm not in the mood for phone sex."

Yvonne laughed. "You suck. Call me in a couple of days, and we'll go to New York."

"Okay, I'll call you." She wouldn't be going on any trip though. "Bye, Yvonne, have fun."

"I always do."

As had she. Amanda. She had always had fun, and it had been fluff and nothing more.

Amanda hung up the phone and picked up Baby and set her on the counter. "Danny was right. I'm like that stupid Barbie, only it's not my bag that's fake. It's the whole me. Everything about me is fake."

Baby looked at her. Baby barked. Amanda stared at her button nose and her luminous brown eyes and scooped her up before Baby broke out a violin and starting playing it.

"Jesus, okay, enough of this self-analysis crap. I sound like Dr. Phil. Let's go call Boston and Shelby and ask about the rent money." She could think it all to death while she slowly wasted away from malnutrition, or she could do something about it.

Amanda was halfway up the stairs, planning to use the phone in her bedroom, since unlike cell phone minutes it was free, when she heard something.

A faint muffled crying. The sound was distant, faded, but grief-stricken. A woman.

Amanda stopped walking and gave a slow look around. She was alone on the steps, and the sound seemed to be coming from upstairs. "Okay, that's weird. All alone in the house. Strange crying. What do you think that means, Baby?"

She was certain it meant that the noise was coming from outside, because obviously it couldn't be coming from the inside.

The crying got louder.

It must be her next-door neighbor. There was a federal blue house on the other side of Amanda's driveway that had a middle-age couple living in it.

"Someone's pitching a bitch." Amanda raised her eyebrow at Baby, a bit annoyed. How could she feel sorry for herself with that racket going on? "Whatever she's crying about, it can't be as bad as my day."

And she was almost certain that sound was coming from inside the house. It had too much clarity and volume to be outside. Following the sound down the hallway, Amanda ducked to enter the tiny third bedroom, the one Shelby had told her used to be a second floor porch and had been enclosed. There was a mirror hanging in that room, a rather overblown baroque job, with proportions better suited to hanging in a great hall than a hobbit-sized bedroom.

"Damn, I was afraid of that." The crying roiled and wailed throughout the room, strongest in front of the mirror. Like someone was in the mirror. With a sigh, Amanda did a cursory search of the room and windows and came to the conclusion that she was experiencing her first encounter with the Crying Lady, the ghost reputed to haunt her house.

It was just her luck that something of actual minor interest happened and she was too tired and hungry to give a crap.

"Okay, chica, what's the problem?" Amanda put her hand on her hip while Baby growled at her ankles. With a deep breath, she turned to look in the mirror.

"Holy shit!" Amanda jumped back and fought the urge to scream.

Good God, her hair looked horrible. She had been shopping with the clip to her extensions showing beneath her left ear. Nice and tacky.

"That's it. I've hit rock bottom." But on a happy note, her curse seemed to have frightened away the Crabby Lady. There was no more crying.

Her phone rang as she was peering into the mirror, fixing her hair. She sprinted down the hall with a burst of energy to answer it. No one called her house number. This was very exciting and a sad testimonial to the state of her life that receiving a phone call got her all hot and bothered.

"Hello?" She was cool; she was calm. She was not alone in the big, bad, wolfish world with a ghost who needed antidepressants, and no one who gave a shit whether she lived or died.

Someone had *called* her. If it were just someone trying to sell her the *Cuttersville Explorer* newspaper she'd slit her wrists.

"Amanda, it's Danny. Danny Tucker."

Like she knew twelve Dannys in Cuttersville.

"Oh, hey, Danny, what's up?" She was just the master of

emotions, currently specializing in nonchalant. Maybe she should hit Hollywood with all this awesome acting she was doing lately.

"Uh, I, well, just wanted to let you know that Hair by Harriet is hiring. If you're really serious about getting a job. I know that's kind of a stupid thing for someone like you to be doing, but I just thought . . ." He trailed off, clearing his throat.

"That I knew hair?" she said, just a little bit touched that he had given her situation any thought.

"Exactly." He sighed in relief.

Without a cosmetology degree, she didn't think she was qualified to do anything at the salon except maybe give advice, but it never hurt to inquire. "Thanks, I'll check it out."

Amanda walked back toward the last bedroom, flipping on all the hall and bedroom lights as she went. She needed another look at that mirror. "How's Piper?" She sincerely hoped Piper would embrace Danny as her father and wouldn't waste unnecessary time punishing him for something he'd had no control over.

Though Amanda thought Piper's mother could stand to be bitch-slapped for never telling Danny he had a daughter. Of course, she was dead, so that wasn't really an option.

"She's in the bath right now, hopefully using lots of soap."

"That's good. You get all her new stuff unpacked?"

"No. There's eight bags lying in my kitchen. But I'll get to it in the morning."

A hazy milky color had clouded the mirror where it hung over an antique whatnot. Amanda ran her finger over the glass, leaving a slight streak.

"Danny, what is the story with the chick who cries in the mirror?" Shelby had told her that story once before, but she had only listened with half an ear, certain it was embellishment designed to boost excitement in the dead, dull country.

Dead was probably the only accurate piece of that assumption.

"Shelby can tell you the full story, but the gist of it is, she cries for her lost love, who was a thief and a murderer. And they say the women who hear her are destined for their own heartbreak in the near future."

That just figured. "Really? How fun. Because I just heard her."

And the last thing she needed to encounter was heartbreak.

Breaking up was hard to do, but it would be intolerable without a credit card for copious cosmopolitans and retail therapy.

Chapter 5

$\mathcal{D}$anny ate his sunny-side-up eggs and picked through the box of junk Piper's stepfather had left.

It told a sad story of what her life had been like.

There was precious little in the box to begin with, but what there was had seen better days. The blanket was worn and faded. The clothes were so·small and dirty and torn up that he took them and pitched them right in the trash. There was a box of broken crayons, a small brown teddy bear with an unraveling ribbon around his neck, and a naked Barbie doll missing half her hair.

Danny gave the doll a shake, and her limp Mohawk twitched. "Who is this? Rogaine Barbie?" He eyed the pitiful hairdo as Piper came padding into the kitchen softly, her hand reaching out for the doll.

"This is *Baywatch* Barbie, but my cousin took all her clothes." She clutched the doll tightly and took a step back from him.

"Maybe next time we're at the store, you can pick out a

new outfit for her." Danny smiled and sipped his coffee, trying like hell to sound reassuring and confident and paternal. Damned if he knew how.

Piper shrugged, her favorite response.

He sucked in a deep breath and reminded himself this was going to take time. He was a total stranger to her. "Want some eggs?"

She eyed his plate with hearty suspicion. "Do I hafta have 'em like yours?"

"No. I could scramble them if you want. Don't you like sunny-side up?"

Her head moved vigorously. "They look like eyeballs."

He grinned. "Okay, then. No eyeballs for breakfast. Scrambled coming right up."

Danny stood and touched Piper on the shoulder as he went past her to the refrigerator. It pleased him that she smelled clean and her skin looked so pink and shiny this morning. Yet at the same time, everything he saw, heard, considered, made him sick that her life hadn't been a bowl of cherries. She'd gotten nothing but the pits.

He hadn't slept a single second of the night before. He had paced and worried and planned until at dawn he'd started the coffeemaker. He was on his third cup and was jittery with caffeine, but no closer to any solutions.

There was a farm to tend to. But he had a daughter now and a million and one things needed to be taken care of in the short term—like bedroom furniture and finding a pediatrician so she could have a checkup.

In the long term, he had to determine the legalities involved in making sure he had full custody, not to mention child care issues. In the fall, he would send Piper to Cuttersville Elementary, but for right now, he had no one to watch her when he was working the farm or out doing a part-time construction job that helped him pay the bills.

"After breakfast I'm going to do some laundry," he said as he pulled out a frying pan. "So why don't you give me that hat you're wearing and I'll wash it with the rest of your new stuff?"

Danny was pretty certain vermin were breeding in that hat.

"I can't take it off. I . . . I don't have any hair," she whispered.

Startled, Danny dropped the pan and turned around. "What? What do you mean?" He moved toward her, and she flinched. He stopped walking, still a few feet from her, not wanting to scare her.

"Mark says no one should have to look at my ugly head." She leaned back against the table, holding her Barbie across her chest like a shield. The grubby hat was clearly a shield too.

It made sense then, at the same time it broke his heart, why he couldn't see her hair falling out of her hat. There wasn't any. Jesus. Danny dropped to a squat in front of her, wanting to cry for the first time in his adult life. For the first time since Shelby had miscarried his child.

"Why did your hair fall out, baby girl?" He was thinking cancer, which was killing him. He couldn't find his daughter to lose her. He couldn't.

"The doctor says its stress. He says maybe it will come back when I'm older." Piper touched her hat, looking a little panicked. "But you can't tell anyone. It's a secret."

While there was relief it wasn't cancer, this answer came with raging, engulfing guilt. Sadness. Fear. How could he ever make this right? "I won't tell anyone, Piper. I promise."

He lifted his hand toward her and saw her wince. He froze with his hand in the air before going with instinct and continuing on to give her shoulder a little squeeze. "Let me get that breakfast started. You must be starving."

Turning to the stove, he struggled to regain his composure, beat back the panic that zipped through his body like the caffeine from those three cups of coffee. This would work out. It would. He just had to be patient.

His front door flew open as he cracked the first egg. "Danny?"

His mother. He should have known to expect her sooner than later. Gossip spread like dandelion weeds in this town.

"I'm in the kitchen, Mom."

He glanced at Piper. She stood frozen in front of the table, her balding Barbie dangling by one leg. "It's my mom, Piper. Bet she heard about you and had to see for herself the little girl I told my father I was so excited about."

His mother came into the room like a semi-truck on an empty highway. Piper flinched, and Danny shut off the heat on the stove and moved to her side to reassure her. His mother wasn't exactly subtle or dainty or soft-spoken. Wilhemina Tucker was descended from strong German peasant stock, and she had made a damn good farmer's wife for the last thirty years.

Tough, tenacious, tender-hearted. That was his mother.

And now he watched her brusque, stubborn face just crumple. Tears filled her eyes, and Danny hoped like hell he wouldn't embarrass himself in front of her by getting choked up too.

"Mom, this is Piper Danielle Schwartz, my daughter. Piper, this is Wilhemina Georgette Tucker, my mother."

"You can call me Grandma, sugar." And his mother bent down and enveloped Piper in a hug that could crack her ribs.

Piper didn't hug back. She just kind of stood there, stiff, biting her lip.

Fortunately, his mother didn't seem to notice. She stepped back and cupped Piper's cheeks with her hands. "I'm so glad to meet you."

Piper's face was enveloped with his mother's tan, farm-worn hands, her little lips compressed into an hourglass shape. His daughter looked nothing short of terrified.

His mother let go of her but started gushing. "We're

going to have so much fun, you and me. I always wanted a daughter."

"Gee, thanks, Mom." Danny rubbed his chin and went back to the eggs, cracking a second along with the first already in the bowl.

She waved her hand at him in dismissal. "Oh, you know what I mean. I wanted a daughter after you." Bending down, she looked at Piper's doll. "Well, she's a sad-looking thing. How about Grandma buys you a new one?"

Danny glanced back and saw Piper shake her head.

"No? Surely you would like a pretty new one with a nice dress and some long hair. And maybe a new hat for you while we're at it." His mother tried to take off Piper's hat, and Danny winced. Now he knew that was absolutely the worst thing to try.

He knew his mother was excited, but he thought she was taking the wrong tact. Piper was sensitive, and the only sensitive thing about Willie Tucker was her teeth when she drank ice water.

Piper was gripping her hat and looking terrified.

"Mom, I think she wants to keep her special things with her." Eventually his mother might figure out something was missing under Piper's hat, but he had promised his daughter he wouldn't tell anyone, and he meant to kept every promise made.

"Oh. Kind of like that grubby little blanket you had when you were little? You know I just kept cutting bits off the end of that until it was nothing but a square of cotton, and you finally lost it."

"And I'm still traumatized from that." He whisked the eggs and gave his mom a warning look. She was not handling this all that well. He wanted to shove an oven mitt in her mouth to shut her up.

"You going out in the field today?" his mother asked him, giving him a bewildered look that suggested she had no idea why he was wiggling his eyebrows.

"I need to. Got to check the soil in the south field, see if it needs watering."

"I can stay with Piper then. Give us time to get to know each other."

He nodded, thinking that was as good of a solution as he could find for now. He couldn't take Piper with him, and his mother would take care of her as well as he would.

Danny was dumping the eggs in the frying pan when Piper said, "No!"

Startled, he turned and found that she was right next to him, sliding between him and the stove like a rabbit wiggling under a fence.

"Watch the stove." He stuck his hand behind her head and pulled her toward his chest, thinking he should have used the back burner on the range to start cooking. The coils were so close to her head, it was a good thing she didn't have hair. It probably would have caught on fire.

Piper looked up at him with big, brown eyes. Doe eyes. Eyes that sucked him in, chewed him up, and spit him out until he felt like oatmeal. Mushy, gushy, sappy, sugary oatmeal.

"Can I stay with you?" she asked in a plaintive whisper.

Danny glanced over his shoulder at his mother, even as he dropped the spatula, turned off the burner, and wrapped his arm around Piper's shoulder blades. She felt so tiny against him, a paradox of soft and hard, smooth skin and bony angles.

His mom was looking bewildered. And a little *overwhelming*. Danny tried to see her through a child's eyes, and decided Willie Tucker could be intimidating. His mother was tall and broad, with big, shellacked hair the color of marigolds. She was wearing plastic pink earrings, a white shirt with pink stripes, and pink ankle-length pants. Her shoes were pink. Her lipstick was pink. The purse slung over her arm was shaped like a picnic basket, with a checked cloth liner in—imagine that—pink.

Not to mention that his mother had insulted Piper's hacked-hair Barbie.

With so much upheaval in her life, Piper was probably just scared again that she would get dumped, left behind, ignored. He had to give her stability, and he couldn't expect her to stay with someone she had just met and wasn't comfortable with yet.

"Of course you can stay with me. Why don't you run along and get dressed while I finish these eggs. Put your old shoes on because we're going to the fields." He gave her a squeeze then stepped back. "Your jean shorts and T-shirts are in the bag on the chair right there. I'll cut the tags off after you're dressed."

Piper gave a last glance at his mother, then ran across the room, grabbed the bag, and headed down the hall.

"You didn't wash the clothes first?" his mother said, with a horror he just couldn't share.

"I just bought them last night. There hasn't been time. And if you'd have seen her other stuff, you'd realize this is the lesser of two evils." Danny turned the burner back on and scrambled the eggs.

"Well, why did you let her run off? I want to see her. She's my grandbaby. And by the way, didn't your father ever talk to you about condoms?"

Danny's head snapped up at her annoyed tone, and he opened his mouth, not sure what was going to come out of it, but certain he wanted to prevent anything else from coming out of hers.

"For God's sake, Danny."

Too late.

"You got two girls pregnant in the same year. I thought we raised you better than that."

Despite being twenty-six years old, Danny felt a prickling of shame and a bucketful of embarrassment. This was still his mother, no matter that he was grown. And he *had* gotten two girls pregnant less than a year apart.

He spoke to the stove. "Mom, can we just not worry about that at this point? It's sort of irrelevant."

About the only thing that might be relevant was the knowledge that he had aggressive sperm, and that when women tell you they're on the pill, an extra measure of security should still be taken. Of course, that would only be necessary if he were having sex, which he wasn't.

He'd only had sex twice since his divorce, and both times he'd walked away thinking that getting naked and joining bodies with a woman he didn't love was a rather awkward experience.

Not that he wanted to share any of that with his mother.

"Of course it's relevant."

Uh-oh. His mother's finger had come out and was shaking at him. "You need to take responsibility for your actions. You need to be careful. I don't want any son of mine shooting sperm left and right like he's using the seed spreader in the fields."

Oh, God, there was an image. "Mom, I'm a grown man now and know all about responsibility. I was just a kid then."

She sniffed. "You weren't that much of a kid. You were having sex, weren't ya?"

He figured there was about no way to win this argument. "Can you keep it down, please? Piper will be back any second now."

His mother had already scared Piper; he didn't want her mentally scarred, too. At least not any more than she already was.

With a sigh, he tipped the pan to slide the eggs to a plate. They plopped in a heap on the hard, very breakable white plate, and he wondered if Piper was too young for a plate that heavy. There was a whole lot he didn't know about kids.

His mother took the frying pan away from him and dropped it in the sink, blasting it with cold water from the faucet. She pursed her lips. She frowned. She took a deep breath. Put her hand on her hip. "I'll send your father over to help you out for the next few days. Then you're going to have to get some kind of child care, or leave her with me."

He nodded. "Thanks. And I think in a few days Piper will warm up to you. She's just dealing with a lot all at once."

She reached for him, cupped his cheek and gave it a pat, even though she had to reach up to do it. "Danny, you're a good boy. Always have been. I'm proud of the way you're handling this."

That meant a lot to him. He was feeling a bit overwhelmed and a lot unsure of himself. He needed his parents on his side. He was about to say thank you, tell her he loved her, when she spoke again.

"But whatever you do, please be careful from here on out." She clicked open her purse and pulled out a big box of condoms. A thirty-six pack, with spermicide.

While he stood frozen in horror, she put them in his hand. "I'm begging you not to get the blonde pregnant."

Feeling dirty even holding condoms in his hand in his mother's presence, Danny tossed them in the closest kitchen drawer and rubbed his jaw. "What blonde?" He couldn't even imagine who his mother thought he was sleeping with. And for the record, he was old enough to know to buy condoms should the situation ever arise.

"Boston's friend. Amanda. Please be careful around her."

Amanda? His mother thought he was having sex with Amanda? What the hell had he done to make her think that?

He did want to have sex with Amanda. Real bad. In an unexplainable, lust-driven way. But his mother couldn't know that, and Amanda certainly didn't know that. He hoped. And he wasn't going to act on it.

Unless she wanted him to.

No, damn it, he wasn't going to act on it. He had Piper

to think about and a whole heap of troubles. Amanda was more than a heap of trouble. She was the *Titanic* of troubles.

"Mom, trust me. I am not going to get Amanda pregnant." The very thought made him break into a cold sweat. Good God, he couldn't even imagine blending genes with Amanda. It would be like breeding a poodle and a Labrador, a mixed breed nature had never intended. They'd wind up with a Labradoodle.

"Umm-hmm." His mother pursed her lips and raised an eyebrow. "I bet that's exactly what you told Shelby and Nina Schwartz. Right before you knocked them up."

Chapter 6

𝒜manda was in a mood.

It had been an entire week since her father had cut her off, and things weren't going quite according to plan.

She punched her pillow and rolled to the left one more time. She was turning and jerking in bed so much she had probably lost five pounds. Which normally would be a cause for celebration. Frankly, right now she needed to maintain her fat stores.

Fifty bucks hadn't bought her a whole hell of a lot of groceries, and she was starving. In agony. Her stomach growled around the clock, and she spent all her time focused on when she could reasonably eat again without depleting her meager supplies. She ate a lot of cereal. She chewed a lot of celery. And her only source of protein was licking peanut butter off a spoon at three o'clock every day.

Samson wouldn't hire her, tight-fisted bastards that they were. They claimed there were no positions available, but she suspected her father had given instructions not to help her.

Finally, yesterday she had managed to wrangle a job at Hair by Harriet as a receptionist, and it had gone reasonably well if you didn't count that little incident over Mrs. Bitterman's perm.

Amanda had tried to keep her mouth shut, honestly she had, but perms were so nineteen-eighty-seven that she had suggested Mrs. B might want some color instead and a kicky little haircut. The next thing she knew, the old lady was leaving in a huff and Harriet wasn't Happy Harriet.

But she hadn't fired her, so Amanda took that as a vote of confidence. Even if she made it through another day, and another, answering the phone and booking appointments, Harriet said she wouldn't get paid for another two weeks. That just wasn't physically possible since she had to eat *something*.

Deprivation didn't suit her.

Neither did lack of sleep, and if that chick in the mirror didn't stop crying all night every night, she was going to find a baseball bat and send it right through the glass.

Loony Lady was at it again tonight.

"That's it." Amanda sat up, her monogrammed tank top and shorty shorts both riding up. The shirt had a large hot pink A on the left side, and the shorts spelled out AMANDA across her ass, which struck her as extraordinarily stupid. Anyone seeing her from behind while she was in her pajamas damn well better remember her name.

Baby yipped to be let down off the bed, so Amanda scooped her up. "We're telling this ghost-bitch from hell to do her crying during daylight hours. That as humans, we still require sleep."

Tossing her hair over her shoulder, she stomped across the wood floor, catching a blast from the floor fan on her way past. Baby sneezed on her arm.

"Lovely." She wiped her now-damp skin on her shorts

and headed toward the back bedroom, where the wailing and moaning had been occurring on an extremely regular basis since that first night she'd heard it.

As usual, there was nothing in the mirror but a cloudy film in front of her own image. But that noise was coming from somewhere, and Amanda figured Miss Maudlin could use a little pep talk.

"Listen, babe, I understand that your husband deceived you, murdered, stole, and yada, yada, yada. But I should think after a hundred years you'd be over it. He's not coming back, and if he did, you shouldn't even consider taking him back. Have some self-respect. Have some dignity."

Amanda realized she was talking a little loud with excessive hand gestures, but of course she was reminded of that dickhead Logan, who had been quite the liar himself. It still rankled that she had let down her guard, that she had retreated into the naiveté of her teen years and blithely trusted him and his feelings.

He had adored her, she had thought, and she had been quite smug and happy in that knowledge. She had even allowed herself to think that maybe, just maybe, there could be a husband and happiness in her future. That she could find some sort of purpose in loving him.

Then she had heard him on the phone, obviously talking to a woman who wasn't a relative or a coworker. The "I can't wait to see you so I can fuck you again" had been something of a dead giveaway.

But worse than that, truly, was that he had then critiqued her, Amanda. And she hadn't scored well according to him. On the sexual SATs she couldn't even get into community college with that pitiful showing. Logan had said she gave lousy oral sex, was too flat-chested, had an annoying habit of raking her nails down his back, and was only tolerable because of the money he expected to siphon off during their relationship.

It had been brutal. Humiliating. And it left her questioning her abilities to read people and doubting if she could ever fully trust someone again.

One thing she knew without a doubt.

Never again would her attention, focus, future be determined by a man, her father or otherwise.

She was Amanda Margaret Delmar—hear her roar, damn it.

The thought of Logan and his deception made her physically ill. Or that could be her empty stomach rebelling. But either way, she forced herself to lower her voice, relax her shoulders.

"Listen to me. Do you think your husband is crying, wherever he is? He probably spent all that money, living it up, and didn't give you two thoughts. Just like my ex-boyfriend isn't giving me two thoughts. And my father hasn't even bothered to call and see if I'm alive or dead."

Stroking Baby's trembling body, she thought the crying softened a little, but she couldn't really tell. "Now I've got to go to sleep, and I'm asking you to please keep it down. I have no money. None. I'm penniless. I need this job to buy food before I start to look like a *Survivor* cast-off."

The pitiful wailing cut off, like the stop button on the CD player had been pressed.

"Thank you." Amanda turned with a yawn and started to count shoes in her head to relax herself. Sheep were so toddler. She got to a sunshine yellow pair by Bebe when something passed in front of her in a blur and dropped onto the floor in the hallway.

"What the hell now? If that was a spider, Baby, I expect you to eat it. I can't handle spiders at midnight when I'm starving and broke." She had her limits, and she had just about reached them.

But it wasn't a spider. It was a penny. A shiny, coppery penny, looking never used and stamped with the date nineteen ninety-seven on it.

"Okay. Where did this come from?" Twirling it in her

fingers, she looked around. It could have fallen off the door frame to the extra bedroom she wasn't using, but it wasn't dusty. Nor could she imagine why someone would put a penny on a door frame, but it seemed like the only explanation, and there was no understanding some people's actions.

Another penny blurred past her as it fell to the floor. Hello. Where had that one come from? "Getting freaked out here."

Baby was tense, her body taut and poised to attack.

Amanda took a glance up, and watched in utter amazement as another penny fell out of the ceiling, dropped all the way to the floor, then rolled to a stop by the bathroom door. She rubbed her eyes, squinted a bit. Maybe she was hallucinating, going into insulin shock from not drinking coffee or eating sugary desserts for the last week.

Because she could swear that penny had dropped right out of the plaster ceiling.

The next one hit her in the eye.

It was very real, and it had very much fallen out of nothing.

"Okay, time for bed." Amanda took one last glance at the three pennies resting on the floor, and dropped the one in her hand to the floor. She padded toward her bedroom.

She hoped her father was happy. She had gone insane.

Next she'd be wearing her thong on the outside of her dress and talking to pigeons.

She was just going to go to sleep, and in the morning those pennies would be gone.

Or not.

When Amanda came out of her bedroom in the morning, thinking only of a hot shower before she had to head to Harriet's at nine, she stepped on a whole pile of pennies.

They stuck to her foot, scattered left and right, and towered so high that Baby had to execute a fence jump to clear the pile.

"Ummm . . ." This was an interesting development.

One that was too strange and unbelievable to think about for any length of time. Amanda squatted down and started counting.

At six hundred and twelve, she sat back on her butt and looked at the little stacks she had made of ten pennies each row. "Hot damn. I have six dollars and twelve cents."

She was going to take these pennies and buy herself a whopping king-size cup of coffee this morning, and she planned to do it quickly. Before the pennies disappeared the same way they had originated.

Unfortunately, Amanda bought too large of a cup of coffee. She couldn't get her hand wrapped around the cup with a solid grip, and while offering a magazine to a customer who was so old she was shriveled like a raisin, Amanda dropped the coffee. Right into the woman's lap.

Slow reflexes, dulled by a century of living, further exasperated the problem, so that the old woman wound up with a huge wet spot across her crotch and an angry red burn on her wrist.

"Oh, I'm so sorry!" Amanda set down her cup on the reception desk and looked around for paper towels or something. Whoops. This might be worse than the whole perm incident of the day before.

The little old lady, who had been sweetly sitting in the first station to wait for her stylist, morphed like Linda Blair in the *Exorcist*.

"Clumsy idiot! Get me a blow-dryer. I can't leave the store like this—it looks like my Depends failed." She craned her neck. "Harriet? Harriet! Where is that fat fool?"

Appalled at her own clumsiness and the woman's nasty reaction, Amanda just stood there wondering what the hell had happened to her life. Maybe if she clicked her heels three times, she'd wake up back in her four-poster bed in her tasteful, understated apartment in Chicago. She could go shopping on Michigan Avenue. Hit Sugar, one of her favorite bar hang-outs.

But she wasn't in Kansas anymore.

Damn it.

Harriet bumbled over, looking angry, flustered, and out of breath. "What on earth happened here, Miss Raeleen?"

"This incompetent spilled her coffee on me. At my age, I could have had a heart attack, or a stroke, not to mention this is my best dress, new only three years ago. I absolutely demand that you fire her." A bony knuckle with dangling skin pointed at Amanda.

She couldn't help but snort. And her father thought she was a drama queen? This biddy had her beat.

"I'm really sorry. It was just an accident." Amanda was trying to think of the proper restitution to offer the old bag, when Harriet turned to her, tight-lipped and determined.

"You're fired, Amanda. I'll pay you for yesterday, but you can collect your things and leave now."

"What?" Amanda just stared at Harriet. She couldn't be serious. And the ruin of that woman's ugly, flowers-on-acid-looking dress wasn't any great loss.

"You're just not up to snuff. I expect superior skills from my employees."

Amanda looked around her at the mottled assortment of aging, overweight beauticians shuffling around in their thick-soled orthopedic sneakers, tissues tucked into the sleeves of their blouses. She just had to wonder . . . superior skill at what? Creating immovable hair that could withstand hurricane-force winds?

"Okay, fine, whatever, Harriet. You can calculate my pay while I get my purse from the back." Baby was probably lonely at home, anyway. She wasn't used to being by herself.

Amanda refused to sigh. She refused to worry. And nothing would make her whine. She got her purse, collected her forty dollars, which seemed so not worth a whole day at work, and went outside to look up her cousin's number on her cell phone. She was so done.

Brady Stritmeyer was in front of the door, leaning on a

pair of crutches, his low-hanging shorts drooping over a leg cast.

"Hey, Brady." Amanda dug in her purse for her sunglasses, the intense sun prickling her skin and making her eyes water. "What happened to your leg?"

Brady was Shelby's cousin and about ten years younger than Amanda. They had struck up an odd sort of friendship almost immediately, though she hadn't seen him since her Time of Troubles had begun.

Hovering on his crutches, he flicked his head, sending a lock of blue hair to the side and out of his eyes. "I'm telling everyone I fell playing basketball."

Amanda smiled at his wording. "But what really happened?"

"I was in Joelle's bedroom, uh, without parental permission, and when her dad started to come in, I went out the window. Got my foot caught in my pants and fell off the side of the house. Went down about ten feet. It hurt like a motherfucker."

She had to laugh. "Oh, my God, you idiot." It wasn't hard to picture Brady lying flat on his back in a bush, groaning. "Did her father figure it out, or did you get away?"

"My leg snapped like a twig, man, of course I got caught. I was stuck there all helpless like the gingerbread boy in *Shrek*." He shuddered and patted his shorts pocket. Brady drew out his cigarettes and offered her one.

"No, thanks." Amanda moved to the side when a customer came to the door of Harriet's. "I'd better sit down. I just got fired by Harriet, and if I hang around she'll probably call the cops and claim I'm loitering or something." She dropped onto the bench next to the door.

"I got an appointment, but I'm really early." Brady pointed to his head, resting on his crutches as he flicked on his lighter. "Going to go red. I'm tired of blue."

"That'll look cool. So are you playing the sympathy

card with Joelle? You can tell her you broke your leg in pursuit of her love." Amanda thought leaping out of a window had been a really stupid thing to do, but at the same time, she wondered what it would feel like to have a boy or a man so enamored of you he would sneak into your room, risking life and limb.

No man had ever risked anything for her, except maybe surpassing his credit card limit. Men always bought her things, but it didn't mean anything. Money was easy. Money was always there, available, to the guys she'd gone out with.

A diamond bracelet from them meant nothing more than Brady Stritmeyer offering her a cigarette from his pack.

Emotion, love—those had never been offered to her. And she had to wonder why. Was she so inherently unlovable that no one would ever climb the side of a two-story house for her?

It sure in the hell seemed that way.

Brady snorted, smoke filtering out his nose in a pungent cloud as he gingerly lowered himself onto the bench next to her. He dropped a knapsack at his feet. "Nope. Joelle gave me no sympathy. None. Told me I was stupid to be sneaking into her room like that and that I deserved everything I got after she told me not to do it." He shook his head. "She was a nag anyway—always talking about getting married. We're done."

Such was teenage love. But it still made Amanda sigh. "I'm sorry."

"Don't be. Joelle was my first serious girlfriend, and I'll always have feelings for her, but it's time to move on." He grinned. "And Abby Murphy's been coming around the house with cookies for me. *She* feels sorry for me."

She wished she could be so prosaic. Logan was a prick, but it was time to move on. Yet it festered and burned and irritated her, the feelings of self-doubt he had inspired in her. Or maybe not inspired, just illuminated. Maybe she had always doubted herself.

Maybe that was why she had never pursued a real job in art.

Maybe that was why right now she was considering taking her forty dollars and buying a bus ticket to Chicago to throw herself at the mercy of her father.

"So what are you going to do, Amanda? If word gets around that the biddy fired you, you'll have a hard time finding another job. I'll loan you the cash if you want to get back to Chicago."

Amanda stared at Brady, at the sincerity in his eyes. He meant it. He would loan her the money, no questions asked, no concerns if he'd see it ever again, all on the basis of a minor friendship.

"That's sweet of you . . ." But how could she do that? How could she take money from a fifteen-year-old, who came from a modest, hardworking family, and slink back home to mooch off her wealthy father?

She couldn't. She just couldn't.

It was time to get serious. It was time to find a job—and keep it this time—and scrape together some money. It was time to see if she could stand on her own two feet, or topple off them.

"But I'm staying." And not because it would be the last thing her father would be expecting, but because she needed to prove to herself that she could.

Right as the words left her mouth, she looked up and saw Danny Tucker crossing the street, Piper's hand in his.

A father and his daughter.

And it made her think that maybe there really was such a thing as hope buried deep inside her, hidden under the layers of disappointment and the calluses around her heart.

Chapter 7

*D*anny hoped he didn't look desperate as he led Piper over to where Amanda was holding down a bench in front of Harriet's hair salon.

But he was feeling a little desperate.

He wanted to do this right, raising his daughter, and didn't want anyone thinking he couldn't handle it. But Piper wouldn't leave his side. And while that thrilled him on the one hand, after a solid week of carting her around the farm, and her showing no signs of ever being willing to let him out of his sight, he was starting to get concerned.

There was work to do, and not all of it could be done with an eight-year-old girl standing next to him.

Part of him wished he could just blow off the work and hang out with Piper. He liked her quiet company and was enjoying getting to know her. She was a smart little thing and eager for love. He was eager to give it.

But the reality was that while a crop could grow on its own, it needed a human hand to harvest it. The corn in the north field was ready to be brought in, and he just couldn't see having Piper around heavy equipment. He'd taken a few weeks off from his part-time construction job, but eventually he'd need to go back, especially with the added expenses of Piper's needs.

He wished none of it were the case—that he could stay with his daughter day in, day out for a good, solid year or two to make up for lost time, but life didn't work that way.

"There's Amanda." Piper pointed and waved, a broken smile crossing her face.

Danny thought there was something cruelly ironic that the one person Piper had said she'd be willing to stay with was Amanda Delmar, probably the least likely candidate for a babysitter in all of Cuttersville.

Seeing her sitting there with Brady only confirmed it. She was wearing white pants and a sleeveless clingy beige top. And the requisite heels, of course. Not exactly nanny-wear. And no one on a farm wore white unless they were getting married.

But Piper seemed to have formed an attachment to Amanda, probably because her first night in Cuttersville they had gone shopping with her. Like when animals bonded with the first creature they saw upon hatching, Piper liked Amanda.

Whatever the reason, Amanda was the only person Piper was willing to stay with, and Danny had to figure out how exactly to ask an heiress to babysit his daughter.

"She must be on a break from working at the hair salon. You can run on over and say hi." Danny had told Piper they were coming to town so he could get a haircut. Which was true, he did need a little trim. He usually went to the barber, not Harriet's, but he had been hoping to accost Amanda and beg her for mercy and babysitting.

Now that he was three feet in front of her, he wasn't sure he could go through with it. Begging Amanda for anything was a bit too carnal for comfort.

Amanda was smiling at his daughter and patting the bench next to her for Piper to sit down. "Hi, Piper."

Then her eyes slid up to his. "Hi, Danny," she said in a totally different tone of voice than the one she'd used for Piper. That had been friendly, cheerful. The way she said his name was . . . sexy.

Which made what he was going to ask her even harder. Why couldn't Piper feel comfortable with his mother, or even a matronly middle-age woman with a fanny pack full of healthy snacks? He couldn't handle a sexy babysitter. He just couldn't. He needed to feel comfortable with the situation, and he had never once felt comfortable around Amanda Delmar.

He usually felt more like his skin was too tight and his pants were too small, which was not the least bit comfortable.

"Hey, Amanda. Brady. What happened to your leg?"

"I broke it two days ago. Playing basketball."

Amanda snorted and draped her arm around Piper's shoulders. "What are you two up to? Is your dad taking you for ice cream? The place across the street has fabulous twist cones."

Piper sucked in her breath and looked at him with beseeching eyes. "Are we getting ice cream?"

"Sure, baby girl, we can get ice cream." That was the closest Piper had ever come to asking him for anything, and there was no way he could deny her. Even though he suspected Amanda had set him up, given the unholy grin on her face.

"Do you work here?" Piper asked Amanda, pointing to the hair salon. "Do you cut hair and paint nails and stuff?"

The interest in the question made Danny stiffen. Was Piper about to go girly on him? He kind of liked her scuffed and dusty, wiping her hands on her jean shorts after she ate each meal. While he thought he was adjusting pretty darn well to fatherhood, he wasn't quite up for painting nails and doing hair clips yet.

But then Amanda said, "No, I don't work here anymore. I got fired for dropping my coffee in some old lady's lap by accident. Know anyone who is hiring, kiddo?"

She nudged Piper with her hip, and Danny couldn't believe his good fortune. Or misfortune, however you wanted to look at it. Amanda didn't have a job. He had one he could offer her.

And he was almost desperate.

Piper shrugged. "I don't know anybody but you and my dad and Shelby and Boston and my grandma and grandpa."

"You going back to Chicago, Amanda?" Danny held his breath as the three of them became distracted by Brady pulling out a pack of gum.

First, the pack had to be passed around. Then everyone unwrapped, started chewing, and the foil wrappers were collected by Amanda, who stood up and dropped them in the trash outside the door to Harriet's.

"No, I'm not going back to Chicago."

Danny moved fast, sliding up behind her, blocking her from returning to the bench. He had to keep Piper from hearing what he had to say. If Amanda said no, he didn't want Piper to hear.

Plus he didn't want Piper to hear her father begging Amanda to reconsider.

♡

Amanda jerked back and hit the trash can with her butt. Jesus, she hadn't expected him to be right behind her like that.

Danny was completely in her personal space. And when a man like Danny moved into your space, there wasn't any air left to even breathe. Nor could she see the sky any longer, given that his shoulders were blocking out the sun.

Assuming he had trash to dump, she tried to sidle past him. He cut her off by moving right in front of her again. She stepped on his foot by accident and bounced her breast off his shoulder.

"Did you need something?" she said, a little irritated. Obviously, he had no idea what he did to her hormones or he would stay back a minimum of twelve feet. Obviously, she did not have the same effect on him, given that her breast could collide with his arm and he didn't even blink.

Of course, he probably hadn't even felt it, since according to Logan, she was two cups shy of a full bra.

Well, she was who she was and Danny Tucker could just get over it—she was not going to put those implants back in for any man, least of all a farmer. Not that he had asked. But the implication was there. Sort of.

"What?" she said, when he still didn't answer her, just sort of rubbed his jaw and avoided meeting her eyes.

"I'm sorry Harriet's didn't work out for you. But I do know of another job if you're interested."

"You do?" Amanda was immediately suspicious. She wasn't milking cows or anything gross like that. Or feeding chickens. She had to draw the line somewhere. "What's the job?"

"Child care and light housekeeping."

That didn't sound too horrible. In fact, it didn't sound bad at all. So why was he looking like a defendant on *Judge Judy*? Guilty as hell.

"How many kids?" She had serious doubts about her ability to handle more than say, two. And she didn't think a baby would be such a hot idea, either. Her experience with infants was limited to Baby's puppyhood, and she didn't think there were a lot of similarities. People probably frowned on you sticking a leash on a baby so it didn't crawl away.

"Just one."

"For who?" The town loon? Drunk? Postmaster General? Why was Danny looking so weird?

"Me. Babysitting Piper and keeping my house clean."

Amanda chewed the gum and sucked back the excess saliva that seemed to have puddled in her cheek. Damn

Juicy Fruit. It had her drooling. Not Danny. He couldn't make her drool.

Much.

"Really? Why do you need a babysitter?" This gig sounded too good to be true. He was willing to pay her to hang around his house and paint Piper's fingernails? It sounded as easy as Britney Spears.

Danny rubbed his chin again, making her want to run and find a razor and shave it so he'd quit touching it, looking sexy.

"Piper is a little, um, uncomfortable staying with just anyone. My mom is kind of intimidating, and I don't really trust anyone else. And well, Piper likes you. She said she'd stay with you while I'm in the fields."

Let's see. Play with the kid. Ogle Danny on his tractor. And get paid to do it. "I'm your girl. When do I start?"

"Don't you want to know the salary?"

That made her laugh. "You can't possibly be paying me less than Harriet. And considering I'm down to my last forty-three dollars, I can't exactly hold out for top scale." A frightening thought suddenly occurred to her. One that made her chest do that funny tingle thing again, and her thong suddenly seem a little too invasive. "You don't want me to live in your house, do you?"

Danny's jaw dropped. "Oh, God, no. You can just work nine to five every day. I'll pick you up every morning."

Nice to see the thought of her being under the same roof as him struck horror in his heart. She was a decent person. A little selfish sometimes, but it wasn't like she was black mold. She wasn't going to *harm* him, damn it.

But pride aside, she really did need the job. She was not going to slink back to her father, hand out. "Can I bring my dog?"

"Sure."

"Then we have a deal." Amanda stuck out her hand.

Danny gripped it, his hand swallowing hers. "Deal. Can you start today, after lunch?"

"Absolutely."

Then they pumped up and down with their interlocked hands, and Amanda struggled for nonchalance. His skin was rough, so masculine, so raw, so goddamn big, and his thumb was moving in a way it shouldn't be moving for a regular, friendly little handshake. It was doing all sorts of interesting wayward strokes and tickles, and she was getting a little hot under the midday sun, and God, what would it feel like to be under a man like Danny Tucker?

Her breath shortened, her shoulders leaned forward, and she found herself fixating on Danny's bottom lip.

"Amanda . . ." he said, his voice low and husky.

"Yes?" *Touch me, touch me, touch me.*

"You'd better take those pants off."

"Excuse me?" Granted, she'd been thinking along those same lusty lines, but they were on the sidewalk here.

"And change into flat shoes. Piper's easy to care for, but heels on a farm probably aren't such a great idea." Danny gave a pointed look at her shoes.

Right. Of course. Uugghh. Amanda willed herself not to take off the spiky heel and ram it up Danny's nose. She was thinking of the tongue tango, and he was worried about her wardrobe. "Daisy Duke always wore heels. If she can handle it, so can I."

Danny looked like he had absolutely no reply to that. Good.

Piper shoved a piece of paper into his face, distracting both of them. "Look what Brady drew."

"Hey, that's you." Danny turned the paper around for Amanda to see. "It's looks just like you, Piper—gorgeous. I didn't know you could draw, Brady."

Amanda sucked in a breath. Holy handbag, he was good. In what—five minutes—Brady had sketched Piper in charcoal. He had completely captured the angles of her face, the melancholy sorrow in her eyes, the aching hopefulness.

Still on the bench, Brady shrugged. "I just fool around with it."

Amanda turned and gaped at him. "Well, you shouldn't. You should get serious. You have real talent."

"How would you know?"

"Four years of college studying art, that's how." If she knew anything, it was discerning value from worthless, whether it was clothes or jewelry or art. The exception to that was men. With men, she was having a hard time distinguishing the fakes from the originals. Which was why it was a damn good thing Danny hadn't acted on her desire for him to kiss her.

Brady just shrugged again. Geez, five minutes with Piper and he'd picked up her body language.

"Do you have anything else you've done?" She would like to send some of his work to her cousin Stuart in New York, who owned a gallery. Well, her dad owned it, but Stuart ran it.

"Not really. I scratch out stuff, but I don't usually keep them. There are some up at the high school, but mostly I just throw them away."

Teenagers. She was about to give him a nasty lecture about taking opportunities given to him, unlike her, and maybe kicking his broken leg if he got lippy, when Piper spoke.

"Can you draw the ghosts?"

Every head turned to stare at her. "What ghosts?" Danny asked.

"The ones who live in Shelby and Boston's house." Piper readjusted her baseball hat. Amanda couldn't believe Danny was still letting her wear that nasty thing.

But Piper's next words ripped her thoughts off dirty headwear.

"I've seen them, you know. And I think they would like it if you drew their picture, Brady."

While they were all staring at her blankly, digesting this,

she added, "They told me no one pays them any mind, and it hurts their feelings."

Amanda thought this was an interesting twist to her life. Not only was it completely and utterly unbelievable that she was going to be a nanny, she was going to be responsible for a female Haley Joel Osment.

"She sees dead people," she told Danny. "Somehow I'm guessing she didn't inherit that from you."

Danny looked about as here-and-now, rock-solid real as any man was capable of.

He made Michelangelo's *David* look like a femme.

And she'd bet her last forty-three dollars he didn't see ghosts, in mirrors or otherwise.

"I don't suppose she did. But it makes her way more interesting than I am."

Amanda wasn't having any problem finding him interesting. Which was a disaster.

If she was going to take this job and prove to herself, her father, the world, that she was capable of earning a wage, then she couldn't be dallying with her boss like a nineteenth-century British chambermaid.

Not that Danny looked like dallying. He looked like he had far more important things on his mind. Like his daughter and his dinner.

But if he did dally, she'd be damned if she'd dally back.

So maybe the dead people thing was a positive, actually. Dead people would probably serve as a great sexual inhibitor.

God, she needed another cup of coffee.

Chapter 8

"Geez, this house is dusty. You should get someone in here to clean it."

For a long second, Danny really thought Amanda was joking. A cute little witticism that seemed right in line with her sense of humor.

But as she continued to survey his living room like she had discovered a three-thousand-strong army of cockroaches marching through a cloud of chemicals, he realized that she was perfectly serious.

Which confirmed that he was out of his ever-lovin' mind to think this could work.

"That's why I hired *you*, Amanda. To clean the house and keep an eye on Piper." He watched her eyes go wide with astonishment.

"But I thought you said housekeeping. I'm positive that's what you said."

Suddenly, he wanted to laugh. "I did. What did you think housekeeping meant? It means cleaning the house."

Piper had scampered off to her room, so they were alone in the living room, though Amanda's gigantic purse took up two feet between them. Amanda was clutching it, her eyes narrowed, her head tilted slightly like she just wasn't getting it.

"I thought you meant I was going to be your house-keeper, and the housekeeper's job is to hire the people who do the gross stuff. The housekeeper doesn't actually do the gross stuff. You know, like *Gosford Park*."

Now he did laugh. She looked so confused, and so deliciously sexy standing there in her fancy striped top and her spotless white pencil-shaped pants, he couldn't help but tease her a little. "Princess, maybe that's what a housekeeper does in *Gosford Park* or in Chicago, but here in Cuttersville, a housekeeper cleans the toilets."

"Oh my God," she said, her cheeks bleaching white under her tan. "You want me to clean the toilets?"

"Well, there's only one. It's a small house."

"But you . . . use the toilet!"

He grinned. "That's kind of the reason it gets dirty. We use it."

Then he realized maybe his teasing hadn't had the right effect. She looked like she might faint or throw up. "Are you okay?"

"No. I'm seeing spots and the room keeps fading in and out." She clutched her bag like it was the only thing keeping her from sliding to the ground.

"Jesus, I'm sorry, I was kidding, Amanda." He reached out and grabbed her forearms so she wouldn't hit the carpet. "I don't expect you to clean the toilets. Just dust, vacuum, wash the dishes. That sort of thing. Light housekeeping."

She took a deep, shuddering breath. "Okay. Dust, vacuum, wash the dishes. I can do that. And I would have cleaned the toilets, that's not what made me dizzy."

With a stubborn lift of her head, she told him, "I didn't

eat lunch, that's all. I could clean the hell out of any toilet. I'd be so good at it that the next time that toilet saw me, it would just clean itself out of fear."

Only by coughing into his hand did he keep from laughing. He could just picture Amanda ordering that toilet to clean itself. "Why didn't you eat lunch?"

"I just didn't get around to it." She waved his question off and dropped her purse onto the coffee table. "Okay, so where's like a rag or something? I'll dust this room, then I'm going to check out Piper's room. She and I can hang while I make like Cinderella."

Amanda's cheeks still looked a little white, and Danny had the sudden sinking feeling that she hadn't eaten because she was out of money. Only he suspected she would never admit that. "Are you trying to impress me? I can give you a tour of everything first."

She snorted. "Just doing my job. It's what you're paying me for. Bring on the dirt."

Though Danny had some real reservations that he'd be getting his money's worth out of this, he went to the coat closet by the front door and pulled out a blue milk crate filled with cleaning supplies. "Here." He plunked it at her feet, still tilted at an unnatural angle in high heels. "Rags, furniture polish, Windex, paper towels. The vacuum is in the closet. I figure it shouldn't take you more than an hour every day to keep the house picked up and clean—I want your focus to be on playing with Piper."

Though he thought things were going well for the most part, it stuck in his craw that Piper still seemed to think living with him was temporary. She didn't want to unpack her clothes into the dresser, and she showed no interest in meeting other kids. It was ridiculous for him to expect her to just move on in with him after eight years—never having met him—and be ready to trust him, but damn it, he wanted it to be that way.

He wanted her to love him right now. He wanted her to throw herself into his arms, not out of fear, but out of joy.

He wanted to turn back time and have her from day one, and give her a proper home, with a family who cared.

Instead, he was giving her Amanda Delmar for a nanny. God help them all.

Amanda was picking through the crate, pulling out bottles and reading their labels. "Okay, hold twelve inches from object and spray for three seconds. Wipe with cloth. Repeat as necessary."

Danny shook his head, half amused, half horrified. He wasn't going to let her anywhere near the laundry. There were no written directions for separating whites from darks. "I'm going to go fix us all some lunch." He didn't think he could stand around and witness her bumbling her way through dusting.

It would either make him laugh, which would insult her, or he'd wind up grabbing the rag out of her hand and doing it himself.

Not that he was any kind of domestic god. And he had let the house go since Piper had moved in, preferring to spend all his time with her, but he could clean as necessary. His mother wouldn't have had it any other way. Willie Tucker didn't approve of gender roles.

"Yes, sir." Amanda saluted him with the Pledge bottle. "Everything is under control."

That was debatable.

Especially when she pushed the button and shot out a three-foot-long vapor cloud of furniture polish in the general direction of the coffee table. A sprinkling landed on the table—the rest scattered all over the sofa and the carpet.

"Whoa, that stuff has a real kickback on it."

He moved toward the table, fingers itching to rip the bottle out of her hand. "You like ham?" Sandwiches were probably all he could manage on short notice.

"Sure. What's a little pig between friends?" she said,

clearly distracted with swatting the cloth around on the table, holding it at arm's length and being careful not to get her white pants dirty.

Danny skirted the coffee table and went down the hall, hoping to draw Piper out of her room and into the kitchen. She had taken to spending long stretches of time in her room, and it made him nervous, like she didn't want to be with him. Like she wasn't happy with him.

"Nice doily," Amanda said.

Danny looked over to where she was shifting a lace thing on the end table under the lamp. It occurred to him that his house must look a little ridiculous from her point of view. Here she was used to expensive hotels and hiring decorators to create the perfect home, and he had a poky little ranch house with plaid sofas and a few girly touches left over from his marriage to Shelby.

He wondered if Amanda had her own house or apartment or if she lived with her father still. "Shelby used to like those things."

"I should have guessed. They're doily-heavy at their house."

Danny hovered in the doorway that led to his three small bedrooms. "You probably have a house that's five times this size."

She shrugged, moving the rag across the table, then swatting the lampshade with enough force to make him wince. He wasn't emotionally attached to the lamp or anything—it was just an old brass job with a beige shade—but it gave good light and he didn't feel like spending the money to replace it. Cash was tight right now while he tried to get Piper everything she needed.

"My father has a big house in Lake Forest. An appropriately pretentious contemporary wonder, with lots of windows and leather and glass sculptures. I don't live there anymore though. Daddy pays for an apartment in the city for me. It's smaller than this house, but I do like it. I've decorated it with nice cozy furniture, sort of shabby chic meets modern. Lots of color, patterns, some art I picked out in Paris."

Art in Paris. Doilies in Cuttersville. It said all there was to say. Even if he were wildly attracted to Amanda, which he was, the doily spoke volumes. She was out of his league. She was so far out she might as well be on the freaking moon.

"I kind of miss my stuff, but there's something to be said for earning my own money. It makes what I buy matter more."

"That's true. Maybe that's why I'm not all that attached to anything in this house. It's not really mine. I got hand-me-downs from my mom and then Shelby picked out a few things. But we didn't have a lot of money in those days, and she didn't have a lot to work with." He looked around the somewhat sparse, definitely haphazard room. "I didn't buy anything for the house, and it's never really felt quite like home."

He knew what he'd been waiting for. Since Tucker farmers weren't exactly known for their decorating skill, he'd been waiting for a woman. He'd been waiting for a wife, and this time around he'd had the idea that they could shop together, pick some things out.

She'd say things like, *I just love this burgundy sofa. What do you think, Danny?* And he'd say, *Looks good to me.* And they'd both be happy.

But he hadn't found a woman he wanted to marry—or hell, any woman who had wanted to marry him—and now he had Piper. Marriage wasn't going to be in his future, at least not for a long time.

"You just need a jumping point." Amanda pointed to his fishing trophy that adorned the mantel. "Like removing this and putting it in the basement."

"Hey, I caught a nine-pound bass."

"How exciting. But it belongs in a den. Maybe it's time to get a big-boy living room. I can help you."

Oh, no, here was her helping hand again. That kind of assistance had almost gotten him kicked out of Wal-Mart. "Yeah, right. You'll have me decked out in flowers or something. And I don't have ten grand to blow on my décor." He gave a fruity little shake of his hand to show her just what he thought about florals.

"As if I would pick florals for you. I would have you so completely styling, on a budget, with a very masculine, very sexy house."

"I don't need my house to be sexy." Damn, did she have to use that word?

"You can't bring women here like this. They'll see that you're a certified bachelor looking for a woman to build his nest. That's too much pressure. And I haven't seen your bedroom or bathroom yet, but if this layer of dust is any indication, you can't be having a woman spend the night."

"It's clean," he said defensively.

Amanda lifted her eyebrow at the same time she lifted the white rag, which was now the color of topsoil.

"And I can't have women spend the night anyway," he hissed in a whisper, then realized plural could imply something kinky. "*A woman* spend the night. I have a daughter."

"Yeah. And I can only imagine how pathetic *her* room looks."

She had him there. "Well, it does leave a lot to be desired. It was a catch-all room before, and I haven't quite gotten everything out of there yet."

"Let me see." She pushed past him, rag held out, hand up. Her hair swished down her half-naked back. When she reached Piper's doorway, she sucked in her breath. "Oh, poor baby, don't worry. Auntie Amanda's here to make it alright."

Piper looked up from playing with her balding Barbie on a comforter that had hound dogs on it. The bookcase stuffed with farming manuals and old copies of *Fishing World* hovered dark and dusty behind her. One lacy, yellowed curtain hung in the window, and the dresser was stacked with Piper's new clothes since Danny hadn't had a chance to empty the drawers yet. They contained old T-shirts that he wore when painting the barn or snaking the pipes.

So it wasn't exactly a little girl's dream room. It wasn't that he didn't want to give Piper the world—God knew he wanted that more than anything—but he just hadn't had *time*. "Okay, it's a little sad, but I haven't had a chance to do anything about it. Not enough hours in the day."

Amanda got a gleam in her eye that sort of scared him. "But now you have a housekeeper. And I'm cleaning house, starting right here."

Which was how twenty minutes later Danny found himself standing behind Amanda eating a ham sandwich while she navigated her way around Potterybarnkids.com on his computer.

This was going to cost him.

But seeing Piper's face light up as Amanda pointed out room after overdone room, he knew it would be worth any price.

♡

Amanda couldn't believe how fabulous she was at this job. She should have never doubted herself.

Aside from the little misunderstanding over the toilets, she was on the job, handling the whole thing like she'd been born to be a housekeeper/child-care-giver. She was Alice from the *Brady Bunch* without the bun and stupid blue dress.

Crumbs rained down on her arm as Danny bit his sandwich.

"Sorry," he said, looking a little embarrassed. He reached down and brushed her arm rapidly. "We should probably be eating in the kitchen."

"This can't wait. This is a shopping emergency."

Amanda lifted her own piece of ham, sans bread, and bit the end of the roll she'd made. "Okay, Piper, what room do you like? What gets you going? Butterflies? Ladybugs? Princess crowns?"

"I don't need a new room." Piper flicked her fingernail over the crust of her sandwich, sitting on a paper plate on the desk next to the computer. Her ankles were crossed, and she was only halfheartedly looking at the screen, which displayed a bedroom with a floral meadow motif.

A minute ago, the kid had been drooling in ecstasy at the picture in front of her. Amanda chewed and thought. Maybe this nanny thing was a little more challenging than the dusting. "Why not? It sure looks to me like you need a new room."

Piper shrugged and cast a wary glance at Danny. "Costs too much." Her finger snaked out and touched the screen where the prices were listed. "That bed costs six ninety-nine. Mark says anything more than two dollars is too much to spend on me."

Amanda heard Danny's breath suck in hard. She could feel his tension, sense the way his muscles tightened, his hands clenching.

"I'm not Mark," he said, his voice surprisingly soft, given the emotion Amanda suspected he was feeling was red-hot anger.

She turned to see him try and pull Piper into his arms. She let him take her to him, but she hung loosely in his arms, not responding to the hug he was trying to give her.

"You're worth more than any amount of money, Piper. My whole life I wanted a family of my own, a daughter I could spoil. Now I've got you, and I couldn't be happier."

Amanda had a clump of mascara in her eye. That had to be why she suddenly needed to blink hard to clear her vision. Or maybe it was because if she had ever doubted Danny Tucker's integrity before, she didn't now. And even though the conversation she was hearing was very private, and none of her damn business, she was so happy for Piper that she had a chance. This was truly the beginning of a new life for her.

Danny would make sure of that.

He didn't wait for an answer from Piper, probably guessing she wouldn't have a response. He pointed to the computer screen. "Now we don't need a bed or a dresser, because we already have those. But we can get a curtain and a bedspread and a few things like that to make the room more yours."

Amanda wasn't thrilled about keeping the oak furniture, but she would approach it as a challenge. How to work around ugly furniture and buy on a budget. "Can we paint?"

"Sure."

Not that Amanda knew how to paint, but she could try it. Slap a roller thingy up and down, and there you had it. "Sounds like a plan, Piper. We can get you a whole new look without breaking the bank. Busting the budget. Weighing down the wallet. Maxing the credit cards." Piper just stared at her, all big, round eyes and confusion.

"We can get a new room for very little money."

"Oh. Okay. I like the butterflies best."

"Excellent choice!" She set her ham back down on Piper's paper plate. Only now her hand was greasy and Danny hadn't deemed napkins necessary to their impromptu lunch.

Slimy fingers and the computer mouse didn't mix, so she looked around for a good place to wipe the sheen of grease off them. Danny's legs were the closest absorbent surface, so she wiped her hand right above the knee of his jeans. There was so much dirt on the pants, he couldn't possibly object.

And it had the added benefit of giving her a feel of what he was hiding under all that denim every day.

A lot of hard muscular thigh, that's what.

Very nice.

"Do you mind?" Danny asked, giving her fingers a pointed look.

"I don't mind, do you?" Amanda took her time pulling her hand away. She realized that from her sitting position, she had a bird's-eye view of his crotch. Too bad he was wearing the pants.

"I could have gotten you a napkin if you'd asked."

Not that he looked all that upset. Amanda was discovering Danny Tucker was like San Diego. Sunny skies and seventy degrees all year round.

"Too much bother. And your jeans are already dirty anyway." She turned back to the computer and started adding the butterfly comforter to her virtual shopping cart.

"That was just dirt. Grease is harder to get out."

"Dirt, grease, crops, pigs—it's all just part of the circle of life, Danny. Chill out."

She could take her own advice. The temperature in her Celine halter and Michael Kors pants had shot up ten degrees. And she was being paid to look out for Piper's needs, not her own.

Needs that were rapidly escalating into urgent.

"I know what else is part of the circle of life," Danny murmured right above her ear, in a low, sexy drawl.

So did her inner thighs.

There was no response appropriate for voicing out loud with Piper hovering at her elbow, so she kept her mouth shut.

"A woman doing a man's laundry fits the natural order of things. You can just wash my jeans for me, Amanda."

Outraged, she turned to give him a lecture worthy of Gloria Steinem, when she saw he was grinning from ear to ear.

"What? I'm just kidding. Chill out."

He threw her words right back at her, and the whole thing made Amanda want to laugh. He was awfully cute, in a brawny, sweet, uncomplicated sort of way. She watched him take another incredibly large bite of his sandwich.

"Pig," she said, with more amusement than censure.

"Oink, oink." He spoke around a mouthful of food, with an appalling lack of manners, but his brown eyes flirted with her, disarming and charming.

Good God, the country air was affecting her sanity.

She was actually falling for a farmer.

Chapter 9

$\mathcal{D}$anny had always liked the end of the day. It was a quiet satisfaction that stole over him as the sun disappeared and the moon trotted out, when his muscles ached from a hard day at work, and his thoughts slowed down.

He sat out on his deck most nights, nursing a beer and listening to the ball game on the radio as he looked out over his fields. The Reds were trouncing the Cubs as he put his feet up on the railing, trying to reassure himself everything was alright.

There were a number of things he believed in, took stock in, felt pride for. He was proud to be an American, tried to live his life without sweating the small stuff, and knew that no accomplishment was greater than the one a man earned through his own hard work, with his own hands.

Wealth was never going to be his unless he won the Powerball, but Danny felt his life was a good one. When he had problems, he usually dug in and stuck it out, thinking it through, taking things nice and slow until they either worked themselves out, he worked them out, or he discovered they hadn't needed working out in the first place.

Raising Piper was going to work out. He just had to take it slow.

"Evening, Danny."

He waved his beer in salute to his mother as she came around the corner of the deck from the driveway. "Hey, Mom. How are you?"

"Fine. Since when do you lock your front door?" His mother climbed up the steps and leaned against the railing, a vision in violet from head to toe.

Her coordinated outfit glowed in the moonlight. Danny couldn't help but smile. "Since I have a daughter. She's in the house taking a shower."

Piper didn't want him anywhere near her when she was changing. At first, he had been concerned that she had good reason to mistrust men, but after talking to the pediatrician, he had decided it came more from having several stepfathers, not from any actual abuse. And she had only been with him a week. There wasn't reason for her to trust him yet.

"What did the pediatrician say when you took her in yesterday?"

There was a rebuke in his mother's voice, that he hadn't called her to tell her. "I told Dad what she said when I saw him yesterday afternoon. Didn't he tell you?"

She snorted. "Get serious, Danny. Daniel has a word limit per day. He probably used them all up on you, then didn't have any left for me."

It was a humorous assessment of his silent father. "Well, fortunately there wasn't that much to tell. The doctor in Xenia said Piper is fine, physically speaking. She's on the low end of the weight chart, which could be just her build or the result of poor nutrition."

Danny took a pull off his beer. He looked straight out at

his soybean crop. "And there was no evidence of abuse, sexual or physical. No bruises, broken bones, or anything . . . worse."

He had almost sunk to the floor in relief when the doctor had assured him Piper was fine. "She said she seemed bright when she could drag a response out of her. Then she recommended calling the school to get an early assessment before the school year starts. And she suggested counseling with a therapist."

His mother's response to that was exactly what he'd expected. "Counseling? She doesn't need some shrink poking around in her head. She just needs some love, which I'd be happy to give her if she'd let me."

It hurt his mother, he knew, to feel like Piper didn't want a relationship with her. But Danny was pretty sure she just needed some patience.

He needed patience. And he hadn't quite wrapped his mind around the counseling suggestion. He'd think it over, let it simmer, watch Piper for signs that she needed to talk to a professional.

Nor could he tell his mother about her hair. He had promised Piper he wouldn't tell a soul other than the doctor, and he meant to keep that promise.

"Just give her time, Mom."

His mother threw her hands up in disgust. "You and your father . . . just once I wish you'd get angry and scream about something. It's damn unnatural."

"You want me to yell and scream?" He shot her an amused look.

"Yes. Even as a baby, you never got good and mad and hollered. You just fussed." Her finger came out, and he knew she was on her high horse. Why a woman would complain that her baby didn't cry, he couldn't imagine, but that was his mother.

"Maybe this will get you riled up. I heard you hired *that woman* to watch Piper. Have you lost your mind?"

Danny figured it was only a matter of time before Willie had heard about *that woman*, or Amanda, as he liked to call her. He had known his mother wouldn't like it. "Nope, don't believe I have. Today went pretty good."

And it had. Piper was comfortable with Amanda, and while her housekeeping left a lot to be desired, her matter-of-fact approach to hanging out with Piper seemed to be working. If he just ignored the fact that watching sometimes gave him a very unwanted hard-on, he could call this arrangement a success.

"She's a spoiled, rich girl!"

"Who needs a job. And Piper likes her."

"She's just trying to get her fake claws into you, mark my words."

That annoyed Danny. Like Amanda Delmar gave a damn about attracting him. If she wanted to sink her claws into a man, it wouldn't be him, a country bumpkin if ever there was one. She probably had rich men panting behind her all the time, begging her to let them buy her the world. What the hell could he possibly have to offer a woman like that?

"And I don't think you should be having sex with Piper in the house."

That was it. "Good night, Mom. You've said enough, I think." He noticed the shower was no longer running. Piper would be coming out. "And I told you before, I'm not having sex with Amanda Delmar. Not that it's any of your business."

"It is my business if you're getting mixed up with some city slut."

His feet fell to the ground. *Slut* was pushing it too far. "Good night, Mom. I mean it."

Willie huffed, but she stepped back down into the yard. "I see how your bread is buttered. Just like your father . . . never listens to me."

Danny shook his head, wondering why he hadn't gotten

any of his mother's drama. She was angry with him, but hey, he was a little miffed with her. She'd crossed the line, yet he knew tomorrow they would be fine. She wouldn't apologize, but she'd bake him a pie.

"Good night. I love you, Mom."

"Good night, Daniel William, I love you too, and remember the condoms."

Oh, Lord. He didn't want her to get on her condom kick again. "I will, Mom, cross my heart and hope to die."

"Smart-ass," she muttered as she went down the driveway.

In relief, he heard her car start up. The only drawback to living five hundred feet from his parents. Easy access. Normally, that didn't bother him—in fact, he liked it, since he enjoyed their company and it gave him a home-cooked meal every night.

But he didn't like discussing his sex life with his mother. Especially since she seemed to think he was a swinging single, and the truth of it was, he was practically a monk. No one had buttered his bread in a good long while.

Even when he had been doing it on a regular basis, he suspected he wasn't all that good at it, which was damn hard to swallow. But Shelby had never seemed all that interested in sex with him, no matter how sweet and coaxing and patient he had tried to be. Finally, he had told himself that she just wasn't as hormonally charged as he was. A lot of women didn't get into sex as much as guys did. At least that's what all his male friends claimed.

Yet now Shelby was married to Boston, and she seemed mighty interested in sex. Danny had been privy to some sights he could have done without, including Shelby doing a sultry little grind across Boston's jock when she thought no one was in the room with them. Danny was absolutely certain Shelby had never mimicked sex with him in public at any time during their five years married.

Which must mean he sucked at sex.

Not an ego boost, that was for sure.

So even if he were crazy enough to think that Amanda might be attracted to him in any way whatsoever, and even if he didn't have an eight-year-old daughter, he couldn't have sex with Amanda.

Nothing could possibly be more humiliating than not measuring up, both literally and figuratively.

The kitchen door slid open and Piper came out, wearing her pink pajamas and her ball cap slapped back on her head. He hoped eventually she would feel comfortable enough to be at home with him without the hat, but he wasn't going to push it. At least she didn't sleep with it on. He wondered if hair needed air to breathe, like feet. Maybe that's why her hair wasn't growing back. The pediatrician had recommended just waiting for now and seeing if a better, stable home environment allowed the hair to grow back. She thought if there was no improvement in six months, they could discuss medication or a hairpiece.

"Hey, baby girl, how was your shower?" He patted his lap, wishing she would just sit on him, just once. Just snuggle against him.

Instead she took the chair next to him and pulled her pj top down over her knees. "Fine. Anita thought the water was too hot, but it was good for me."

The whole imaginary friend thing was a little foreign to him, and he didn't suppose the rules for that followed normal adult morals. He would not freak that Piper was sharing a shower with a fake female friend.

If she was still doing it at twelve, he'd be in trouble, but for now, it was normal. He thought.

He slung his arm around her, pathetically trying to steal some affection from her. The night was warm, humid, and Piper's skin glowed rosy from her hot shower. Her cheeks were pink, her shoulder sticky and warm beneath his fingers. He could smell her body wash, a fruity strawberry mix that Amanda had gotten in their Wal-Mart spree. The tips of her fingers were pruney from staying in the water so long.

It was love he felt for her, in a way that surprised him. It was intense, powerful, laced with worry and anxiety, and topped with pride. He loved her, and he would do anything for her.

"How long is Amanda going to babysit me?"

"Until you start school." That had been his requirement of Amanda—that she stick it out until the end of August. Then she should have enough money to get home, and he would have had enough time for Piper to get used to her new life. "That's five weeks from now. And then when you get off the bus, I'll be here, so you won't need a sitter."

"I don't need a sitter at all, you know. Anita and me stay home alone all the time."

He had a hard time swallowing that an imaginary friend would be any sort of protection against fire and abduction. For the ten thousandth time he wanted to track down the stepfather from hell and pound him. "Well, I'm sure you can, but Amanda needs a job, you know. We're sort of doing her a favor because she's having a hard time paying her bills."

Piper glanced over at him, rolling her bottom lip completely over the top one. She popped it back with a wet slurp. "She should move in with us. Then she wouldn't have any bills at all."

Sure, but he would go insane from unfulfilled sexual need. "I think Amanda is used to a lot of space. Our house is kind of small, and I've got the extra bedroom set up like an office, with the computer and bookshelf."

"She could share your room. Grown-ups share a bed all the time." She blinked at him innocently.

He wasn't touching that one. Not even getting close to it. "Do you miss your mom, Piper?" It had occurred to him that maybe there was a valid reason she had bonded with Amanda. Her mother was about the same age as Amanda.

Piper sighed. "I miss her a lot. But she's dead."

His heart squeezed. "I'm sorry, baby girl, I really am." He tightened his grip on her shoulder, tried to draw her toward him. She stiffened a little but didn't pull away. "Tell me about your mom. What was she like?"

"Don't you remember her?"

Danny had memories of a loud, brassy laugh; light brown hair with blond streaks in it; and a healthy cleavage well displayed in a tight T-shirt. He remembered Nina as flirtatious, inviting herself to ride the Ferris Wheel with him, and squealing with fake fear when they rounded the top.

And he remembered getting hot and sweaty, breathing hard in the backseat of his car, fumbling his way over those perky breasts, and sliding himself into her with more enthusiasm than skill. Not the sort of memories he was willing to share with his daughter. Or anyone, ever.

He had been a kid, lumbering along toward adulthood, confident and overflowing with energy. It had hurt when Shelby had broken up with him, especially since he hadn't seen what the big deal was, why she wouldn't just have sex with him. He had felt entitlement toward her body, and so he'd gone and taken that from someone else, and he had made a baby with that girl.

A girl he hadn't known at all, and never would. It was humbling and hard to stomach at twenty-six, when he was more mature, calmer, his body not aching with misunderstood urges, overwhelmed with sexual need.

Or at least, that's the way he usually was. Amanda had a tendency to make him urgent, but all he had to do was think about Nina to remind himself that decisions based on sexual want were bad ones.

"Of course I remember your mother. She was a nice girl when I knew her—always smiling and laughing. But I didn't know her when she got older, grew up a bit. Most people are a bit different once they get married and have kids. I was just wondering what she was like with you."

"She still laughed a lot." Piper twisted her cap on her head and dug her toes into the hard white plastic edge of the chair. "But she yelled sometimes too. I have a little brother, you know. He's two. She yelled at Marcus a lot because he cries all the time. I don't think she ever yelled at me that much, but maybe I don't remember."

Danny reached for his beer, picked at the label, his throat tight with guilt. "I didn't know you have a brother."

"He's pretty cute, 'cept he can get on my nerves too. But that's the way it is with brothers, you know."

"No, I don't know. I'm an only child."

Piper looked up at him and frowned. "That's sad." And she leaned just a little closer to him.

Danny's chest tightened even further. "But now I've got you, so it's okay."

"My mom never minded Anita. When Mark used to yell at me and tell me to stop talking about her, Mom would tell him to leave me alone. That Anita didn't eat much so why was he complaining?"

Danny laughed. So Nina had had a sense of humor.

"And she used to sing to me sometimes at night. I miss that."

Unable to resist, he shifted her, lifting her with his right arm until she was on his thigh, settled in the crook of his arm. When she didn't protest or wiggle away, he spoke in a low voice. "I'm not much of a singer, but maybe if you teach me the songs, we can sing them together. I bet your mom would like that."

"You think so?" Her eyes were so solemn, her voice soft, her cheeks stark white in the glow of the moon and the kitchen light from the house.

"I think so. And maybe we should go visit your mom where she's buried. Take her some flowers. I need to thank her for giving me you. Would you like to do that?"

"Maybe." She shifted on him, settled in a little more against his chest. "Are you really my father?"

Danny spread the palm of his hand on her warm back, stroked his thumb back and forth. He nodded, never so sure of anything in his whole life. "Yes, I really am."

"That's good," she whispered.

That it was.

♡

Amanda bit a French fry as she walked into her kitchen. It tasted so damn good, she had to close her eyes for a second.

"Aaahhh. Good thing I'm alone. I think I just had an orgasm," she said to her Burger King bag.

Never again would she take fast food for granted. When Danny had dropped her off at the end of her first day nannying, she had gone into the house and found another four dollars and seventeen cents in pennies. And promptly turned on her heels and walked the block to Burger King, where she had gotten a sandwich-fry-gigantic-soft-drink combo.

Perhaps not the wisest use of her unexpected windfall, but man alive, she was hungry. The ham and pretzels at Danny's hadn't even dented her appetite. She had a whole week's worth of eating to make up for, and a Whopper was a big lead on accomplishing that.

Besides, Baby had needed the walk after being stuck in the house all day. Jamming three more fries in her mouth, she picked up the phone and dialed Brady Stritmeyer's number.

"Hey, it's Amanda," she said, chewing her fries, when Brady answered. "How's your leg?"

"Annoying. What's up?"

"You need some cash? I've got a job for you." She was still pleased at her brilliance in coming up with this scheme. Bedroom on a budget, she was all over it.

"Cash is good. But I'm kind of incapacitated right now. What's the job?"

"Painting butterflies on Piper's bedroom wall. We'll sit you in a stool, you'll be fine."

"Sure, I could do that. Butterflies, huh? Realistic or cartoonlike?"

"Pink and purple in whatever style you want. You tell me what supplies you need, and I'll get them."

"Cool. What's the pay?"

Like she knew. Nor had she discussed an actual budget with Danny, but surely he wouldn't begrudge a little paint. He seemed pretty eager to make Piper happy.

"What do you usually charge?" There, that sounded like she knew what she was talking about.

"Ten bucks an hour. It will probably take me about eight hours to sketch it out and paint it."

"Ten bucks! Are you sure?" She was fairly certain her mother's decorator would charge a thousand bucks to have a wall mural painted. It seemed cruel to have Brady do it for only eighty, with a broken leg besides.

"Is that too much? I'm not trying to stiff Danny or anything. I can take eight bucks an hour."

Amanda reached for another fry. "No, no, ten is fine. I just thought you might want more."

"Oh."

There was a silence where they both seemed to be trying to figure out where the other was coming from, before Brady let out a snort. "Ten is good. And if you want the walls painted first with a color or a base paint, you'll have to do that. I'm not up for standing on a ladder or anything."

"Paint the walls first. I can do that." She had thought maybe they would use a crisp white instead of the dirty beige that was on there now. That way Brady would have a blank canvas to start with. "Thanks, Brady. I'll go to the paint store tomorrow, so I'll call you when I'm there and you can tell me what to get. I'd like you to get started over the weekend or Monday. Sound good?"

"Cool. Talk to you later, A."

"Bye."

She liked that kid. He was flaky, yet all there at the same

time. Sort of like how she saw herself. And damn, could Brady draw.

Well enough that she was willing to eat up some cell phone minutes and call Stuart in New York.

"Hey, I have an artist for you."

"Well, hello to you too, Miss Fell Off the Face of the Earth."

"Miss me? Guess what, you're the only one." She shoved another fry in her mouth. These things were addictive. Every time one was in her mouth, she felt just a little bit better.

"Uncle Brett put out the word that no one is to assist you, my little debutante, in getting yourself *anywhere*. What gives between you two? That's a little harsh even for him."

Rolling her eyes, she licked salt off her lip. "He's just in a mood, that's all. This too shall pass, I'm sure. But in the meantime, I'm hanging out in Cuttersville."

"Oh, God." Stuart sounded horrified. But then again, he thought leaving Manhattan was indulging in the primitive. "Why don't you call one of your sugar daddies and ask for a plane ticket? Uncle Brett said family couldn't help you, but he has no control over the men you sleep with."

Amanda reached for her eighty-seventh French fry. "Apparently you've confused yourself with me. I don't sleep with sugar daddies."

"Well, shit, why not? It's vaguely like prostitution, but it's such naughty fun. And then you wouldn't find yourself rusticating where fashion hasn't ventured."

"The reason I'm calling," she said loudly, so he would snap out of his sexual musings, "is because I met a kid here who is talented. I want to send you a sketch he did."

"Sure, gorgeous. Send it my way. But make sure it's not a sketch of a hound. I hate dog pictures."

She laughed. "I promise—no pooches."

"*Pooches.* Now there's a word you don't hear every day. I like it. It almost sounds dirty."

"You're a nut." He was the closest thing she had to a sibling, and she loved him in all his quirkiness.

"No, a fruit." Stuart cleared his throat, and his voice got serious. "If you need money, I'll give it to you, you know that. I don't give a shit what Uncle Brett thinks."

She swallowed the lump in her throat, and it wasn't from a fry. "You're sweet, Stuey, but I'm fine. I'll keep in touch."

"Alright then, you know how to reach me. Kiss, kiss."

"Hug, hug." Amanda hung up the phone and reached for her burger.

The cell phone immediately started ringing, and she eyed her food with longing. Probably Stuart calling back. Or it was one of her friends or her father, though that seemed unlikely. He hadn't exactly been anxious to get ahold of her.

But it was him. His name flashed boldly on her caller ID and Amanda drew a deep breath. "Hi, Daddy. Long time, no talk."

"Where are you?" he demanded, sounding brisk and impatient, adjectives he owned most of the time.

"Standing in my kitchen, watching my burger get cold while I talk to you."

"You're at the apartment? But the doorman said you haven't been back."

At least he cared enough to spy on her. She'd been starting to wonder if he wanted her to disappear. "I'm in Cuttersville, where I was when you cut off my credit cards. How do you think I could have gotten back to Chicago?"

"You don't have any money at all?"

"No!" Where had he been, Mongolia? "I told you that."

"I thought you were exaggerating."

"I wasn't exaggerating. I had fifty bucks and change a week ago."

"How much do you have now?"

"Two dollars. Fifty bucks doesn't buy what it used to." She took a bite of her sandwich and chewed in his ear.

"So you can't get back to Chicago?" The distinct sound of computer keys tapping came through loud and clear. Dad was multitasking. "I thought you would have enough to get home, and we could talk when you got here."

All that drama and he just wanted to get her home so they could have a daddy-daughter lecture? Her father was always about control, always had been, always would be.

He sighed. "I'll get you a flight home this afternoon. I mean what I said about the money, but I'll get you home and set you up with some job interviews."

With her father's quote, unquote friends who would hit on her. Most of them were divorced and on the lookout for a new, younger model of trophy wife. And any job he secured for her meant she was indebted to him as usual.

"I already got a job. Here. In Cuttersville."

The typing stopped. There was dead silence. "What do you mean?"

"I mean I got a job. What did you expect me to do? Starve? Beg for food?"

Wiping a little ketchup off her lip, Amanda watched Baby running back and forth across the kitchen floor, playing with a sock she had given the dog after she'd popped a hole in it with her puppy teeth. "Daddy's shocked speechless," she whispered to Baby, hand over the mouthpiece.

"You're not stripping, are you?"

Her amusement disappeared. "You so did not just say that."

"Well, what are you doing?" He didn't sound the least bit remorseful for accusing her of dancing naked for cash.

Pissed off, she didn't temper the sarcasm. "I'm a nanny. I have the complete and total care of a small child. And I'm good at it. I rock. I'm like Mary Poppins and Jane Eyre all rolled into one. But better looking."

"A nanny? Jesus Christ, that's scary. You can't even take care of yourself."

The insult was so unexpected, so brutal, that it ripped

through the thin veneer of nonchalance Amanda wore like a mink coat. She felt the unmistakable, embarrassing sensation of tears in her eyes—tears she had thought she'd seen the last of.

But he still had the power to hurt, deep and biting, aching, hurt that had her sucking in a shuddering breath and striving for control. She despised that after everything, at twenty-five, she still needed and wanted her father's approval.

He would never give it.

That was the reality of the situation.

He had spent thirty grand on fertility treatments for her mother and had wound up with Amanda instead of the son he had dreamed of. And she had had the pleasure of hearing him tell her mother just how disappointed he was with his investment when they had a fight over the cost of Amanda's tenth birthday party.

So she had never had any delusions about his feelings for her.

But it still hurt. And she hated that.

There were a lot of things she'd like to say to her father, including the fact that he'd gotten exactly what he'd created, but she didn't trust herself not to splinter and crack in front of him. She wouldn't give him the satisfaction of breaking down, and she wouldn't sacrifice her pride.

"Thanks for the call, Dad, but I have to go. Burger King tends to congeal if you let it sit too long. But I'm sure you have plenty to keep you busy. Maybe you can call cousin Stuart and cut him off, too, just for fun. And maybe put a red flag on Mother's credit card. That would be a good joke."

"Stop acting like a child, Amanda."

"Stop manipulating your family."

"Call me when you're ready for the plane ticket."

She'd accept his ticket when her mother let her natural gray show—not in this lifetime. "I don't want your ticket.

I'm staying here. You can close up my apartment and do whatever you want with the furniture, since you paid for it all. But if you could pack up all my clothes and personal items and ship them to my Cuttersville address, I would appreciate it."

"Your teenage rebellions are getting a little tired."

"And so is this conversation. Good-bye, Dad." Amanda hung up the phone, her hand shaking and her stomach churning.

Anger sizzled and popped and snapped inside her, making her skin hot and her mouth dry. She pushed her hair back and watched Baby, who had flopped on the floor, resting her chin on her paws.

"Well, Baby, that went well. Dad and I should talk more often."

Baby yipped, looking like she knew Amanda was full of B.S.

Which she was. And she had just given up possession of her Chicago apartment.

She really was stuck in Cuttersville.

A wail went up from the bedroom upstairs.

"I know what you mean, honey. I know what you mean."

Chapter 10

*D*anny stopped back at the house to see if the lawyer had returned his call. He had left a voice mail that morning to see if the lawyer had made any progress in tracking down who exactly had custody of Piper and filing the necessary paperwork for Danny to request full custody.

He wanted things locked up, nice and tight, with all the legalities taken care of. He didn't imagine anyone would contest his request for custody, but he'd feel better when everything was said and done and no one could ever take Piper away from him.

There were no messages in the kitchen tacked to the bulletin board above the table. Nor was the answering machine light blinking. But Danny wanted to make sure Amanda hadn't taken a message for him.

Having Amanda around the house was going much smoother than he had imagined. She was definitely high maintenance, and he was always incredibly aware of her presence in the house, but she and Piper got along real well. She played along with the whole imaginary friend bit and didn't patronize or smother Piper.

It had only been three days, but he was cautiously optimistic.

And truthfully, he enjoyed Amanda's company. She was witty and sharp, sometimes achingly vulnerable when he least expected it. She just had something about her that made him smile. It felt comfortable to eat lunch with Amanda and Piper every day, and if the occasional lust-filled thought snuck in when he wasn't looking, he just booted it back out.

Danny headed toward the living room to find Amanda and confirm the lawyer hadn't called. He drew up short in the doorway and swallowed hard.

Amanda was on the floor playing Barbie dolls with Piper. Which was sweet and good and all of that, but Amanda hadn't adjusted her wardrobe for babysitting. She was wearing an incredibly short white skirt.

Lying on her stomach, propped on her elbows, she was all long legs and excessive blond hair. Her backside was barely covered, and he could see the little curve of her ass, tight and tempting as hell.

He was in trouble.

Not even the sight of his daughter and Amanda's poodle could change the very obvious fact that he was attracted to her. He instantly had a woody to rival his corn silo in size.

He didn't dare call attention to himself now. She'd turn and be eye level with his tented jeans.

Concentrating on relaxing his body from the shoulders on down, Danny tried not to look at any part of Amanda. Especially her ass, which was so firm and curvy, and wiggling a little as she used her arms to maneuver the doll around, and . . . and damn, he was staring at it again.

Forcing his eyes to his daughter, he saw that she had her half-hair Barbie dressed in a wedding gown. Shelby had dropped by the day before with a Ziploc bag full of Barbie clothes her thirteen-year-old cousin didn't want anymore. Piper's doll walked on her tiptoes back and forth in front of Amanda's. The poodles, both real and the plastic minia-ture toy, slept tucked up next to the couch, ignoring the fashion show.

"Definitely this one," Amanda said in a voice slightly higher than her own. "It's a Monique Lhuillier and perfect for an unconventional woman like you."

Maybe she wasn't referring to the Mohawk hairdo, but either way Danny was amused. He leaned on the door frame and watched.

Piper used a falsetto voice that sounded like a manic squirrel. "Do you think Ken will like it?"

"Who cares? A wedding is all about the bride. If Ken can't appreciate what makes you happy, maybe he's not the man for you."

Danny wondered what made Amanda happy. At first, he would have said money, but he didn't think that was what defined Amanda, even if she was floundering a little with-out her trust fund. She was a lonely woman, a bit lost and insecure, and yet, she was so smart, so scrappy, so incredi-bly sweet when she wanted to be.

"Skipper's been trying to steal him away from me," Piper said in her Barbie voice-over.

"A good man can't be stolen."

The hard edge that crept into Amanda's voice had Danny wondering if she had personal experience with hav-ing a boyfriend betray her for another woman. It also made him wonder what man would be crazy enough to cheat on a woman as sexy as Amanda.

"Now we have to pick out flowers and a caterer and find a tux for Ken," Amanda said. "What kind of wedding cer-emony did you want?"

Piper bit her lip and pondered. "A big one. In a church."

Sounded good to Danny.

Amanda nodded her Barbie's head. "Perfect. A traditional wedding. Vegas is so last year."

Piper sat up, dropping her doll on the carpet. "I'll be right back. I have to go to the restroom." She saw Danny as she stood up and said "Hi" before heading down the hall.

Amanda rolled onto her side and glanced over at him. "Hey. How are you?"

"Fine. Just came in to see if anyone called for me. I'm expecting the lawyer."

"No one called that I'm aware of. But we've been busy planning a wedding. Maybe I didn't hear the phone ring." She propped her head up, blond strands spilling over her shoulder and her tight tank top riding up.

Amanda was tall, long, and lean, and there was a lot of skin showing right now. It didn't take much imagination to picture what she'd look like totally naked, lying on the floor like that, a small smile on her face, ready for him, mischievous.

Temptation was growing by the second, and he had to stay strong. He could not get involved with Amanda, not when she was leaving in four weeks, and it would do nothing but confuse Piper. Not when it would be a distraction he didn't need, when he needed all his brains and emotion focused on his daughter.

But it was like going three weeks without food and having a banana split set down in front of you in your own kitchen. It was really hard not to grab the spoon and just eat.

"There wasn't a message, so I guess he hasn't called yet. Having fun playing Barbie?"

"Yep." She smiled, rubbing her ankle across her leg. "Barbie has changed a lot since I was a kid, getting better accessories and clothes. And she now has two little sisters, Stacy and Kelly, who are so much younger than her I suspect Barbie's parents got divorced and her father started a second family."

"I'm not that familiar with her family tree. I played with G.I. Joe. And a lot of times I just played in the fields." His childhood had been one of both utter wild outdoor freedom and farming responsibilities from the time he could lift a bucket.

"G.I. Joe is sexy. We should get one of those for Piper instead of a Ken. He's too manicured, too narcissistic. That smarmy smile he wears says it all—he's out for number one."

"But Ken is cultured. G.I. Joe is rough around the edges." He would have thought Amanda would go for the expensive clothes, thousand-dollar watch, fancy car kind of guy. Like Boston Macnamara.

Her mouth had slowly sunk open, and her tongue trailed across her bottom lip. "Sometimes a woman wants a real man, one who could protect her from danger with his bare hands. One who could just pick her up off her heels and carry her to his bed."

Danny liked to think he was a real man. He certainly wasn't the aggressive, successful, wine connoisseur type.

This was either flirtation or she'd given a hell of a lot of thought to the social and sexual dynamics of inanimate twelve-inch dolls.

Piper ran back into the room, saving him from a reply.

"Have fun with your wedding planning. I'll be making hay in the north field." He backed up and tried to beat a fast retreat.

"I'll let you know if the lawyer calls."

Oh, right, the whole reason he'd come in the house. "Thank you."

"I'll stand in the yard and wave a scarf or something so you can see me as you go by on your tractor. You know, communication would be a lot easier if you'd just get a cell phone like every other person in America."

He was perfectly content without one, like every person in America had been before the things were invented in the first place. He gave her a grin. "But then I wouldn't get to see you standing in the yard waving a scarf like a weird car commercial. Bye, ladies."

Danny waved at them on his way out as Amanda gave a healthy snort. What she thought was weird was that Danny didn't seem to need or want all the electronic devices and conveniences Amanda could have sworn she couldn't live without six weeks earlier.

He was content to live on his farm, sweat all day long, then return to a small house with no air-conditioning.

It even went beyond content. Danny Tucker was happy, in a way that Amanda had never been.

She had everything in the world money could buy, but she hadn't figured out how to make herself happy. She hadn't figured out how to make someone care about her, love her, in the way that Danny already cared about Piper.

Of course, Piper was easy to love. She was quiet, respectful, eager to please, compassionate, and sincere in her appreciation. She had seen too much, heard even more, known pain that an eight-year-old shouldn't.

Yet her old soul marched side by side with youthful innocence, and Amanda was getting attached to her.

If she did one useful thing in her life, bringing security to Piper's world would be it.

"What happened to your doll's hair? Did you or Anita give her a haircut?" Amanda didn't think it was odd that Piper had an imaginary friend. Something told her she had had one at one time too. A little girl who got messy and dirty and urged Amanda to roll in the grass regardless of her Easter dress *that had an Italian label, young lady*.

Piper shook her head. Then she chewed her lip, tears suddenly forming in her eyes. "My cousin did it. She's ten and really mean."

"I'm sorry, sweetie," Amanda whispered, her heart clenching at the sight of Piper, usually so stoic and proud, giving up the first tears she'd seen from her since she had arrived in Cuttersville. "Cousins can be like that. I have a cousin, Sterling—which is an awful name—who used to throw my favorite doll down the stairs."

And Sterling was now married to the ugliest man in creation, twenty years her senior, because she'd blown her inheritance by twenty-five and Richard was filthy rich. But he was also lecherous and criticized Sterling's butt firmness at dinner parties, so Amanda couldn't be angry with her anymore. Her life was a horror film.

"Jasmine said she just made her look like me."

Amanda frowned. "What do you mean?"

Piper looked away, hesitated. Then she locked eyes with Amanda. "Can I tell you a secret?" she said in a ragged whisper.

"Of course. I won't tell anyone, ever. Pinky swear." She held her pinky finger up, heart racing, hand trembling. God, she hoped she had the ability to deal with whatever Piper was going to tell her. She did not want to hurt this child any more than she already had been.

Swallowing hard, Piper pointed to her head. "I don't have any hair. It started falling out two years ago, and now there's just a little bit left."

So that explained the constant presence of the baseball hat. And the sometimes naked need for approval on Piper's face. She strove to be casual, not betray Piper's trust with gushing pity that wouldn't help make her feel better. "Why did it fall out?"

"Stress." Piper shrugged her shoulders. "Though I'm not really sure what that is. Mark said the doctors were full of shit, that they just didn't know what was wrong with me. And he said I can't go anywhere without the hat, because people will stare at me."

Amanda understood that pain, that hurt, that inability to measure up. The same feelings were mirrored in her at eight years old, and she remembered them only too well, raw and stinging, like sand kicked up in the eye.

"I don't think that Mark is someone whose opinion matters. He doesn't sound like a very smart man." Amanda wiped her hands on her skirt and struggled for composure. She ached with the need to hug Piper, pull her into her lap and give her comfort.

But she knew instinctively that would scare Piper, so she just said as calmly as she could, given that her heart felt kicked, "I have a secret too, Piper. Can I tell you?"

The little girl's eyes widened. "Sure. I can keep a secret *forever*."

"This isn't my real hair." Amanda pointed to her own head. "The bottom half of it is fake."

"Really?" Piper asked in awe, her eyes shifting to Amanda's hair.

"Really. I got my hair dyed different colors too many times and some of it fell out, and the rest got kind of thin. So I wear extensions to make it longer and thicker." Reaching up, she fiddled through her hair until she found the clips attaching the piece to her existing strands.

Weaves were more reliable and blended better, but her stylist had advised against them, thinking they would strain her already damaged hair fibers. So she had little plastic teeth that slid toward her scalp, under the weight of her hair, securing it in place.

She started to tug it off, having a little trouble without a mirror. It stung like hell, but she jerked harder until the thing came free. She shook her own hair loose and dropped the piece in her lap.

Piper gaped at her. "It's like a wig! But it looks so real."

Amanda handed it over to Piper, who curled her lip but took it, tipping it left and right and watching the fake strands spill over her legs.

"Yep. It's real human hair." She ran her hand over her head, making sure there were no stray pieces sticking up and looking tacky. Her hair only went to just below her chin, giving her a boxy, businesswoman look she hated.

Treading lightly, not sure she knew what the hell she was doing, she pointed to her head. "Do I look funny like this? Bad?"

"No." Piper shook her head hard. "Just different, but still like you. Still pretty."

"I bet that's just what you look like without your hat. Different, but still you. Pretty." Amanda took Piper's hand, the hairpiece clutched between them, and stroked her hand, her arm, her shoulder the way she had wanted to since she'd first met this little girl. "If you want to go without your hat when you're with me, you can. I'll like you just the same both ways."

Piper looked at the carpet and bit her lip. "Can I go out and play on the swings?"

That was an abrupt change of subject, which meant Piper wasn't ready to take off her hat, to totally trust her yet. But Amanda figured the important thing was that Piper had heard her, really listened, and hopefully knew that she would be here when Piper did want to take that big step.

"Sure. Stay right in the yard, and I'll be there in a second." She needed that second to get control of her emotions. And to put her hair back on.

"Okay." Piper ran toward the front door, heading toward the grassy area to the right of the driveway that had a few hardy flowers and a metal swing set that had been dropped off by one of Danny's cousins the day before.

It amazed Amanda that his family and friends had just come to his aid, no questions asked. Nothing was brand-new, but they had all cleaned out their closets and garages and given him clothes and toys for Piper.

Piper paused at the door and turned toward Amanda. She reached up and lifted her hat off so quickly, Amanda wasn't even expecting it.

Then she stood there, exposed, vulnerable, and let Amanda look at her.

The sight of her rounded, pink skull covered randomly

with little tufts of baby-fine hair hit Amanda hard. Some of the remaining hair was short and thick, like a baby chicken, others pieces long and thin, like a comb-over trying to hide a balding spot.

"Yep. Just different. But still pretty," she said in a low voice, absolutely awed to have Piper's trust. She didn't think she'd ever been given such an amazing gift.

Piper jammed the hat back on her head and ran out the door, the screen slamming behind her.

Amanda stood up, her eyes blurring with tears, her breath coming in anguished little gasps. She wanted to weep for Piper, she wanted to take it all away, make it all right, love her.

"Hey, Amanda, have you seen my sunglasses?" Danny's voice came from the kitchen. "I can't find them, and I'm going blind out there."

Swiping her eyes, she turned right as he came into the living room.

And burst into the tears she'd been trying to hold back.

Chapter 11

It took Danny a full ten seconds to figure out what he was looking at.

Amanda was standing there, crying, and something about her appearance was off, different, though he couldn't place it. He crossed the room to her, looking frantically up and down for an injury that would cause tears. "Hey, what's wrong? Are you hurt?"

Amanda wasn't the kind for big emotional displays, so he was a little panicked. "Where's Piper?"

She sniffled, reaching up to wipe her eyes, mouth trembling a little. "She just went outside to play on the swing set, and she's fine."

Relief coursed through him. Piper wasn't hurt, and Amanda seemed to be trying to stem her tears. "Well, what's wrong?" He reached out and rubbed her arms below the shoulder, studying her face.

There was something about her, besides the tears . . .

He blinked. Half her hair was gone. "What the hell happened to your hair?"

Not that it looked bad. In fact, he kind of liked it. She looked softer, more natural, with her hair falling just below her chin. It was less showy, less blond, or something, and her face was pale, streaked with tears. At some point over the past few days, she had taken off those plastic claws she'd called fingernails, and if she had been gorgeous—hot—before, now she was beautiful.

The New York skyline was dazzling, but Niagara Falls was breathtaking.

Amanda had just become breathtaking.

"I took my hair extensions out." She sniffled again, another tear squeezing out of each eye. "Did you know, Danny, about Piper's hair?"

Danny dropped his arms. So she'd figured it out. Not wanting to betray Piper's confidence, he said carefully, "What are you talking about, exactly?"

"She told me that she lost her hair. She showed me." More tears rushed down her cheeks.

Her reaction warmed his heart, even at the same time he felt the pain all over again that Piper had suffered without him. She had lived a hard life, and damn it, he hadn't been there. "I think it's good that she trusted you enough to tell you."

"I just can't believe that anyone would tell her she had to wear a hat . . . those people who had her—I'm sorry, but they were fucked-up, selfish, jerk-off assholes, unfit to be parents. She's just a child."

God, did he know that. "I know. And I couldn't tell you, because I need Piper to trust me, know I won't betray her, and she's convinced having no hair makes her ugly. She needs time." And he needed patience and forgiveness. He needed to forgive Nina for her lackluster mothering.

And most of all, he needed to forgive himself for not being there.

But that wasn't going to happen any time soon. He couldn't forgive. He couldn't forget. He couldn't get over the fact that this was all his fault, for not being man enough to take responsibility for his actions. For not being a real man, any more than Mark.

And he wasn't sure why, but he found himself confessing all that raw sewage sloshing around inside of him to Amanda. "It breaks my heart all over again, every time I look at Piper. It makes me sick. Not because she's not pretty, but because she is. Because she's precious and fragile and damn adorable, and because I didn't stop any of this from happening. I should have stopped it, I should have been there. I let my little girl down."

Amanda's hand pressed over his lips with a tenderness that startled him almost as much as her disappearing hair. She took a step closer to him, shaking her head, her green eyes bright with unshed tears and emotion.

"No, don't say that. You didn't know, plain and simple. You can't change the past."

"I want to."

A small smile glossed over her lips as her hand slid over to cup his cheek. "You, Danny Tucker, are a beautiful man. You know that?"

"What do you mean?" Men weren't beautiful, and he was too big and bulky to be considered anything but lumbering. And even though he was the man and should be doing the comforting, he suddenly liked that she was touching him, soothing him. He stared at her, stood perfectly still, afraid that he wanted too much.

Her hand was satin smooth on his rough, stubbly skin, and he could smell her as she leaned toward him. She was like wildflowers, fragrant and riotous, bold and attention-grabbing with their scent, height, color.

"I mean that you are a good guy. One of a very few. And I'm glad that I met you, and that you're Piper's father."

And she kissed him. A light press of her mouth to his, lips cool and soft on him, then quickly gone.

She sighed. "Thank you."

He wasn't sure what the hell she was thanking him for, but he wasn't above accepting a little more gratitude.

Amanda was willowy, tall enough to meet him face to face, to lock eyes with him, to stand shoulder to shoulder with him. And he wanted more from her—he wanted more than just that teasing taste she'd given him—he wanted her, and he wanted to share a moment of pleasure, escape, comfort.

Without thinking over whether it was wise or not, he closed the distance between them and kissed her back. A tentative, questing kiss that quickly shifted into long, lingering, luscious.

She gave a little gasp of surprise somewhere along the way that opened up her mouth and let him pull her bottom lip into his mouth and suck gently. He'd closed his eyes at the first salty taste of her, and somehow he wrapped his arms around her back, tugging her closer into him.

Amanda's hand snaked from his cheek around the back of his neck, and he cupped her bare flesh above her waistband, drowning, aching, burning. It was more than a kiss, it was a conversation, and she was telling him that she hurt for him, for Piper, for himself, and his emotions echoed hers. It felt good to unburden, to share his pain, to give in to the attraction he had felt since the first time he'd spotted Amanda.

Sometimes it was hard to be slow and steady and not worry. He'd been doing nothing but worry for the last ten days, and Amanda understood that, didn't fault him for it, and she recognized how beautiful and special Piper was.

And she was so amazingly gorgeous, so hot in his arms, so passionate.

Their kiss was going deeper and deeper, leaving behind

any doubts that this was a friendly kiss of compassion. The living room was filled with the sound of their desperate breathing, their little gasps, and he was really, really thinking that no woman had ever tasted quite so good. So eager. So delicious.

He didn't understand Amanda and her world, and he didn't understand his own attraction to her, but he understood that there were some things that weren't going to make sense, and he and Amanda Delmar were very compatible.

At least their lips were.

And their thighs seemed to have a nice fit.

Everything fit, and everything felt so goddamn good, and he was shifting his hands down lower, lower while his mouth moved over hers.

"Danny," she whispered, clutching at his shoulders when he found her backside and stroked across it.

"Hmm?" She had a really wonderful neck, long and graceful and smooth, and his lips slid across it with little effort. Her firm little ass rested in his hands, and he indulged in a squeeze, enjoying the way her breath caught.

Amanda was a mysterious mix of tall, yet thin, strong, yet fragile, sassy, yet vulnerable, and he was losing his grip on reality. He just wanted her—fast, slow, some, all—whichever way she was willing.

"I told Piper I'd meet her in the yard." And she wrenched herself out of his arms, smoothing down her skirt, and clamping her swollen, shiny lips closed.

Nothing like the mention of one small, impressionable child to douse his dick in ice water.

"Oh. Okay. Sorry." For taking a nothing of a kiss and turning it in to mating season for tongues.

"Don't be sorry," she said, though her eyes were focused somewhere over his shoulder.

He knew the rooster painting hanging on the wall behind him was not that exciting. It shouldn't be pulling her attention away from him at this particular moment. Unless she wanted it to, because he had kissed where a kiss wasn't wanted. "Look, I don't want you to feel uncomfortable here. Piper cares about you, and you obviously care about her. You're doing a great job, and, I'm, well, sorry if I got . . . carried away."

Shit on a shingle, he was blushing. He could feel it. Heat rising in both cheeks. Damn. "Just forget it happened, Amanda."

He had taken a moment of vulnerability on her part and taken advantage of it. He had taken one teeny itty bitty little old kiss and gone down and dirty on her. He was pathetic. He was a dirtbag.

He was horny.

"You want me to forget it?" Her eyes had narrowed, and she looked a little put out.

God, he could not chase her away because he couldn't keep his horse in the barn. Piper would be devastated. "Yes, absolutely. Just forget it, and I'll forget it, and we can forget together, so that we're just the way we were an hour ago."

There was a long pause.

Then she said, "You're an idiot," with a disdainful toss of her shorter hair. "I'll be swinging on the swings with Piper, Mr. It Never Happened. I saw your sunglasses on the kitchen table. And put on some sunscreen. The tips of your ears are red, and skin cancer is so preventable."

Amanda turned and walked toward the kitchen and the back door, her hips swaying in her sassy skirt and her chin up in the air.

Well. She was staying. That was good.

Except he had the strangest feeling she was mad at him.

Danny touched his red ears and went for the sunscreen, though he didn't think it was ultraviolet rays that had caused the flush.

He *was* an idiot. An idiot to kiss Amanda Delmar and to think she could ever be interested in a redneck like him.

♡

Willie Tucker wasn't happy.

Her son had given her a granddaughter, eight years after the fact, gypping her of baby clothes shopping, and now he had taken that blond bimbo into his house and was letting her babysit Piper. Instead of her, Willie, the child's very own grandmother.

It rankled severely that Piper could ever prefer Pampered Princess with a Tan over her, her own flesh and blood.

But she was smart enough to face the facts, and the truth of it was, Piper preferred Amanda. And Willie figured if she wanted the kid to get comfortable with her, she was going to have to spend time with her.

With the blonde.

They'd have fun together, all three of them, if it killed Willie, and she was fairly certain it would. But for the love of her grandchild, she would put up with the plastics princess.

"Where you going?" Daniel called from his chair in the parlor as she kicked the mahogany front door open with her foot. "And isn't that my lunch?"

Willie shifted the basket under her arm, the scent of chicken rising to her nose. "Your lunch is on the counter. This is for Danny and Piper. And Amanda," she added grudgingly.

"She's a nice young lady," Daniel said, like a total male fool. It just figured he'd be taken in by an eight-foot-long pair of gams. "Piper seems real fond of her."

Willie gritted her teeth. Daniel had no sense of self-preservation. "Let's hope she doesn't get too attached to her. Amanda won't be staying, Daniel. The minute she gets bored, she'll be out of here."

"I wouldn't be too sure of that, Wil. Seems to me like there might be some sparks flying between her and our boy."

Willie rolled her eyes and tried not to lose her breakfast on the antique throw rug that had been Daniel's grandmother's. "A girl like that doesn't stay in a town like Cuttersville."

"My great-grandmother was a rich woman from Boston. She was visiting relatives here on the adjoining farm, the Wiesels, remember them? Sold their acreage to the Murphy boy. Anyhow, she stayed, and she was happy here. Brought most of this furniture in the house with her from back East when they married."

Willie stared at her husband of thirty years. He looked just as mild and calm and strong as he always had. She loved Daniel, adored his steadiness, and a lot of the time wished he would talk to her just a little more.

This wasn't one of those times.

"The chicken's getting cold while you give your family history. I'm leaving."

Daniel was standing up, tucking his T-shirt into his jeans. "Aren't I invited? If you're all going to be eating lunch together, why should I eat alone in my kitchen? That's downright hurtful, Wil."

And she didn't feel the least bit guilty. "You just want a gander at that plastics princess."

"I just want to spend time with you," Daniel protested, a twinkle in his eye.

She snorted and started out the front door.

And nearly jumped a foot when Daniel squeezed her butt. "What? . . . Daniel!"

He laughed, clearly pleased with himself.

And secretly, Willie was too.

Chapter 12

If Danny could pretend that kiss had never happened, Amanda could do the same.

Yeah, right. And Donald Trump's hair looked good.

She was furious with Danny, absolutely eye-poking irritated that he had kissed her with a sweetness and a passion that she had never experienced in her whole life—and then had apologized.

Apologized.

Amanda stared into the refrigerator, wishing tuna rolls would magically appear on the shelf. Danny was busy avoiding her since yesterday, and he clearly wasn't coming in the house for lunch. Which meant she had to fend for herself.

So, okay, maybe she had been the one to break off the you-know-what the day before. But she had started to worry that Piper would be sitting in the yard with her feelings hurt since she had shown Amanda her hair and then Amanda had no-showed on the swings. Or that she would come in the house in search of her and find her sitter lip-locked with her father.

Neither seemed like a good plan, and so Amanda had pulled back, but with every intention of making arrangements to pick that kiss back up later. But Danny had opened his mouth and said he was sorry, it hadn't happened, blah, blah, blah, until she felt about as sexy and wanted as a llama. With bad hair.

And now he had spoken all of two words to her in the twenty-four hours since.

And there was no freaking food in the refrigerator. How could a man as bulky as Danny live off of Velveeta and Bud Light?

She slammed the door shut. She wasn't going to have the energy to start painting Piper's bedroom this afternoon if she didn't get something to eat.

"What's for lunch?" Piper came loping into the room, an orange stain on the front of her white T-shirt, a reminder of her midmorning Popsicle snack.

"Nothing. We're going to starve." Unhappily, Amanda had already discovered that Pizza Hut didn't deliver. They had a five-mile delivery radius from the center of town, and Danny's farm was about a fingernail outside of that. She'd tried bribery, but the teenager on the phone had said it was against the rules and had hung up on her.

Rude country kids.

"Knock, knock." The back door swung open and Willie Tucker's booming voice filled the room. She came into the room like an avocado green tidal wave, earrings dangling like sliced lime wedges.

Amanda tried not to grimace. She got very distinct vibes from Danny's mother. The *I hate you* and *stay away from my offspring* kind.

"Hi," Piper said, though she shifted onto Amanda's leg, gripping the terry-cloth of her tangerine-colored mini-dress.

"You two had lunch yet?" Willie held up a big basket.

Amanda forgave her for every dirty look she'd shot her way in the last week. "No, we haven't. We were just contemplating heading to town to get something."

Danny's father strolled in beside his wife and went right to the fridge for a beer. He popped the top. "Willie made us all some chicken and potato salad. Where's Danny?"

As if she knew. He was probably hiding in the barn or behind the wheel of his tractor. Anywhere he didn't have to look at her. Probably afraid she'd attack him and kiss him again. Cling to his leg or something.

"I have no idea." Her voice sounded like evil personified. She was Cruella De Vil, that creepy rich woman in the *101 Dalmatians* video Piper kept having her watch. Except she would kill for coffee, not fur, because Danny had nothing but cheap, crystallized instant, which was like Tang for adults.

Hunger made her cranky. As did being ignored by a man she had made out with.

It wasn't every day she cried in front of a man, damn him. In fact, it was safe to say she had never done that.

For a minute there, she had thought that there was something real and honest happening between them, and his eyes, his mouth had all . . .

"I like your hair like that, Amanda," Daniel said, lifting the chicken out of the basket with a smile. "We can see your pretty face better."

Amanda touched her hair. She hadn't put the extensions back in, not wanting to imply to Piper that she was self-conscious about her ugly, boxy hair. Which she was. But Daniel's comment made her feel a bit better. "Thank you." She reached to the cabinet for six plates.

Willie scowled at her husband. "Daniel, why don't you see if you can find Danny? And you only need five plates, Amanda, not six."

She felt like sticking her tongue out, but restrained

herself—which was amazing considering she was starving and without coffee. "One is for Anita, Piper's friend."

"Is that a friend from around here?" Willie looked surprised. "What's her last name?"

"She doesn't have one," Piper said, still clinging to Amanda's leg like a bony Post-it note.

"She's invisible," Amanda explained.

Willie's jaw dropped. She looked ready to speak. Then thought better of it. "Well. I see. What part of the chicken does she like? Leg or thigh?"

"I'm a breast man, myself," Daniel said from the doorway, on his way out.

Willie looked even more astonished, if that were possible. "Daniel Tucker, what has gotten into you?"

"What?" Daniel turned and gave her an innocent shrug, but he ruined it by winking at both Amanda and Piper.

Piper giggled. And Amanda smiled, despite her determination to be miserable.

This Daniel Tucker was just as cute and charming as his son.

"Look at that." Daniel stepped to the side. "Found him already."

And Daniel Tucker, Jr., filled the doorway.

He was sweaty, lifting his baseball cap off his head to mop his forehead with a T-shirt sleeve.

Piper left Amanda's leg and ran over to him. "Hi!" she said, with an enthusiasm Amanda couldn't have imagined she'd show a week ago. "We're having lunch."

Danny's face lit up at the sight of his daughter. He smiled, wide, all the way from one side of his tanned face to the other. And despite his sweat, and standing in the doorway, Danny bent over and grabbed her at the waist.

He tossed her up in the air and settled her against his chest, her legs straight down and his arms resting at the back of her thighs. "Did you save any for me?"

Piper wiggled her loose tooth with a finger and giggled. "We didn't even start yet."

With a loud smacking kiss on the top of her head, Danny set her back down. "Good."

And Amanda had to look away, had to busy herself with grabbing paper napkins out of the little wooden holder on the counter. She was happy for Piper and Danny. Painfully happy for them.

But she was also suddenly aware of how completely and totally alone she was.

They were a family, and she was the rich girl intruding in their lives. She was temporary, just a small, tiny part of one short summer, and ten years from then no one would even remember her or give her a second thought.

And God, that hurt. That hurt more than she could have ever possibly imagined.

She wasn't important to anyone.

Except maybe her personal shopper at Neiman-Marcus.

♡

Danny was still embarrassed about that kiss. Part of him wanted to take it back. Part of him wanted to forget about practicality and repeat it, without clothes this time.

But considering that Amanda looked like she could chew through a tractor tire, he didn't think she'd go for a repeat performance.

It was an odd experience, eating lunch with his parents and his daughter, her imaginary friend, and one very pissed-off heiress.

Equal parts elation and agony.

Piper was in a really good mood, putting away a whole chicken leg and picking all the potato chunks out of the potato salad, carefully avoiding the onion bits. He felt warm and fuzzy every time he looked at her.

Then he'd glance at Amanda, and she'd freeze him with an arctic glare.

Clearly, he needed to make some kind of amends.

"So, Mom, did Amanda tell you she's going to paint Piper's bedroom? Pink, right, Amanda? Then Brady Stritmeyer's going to paint butterflies on it to match Piper's new comforter that arrived this morning."

"White," Amanda said.

"Huh?" He just stared at her, sitting across the table from him. She was between his parents, definitely leaning toward his father and away from his mother.

"I'm painting the walls white."

It was hard to get that out through those pursed lips, but she managed it. Then she shot him a glare before giving Piper a brilliant smile.

"That sounds like something special," his father said to Piper. "You'll have to show us your new things after lunch."

Piper looked up from carefully skinning her second chicken leg and nodded. Using a knife and fork, she slit with the precision of a surgeon.

Danny glanced back at Amanda. She was wearing that orange dress that looked like a bathing suit cover-up to him. It was a soft, towel material and just came to the top of her breasts. He wasn't really sure what held it in place, but he was pretty damn certain she couldn't be wearing a bra.

That wasn't a good road to travel down with his family sitting around the table. He focused on the color. It was a really bright melon orange. His mother was wearing lime green to Amanda's left.

"You know, Mom, you and Amanda look like a couple of scoops of sherbet sitting next to each other."

His father and Piper laughed, but neither of the women looked all that amused by his wit.

Willie stood up. "I'll get the dishes."

Amanda still had a piece of chicken in her mouth when his mother whisked her plate out from under her.

"Mom, I don't think . . ."

"You *think*?" Amanda said under her breath.

Now that was uncalled for. What had he done, besides kiss her? He tried to take it back—what more did she want?

"Danny, why don't you take Amanda with you and feed the chickens some of these scraps?" His father rested his arm on the back of Piper's chair and drilled his eyes into him. "Your mother and I are going to see Piper's new things, then we'll walk over to the farmhouse and get some dessert."

"I don't think . . ." Danny said.

"That's a good idea," his mother chimed in, looking a little gleeful as she started to scrape the leftover food off their plates and into an empty coffee can she'd unearthed from under the sink.

"Chickens?" Amanda said, lip curling up to reveal a hunk of white meat between her teeth. She took her napkin and spit it out, as delicately as was possible given it was a paper napkin and she'd been chewing for a minute or two already.

Piper jumped up. "What kind of dessert?"

"Peach cobbler and vanilla ice cream." His mother shoved the coffee can at him. "Watch out for Rudy. He's been cranky lately."

"Are you okay if I walk over to the chicken coop with Amanda?" Danny asked Piper. "You'll be able to see us out the window the whole time." He couldn't imagine Amanda wanted to toss rolls at a bunch of hens, but it would give him a minute alone with her to try and clear things up between them.

He absolutely did not want her leaving Piper before school started.

But he didn't want to scare Piper either. She chewed her lip for a minute but finally nodded. "It's okay." She turned to his father. "Can we get dessert now?"

"Sure. We'll just walk across the field to our house. Your

grandma made that peach cobbler fresh this morning, so it will still be warm. Delicious."

Piper ran out the door without a backward glance at him or Amanda.

"Well, see you later too," Amanda said with a small smile, as Piper's skinny legs pumped hard to take her across the yard. "But hell, I've been known to run for dessert myself."

"I'd never guess," Danny said, preoccupied with the hope that had risen when Piper had agreed so readily to go with his mom and dad.

Her smile fell off her face. She turned back to him and gave the coffee can a suspicious glare. "So who is Rudy?"

"The rooster."

She snorted. "I'm sorry, but I'm not feeding next week's dinner-on-legs. I'm going to go start taping Piper's bedroom. The paint store guy said you have to cover the woodwork with tape to make the job easier."

"Amanda." He grabbed her arm when she started past him. "Just . . . just walk with me for a minute. I want to talk to you."

"Can't you just talk to me now? In the kitchen, far away from anything that smells? Besides you, I mean."

It took him a minute. "I smell?" Shit, he should have taken a shower before sitting down to lunch. But hell, if he stopped and bathed every time he broke a sweat, he'd spend half the day in the bathtub.

"You're a little . . . earthy." Amanda tucked her hair behind her ear and crossed her arms over her breasts.

Danny wasn't sure what a man was supposed to say to that. "I'm a farmer. I sweat. I'm sorry if that offends your little nostrils. I guess men in Chicago don't sweat. They stay in shape lifting their wallets instead of doing manual labor."

"Don't get your flannel shirt in a bunch. I didn't say you smell *bad*. I said you smell *earthy*. Huge difference. One is gross, one is . . . not gross." Her cheeks got a little pink, which surprised him.

Amanda wasn't a blusher.

"So you don't find me gross? Smelly? Disgusting?" Danny took a step closer to her, charmed by that tint to her face. He wondered how she'd feel about kissing a smelly farmer in his kitchen.

"No." But she seemed to have caught onto his intent, because she stumbled back and grabbed the coffee can off the table. "Let's go feed the chickens before Rudy has a cow." She hit the screen door with the palm of her hand. "Get it? Has a cow? That's farm humor."

He got it.

And he liked it.

He liked every inch of Amanda, from top to bottom, inside and out.

Chapter 13

*N*ot wanting to risk her Kate Spade sandals getting pecked, Amanda took them off as they stepped into the yard. Of course, that left her feet bare and completely vulnerable to any rogue chicken who might get carried away.

Better her feet than her five-hundred-dollar shoes. It was doubtful she'd be able to buy replacements any time soon. She tugged on Baby's leash. "Come on, sweetie, we're going to meet some chickens."

Danny glanced down at her feet. "Umm, do you want to borrow a pair of my gym shoes? The grass is kind of dry this time of the year."

She pictured putting his clunky, dirty shoes on with her Juicy dress and shuddered. "No, thank you. I'm tough. I can handle it."

He coughed into his hand. "*Tough* is not the word I would have chosen to describe you."

"What word would you use?" She could only imagine. *Rich, spoiled, irritating, flat-chested* were probably in his primary grouping. Followed by secondary adjectives such as *lazy*, *unskilled*, *stubborn*, and *hawk-nosed*.

Danny walked beside her with his hands in his front pockets. He wasn't looking at her, which wasn't promising. But then he said, "Fascinating. That's how I'd describe you."

What, like freak-show fascinating? Or like, really cool and interesting kind of fascinating?

"Complex. Generous."

He thought she was generous? That was a switch. One that rendered her speechless.

"Beautiful. Provocative."

Danny glanced over at her, and she was instantly reminded of that hot kiss they had shared.

Which she was so over.

Her terry-cloth dress was just rubbing her nipples, causing them to rise, that was all.

Danny continued with his Portrait of an Heiress. "Sweet. Lost."

Now he was too close to home. He was wiggling inside her head and under her defenses. He was seeing that part of her she hated, that she hid and pretended didn't exist.

"I think you've got me confused with Dorothy in *The Wizard of Oz*. Maybe the little dog threw you off."

Baby was jumping and leaping, clearing the brown tufts of burned out grass like they were boulder-size bushes.

"So where are these chickens, anyway? All I see is dead grass and a dilapidated shack. If that's where the chickens live, I'm already feeling more charitable toward them. That's an appalling structure. This is like the ghetto for chickens." Amanda shifted, the sun beating down on her. The grass did hurt. It was like walking on broken glass.

"Chick, chick, chick," Danny said, rattling the coffee can.

There was something about a grown man calling "chick, chick, chick" that cracked her up. Amanda laughed. "Don't tell me that actually works."

Then she let out a squawk and ducked behind Danny.

The chickens—dozens of them—had swarmed out of the chicken house and were pouring toward them, clucking wildly. Baby barked with all the ferociousness a two-pound poodle can muster.

"They're going to attack us!"

"They want the food, not us." Danny tossed bits of dinner rolls and potato salad out into the yard. The chickens turned up the speed, running hysterically toward the food.

Safely behind Danny's bulk, Amanda peered around at them. "Oh my God, that's the freakiest thing I've ever seen. They look like three-hundred-pound men running with their hands in their pockets."

Danny laughed. "That's a pretty accurate description." He tossed chunks of fried chicken after the rolls.

"You're feeding chicken to a chicken? Eeewww."

"They'll eat anything."

Amanda pulled Baby a little closer to her. "I had no idea they were cannibals. I feel a little sick. I mean, that was probably like their cousin or something, and they're just pecking away at her cooked flesh. Maybe they're saying 'That Becky always was a bitch. Glad she's gone.' "

"I think you're giving them too much credit. I don't think there's really a lot going on in a chicken's head."

A wild flapping and squawking commenced, and when the dust settled, Amanda saw a puny little chicken had taken a choice spot in the middle of the pack. The others cut a wide swath around the bird, and it pecked the ground arrogantly, grabbing a piece of roll, holding the food in its beak, and checking out the crowd. With a strut, it swallowed the food and took three steps to the next crumb.

"Who is *that* little bitch?"

"Actually, not a bitch at all. That's a cock."

"Excuse me?" Amanda widened her eyes at Danny.

"A boy chicken. The rooster."

Right. Of course. Cocks. Bitches. Slightly different meaning on a farm than they had in a nightclub in Chicago.

"That's Rudy. He's the only male. The rest are hens."

"He's like half their size! Doesn't he find that intimidating?" She was getting weirded out just thinking about it. Chicken sexuality had never occurred to her before, and she was getting a visual she could do without.

"Rudy isn't intimidated by much."

Obviously, given the chicken strut he was doing around the yard. Male arrogance wasn't unique to humans. "Typical. The smallest cock has the biggest swagger."

Danny laughed and tossed more food in a wide arc. "He has thirty girlfriends. I guess that would make any guy feel like bragging."

"Yuck. Thank you for ruining chicken for me forever. Here I had myself convinced chicken just appears on the table with a nice lemon sauce on it, and you had to go and shatter my intentional delusions."

"While they're eating, let's duck into their coop and scoop out the eggs."

"I'll wait here, but thank you for asking."

Danny grinned at her. "You really want me to leave you out here by yourself with all these chickens?"

There was a very valid point. "Okay, I'm coming."

At the door of the squalid shack, Danny pulled a pair of rubber boots off a hook. "Just slip your feet in these."

"Why?" Not that she wanted to hear this answer, because she was pretty sure it was going to have to do with something gross.

"Trust me. Put the boots on."

They were huge and they were gray. They went above her knees. "You know, if these were orange with some polka dots this wouldn't be a bad outfit. Farm fashion. It could be the newest market."

"I don't think there'd be much of a market for that. But you do look pretty damn cute."

Danny ducked and disappeared into the chicken house. Cute. She was cute. Chicks were cute. Puppies were cute.

She wanted to be sexy, sultry, classy, elegant. Choose one of the above. Not cute. Ugh.

The chicken house was a house of horrors. Starting with the smell. "Ugh, nasty! It smells like the restroom at Wrigley Field in here."

"Watch the droppings." Danny pointed to a pile of . . .

Sick. No wonder it reeked.

Danny had a bucket in his hand, and he started digging through a row of nests, pulling up eggs.

"Can't you clean this place out a little? This is a labor and delivery room, you know. I'm sure the hens would appreciate some cleanliness." Maybe an air freshener for starters.

Danny didn't glance up, though he did shake his head and swear under his breath. "Start grabbing eggs before the food is all gone and they storm back in here."

That would be bad. Amanda shot a nervous glance out the door. They were still pecking like mad at the ground, but who knew how long the food would hold. She clomped to the opposite side of the shack from Danny and almost lost a boot.

"Damn!" Amanda just about pitched over into chicken poo-poo trying to maintain her balance with her legs spread three feet apart, mid-stride. She didn't spend enough time with her legs apart to be good at it, and really almost never standing up.

"You okay?"

"Yes," she said, flicking her hair off her face and bringing her feet back together. "But I dropped Baby's leash. She's over in the corner sniffing something—something nasty, I'm sure—but don't step on her."

The first nest had two eggs sitting in it. Amanda reached out gingerly and lifted them out. Her conscience pricked at her. "Ooh, I'm not sure I can do this, Danny. That poor hen is going to come back, and her nest is going to be empty."

"It's empty every day. I'm sure she's used to it."

"Even worse. She lays each egg, hopeful, and then they're gone. We're kidnapping her chicks. We're thieves, we're scum."

"We're capitalists." Danny moved to her side of the chicken coop and took the two eggs out of her hand. He held each one up to the window and glanced at it before putting it in his bucket.

"What are you looking for? What separates a good egg from a bad egg?" Amanda reluctantly moved to the next nest. "Major producer here. Six eggs, wow. She must have taken fertility drugs."

Danny laughed. "I'm making sure none of the eggs have been fertilized. We can't eat those."

"Why not?" She was trying to keep up, but animal husbandry courses hadn't been offered at her boarding school.

"Because they will have embryos in them if they've been fertilized. The ones we eat don't. If they've been fertilized, we let them hatch into chicks."

She didn't really care, honestly she didn't. But she couldn't help but be curious. "Sooo, how come some are fertilized and some aren't?"

Danny stopped and looked over at her. His ruddy cheeks split into a grin, and his brown eyes had a sexy little glint to them. "If they're fertilized, it means Rudy had a little midnight visit to that hen's nest, and not to play checkers."

Amanda froze with her hand reaching for an egg. "Oh my God. You mean, rocking the nest? That's so frightening. Chicken sex. I'm getting a whole world of information I could do without."

"There's a lot of sex on a farm, Amanda." And he winked at her, the dork. Like a chicken coop was a place to be flirting with her.

"Spare me the details."

When she turned, she almost dropped the two eggs she was holding. Danny was right behind her, preventing her from going left or right. He always prevented her from breathing whenever he got that close to her.

"Jesus, what? Give me some room."

But he didn't back up. "Why are you upset with me, Amanda? You've been avoiding me ever since . . ." Danny adjusted the bill of his baseball hat and cleared his throat.

"Since we kissed? Sucked face? Swapped spit? Is that what you're referring to?" *Upset* was an understatement. She felt *stupid*. Like a big dumb blonde who had thrown herself into the strong, silent type's arms and trembled over his touch.

Gag.

"Yes. Since we kissed. I already apologized . . . and I meant it. I really am sorry if I made you uncomfortable."

She had no idea what he was talking about, and it was absolutely ridiculous that they were having this conversation in a chicken tenement.

"What supposedly made me uncomfortable?" And why couldn't he back up? She could smell him, and it wasn't sweat. It was musky man, and a lingering hint of soap. The urge to squeeze his pecs was starting to make her twitch.

His brow furrowed. "When I kissed you. Here you gave me this sweet little comforting kiss, and I came back at you with tongue. It was rude and tacky. I'm sorry."

Her every instinct screamed for her to deny her reaction. To just accept his apology and consider the whole embarrassing little episode closed. She did not want to give another man emotional ammunition to use against her.

But Danny was different. Just different. And she couldn't let him think he had mashed mouths with her for no reason. Even if he had turned the first kiss into something more, she had been just as responsible. She had given him signals, and she couldn't believe that somehow now he had it all twisted around that he had taken advantage of her.

She was no innocent maiden. "I wanted you to kiss me, Danny!" Hello.

"You did?"

"Yes. That could explain why I was kissing you back, or didn't you notice?"

He scratched the side of his head and frowned. "Well, sure, I guess . . . yeah, I noticed. So you really wanted me to?"

"Yes. Duh."

"So why did you pull away?"

"Because Piper was in the yard and I didn't want her running in and seeing us tugging each other's clothes off."

"Oh." His eyes darkened. "*Oh*. Would we have been tugging each other's clothes off?"

Given the husky tone of his voice, he knew the answer to that. Danny plunked the bucket down next to the sextuplet's nest and took another step toward her. Which there was no room to do.

"Maybe. I might have considered it," she said. He kissed the side of her neck. Just like that, he was there, doing warm and sexy little things with his tongue. "Oh, yes, I was definitely considering it."

And move lower, lower, *yes*. Danny hit the swell of the top of her breast, peeking up out of her dress. He sucked her flesh into his mouth, and she bit her lip to keep from crying out.

Then suddenly he jerked back and swore, while Amanda stood there with a wet boob and a raging case of confusion.

"I can't believe this. I don't understand what you do to me." He grabbed the bucket of eggs and starting scooting back. "This is insane. I'm standing in chicken shit, and I'm turned on."

Amanda looked down. First she saw the big bulge in his jeans. Turned on, yes, that was clear. Then she went farther. His hiking boots were stuck in something . . . chicken shit. Yep, even she could tell that.

"Well, I don't think it's the chicken shit that turned you on, so there's no reason to get so upset. Let's just get the hell out of here."

She grabbed two eggs and left the other four in the nest. Poor hen deserved something for all her trouble. The thought of shooting out an egg every day just made Amanda want to cross her legs.

"I can't have sex with you, Amanda."

Since her back was to Danny, Amanda just froze for a second and stared at a gigantic cobweb forming in the cloudy little window of the coop. She did not just hear another man say he couldn't stand the thought of having sex with her. Surely, that wasn't what he meant.

"Or get involved with you or anything." His hands landed on her arms, and she flinched.

"Quit touching me, or I'll shove an egg up your nose." She couldn't take his friendly, pal-sy, cheerful touching right now. Not when she was feeling humiliation she had sworn she would never allow again.

"I want you, Amanda."

Yeah, right. She closed her eyes. There was something wrong with her. She was unlovable, unsexy, and dumb enough to fall into the same bad pattern every time. She was still trying to prove she was worthy of a man's attention and affection.

"I want you so bad I can't stand it," he whispered from behind her ear. "But if I sleep with you, I'm going to want all of you, all of the time. I'm going to want you to stay."

It sounded so sincere, so sensual, so compelling, that voice murmuring to her while her vision went spotty behind her closed eyelids and her body went warm in the confines of Danny's strong hold. If she slept with a man like Danny Tucker, there would be no hiding, no preening, no protective distance. It would be sweet, emotional, consuming, like that kiss had been.

"I'm going to want you to be mine, and you can't be. You won't stay, and I can't ask you to . . ."

Amanda sighed, letting her eyes drift open. No, she couldn't stay, and he wasn't asking her to. For a split second she had thought that there might be something to be said for staying with a man like Danny, but that was the chicken fumes going to her head. Making her light-headed.

"And I can't do that to Piper, I can't let her think there could be a chance . . . I can't let myself be distracted from her. She's my priority right now."

"I understand. I agree." Her voice sounded calm and rational, even though she felt anything but. She felt like kicking the crap out of some hay in these clod-hopper boots she was wearing.

Amanda turned a little so she could see Danny's face. She gave him a tight smile. "I care about Piper. I don't want to hurt her—I would never hurt her."

"I know that."

His lips were so close to her face as they stood, her back still to him. She could see the bristly stubble of his blond beard. His breath was intermingling with hers.

"That's why we can't." He kissed her lightly. "Do this." Another brush. "At all."

Something was pressing into her butt, and it wasn't a bucket. It was harder, and totally the wrong shape.

He was going to make her be the bad guy again. Which should tick her off, and did, in theory, but while she was simultaneously upset that they couldn't explore anything between them, she was pleased that he really did want her.

Which was lame, but there it was.

But they couldn't do this, he was right. There was absolutely no future for an easy-going farmer and a high-maintenance rich girl.

And she was going to have to be the one to stop it, since he was slipping his tongue into her mouth.

Not to mention her head was about to snap off from the position she was in.

It was such a shame, since it really felt so wonderful. But she could be the bitch, for Piper's sake. She absolutely did not want to hurt Piper in any way.

Amanda yanked her mouth back from his and turned to face front. "Danny."

His lips connected with her hair. His hands were trying to turn her back around. "Just once, please, just one time."

Damn her body for leaping in excitement. Every cell revved up and waited for the starting gun.

Sorry, folks, there wasn't going to be a race today.

"No."

God knew she wanted to, but there were so few things in her life Amanda could point to and claim were done out of selflessness. But this was. This was freaking noble. She had to do what was right for Danny and Piper, and that meant keeping her distance.

Both of them deserved someone better than her in their lives. She was a helpless, hopeless, spoiled woman with nothing endearing about her at all.

Danny would figure it out soon enough, but by then it would be too late. Someone would have gotten hurt.

And if it wound up being her, she wasn't sure she could recover.

"No? Do you really mean that?" His thumbs were rolling back and forth across the top of her dress, peeling the fabric down so he could see the tops of her breasts. His lips nuzzled her neck.

"I mean it." Even if it was hard, hard, hard, damn it, and her fingernails dug into the flesh of her palms.

"Bwack!"

The chickens had returned from their all-you-can-eat buffet.

Chapter 14

*D*anny's answer, which he was pretty sure was going to involve begging, was drowned out by the screeching of half a dozen hens tumbling home engorged on carbs, only to find humans making out in their house.

Amanda wrenched away from him and clomped toward the door, frantically shooing a hen that ran toward her. He sighed and reached for the bucket. He should be grateful for the interruption and for Amanda's resolve.

Instead, he was just chock-full of regret, and horny besides.

"Oh my God, where's Baby?" Amanda sounded hysterical as she scanned the coop for her dog.

Danny didn't see the poodle anywhere, sure her white fur or her red leash would be easy to spot in the coop.

"Danny, what if they ate her?" Amanda took great gulping breaths and lurched toward the door.

"They won't eat her." He didn't think. Another thought occurred to him. "They might peck her to death, though."

Fortunately, Amanda was way out in the yard already and didn't hear him. He realized the minute it was out of his mouth that it wouldn't be a good plan to stress her out any further. She was standing in the middle of the yard, walking backward, looking around desperately. "What did you do with my dog, you nasty, ugly, stupid birds?"

The chickens clucked and kept moving toward the coop. Danny stepped out onto the grass and lifted the bill of his baseball hat. There was a lot of space on a farm for a little spit of a dog to get lost.

"Oh, there she is!" Amanda pointed toward the gravel driveway. "Baby, honey, are you okay? Don't move, Mommy's coming to get you."

The dog yipped, and Danny let out a sigh of relief that he cut short when he glanced at the sky. Not good. "Uhh . . . Amanda, you might want to hurry."

"What? Why?" She picked up the pace in the rubber boots.

Danny started to run, though he was a good hundred feet behind her. "The hawks!" They were circling, three of them, probably thinking Baby was a big mouse or a rabbit.

"Hawks?" Amanda screamed, already running with an odd loping sort of gait before she stumbled to a stop, kicked the boots off and started running like an Olympic track star.

She was an orange blur, screaming the whole way with some sort of warrior cry. Danny might have admired it except he was afraid Amanda was going to get one nasty initiation into farm life and see her puppy snatched up right in front of her by a predator.

His boots ate up the distance between them, and he was only two steps behind her when he saw one of the hawks dive. "Get down!" He tried to push her aside, but she smacked at him.

The dog was barking, Amanda was screaming, and Danny was trying to reach Baby around Amanda's flailing arms, when she suddenly launched herself through the air and landed on the gravel with a loud crunch and smack.

Her body covered Baby in a cocoon right as the hawk descended, talons open, and screeched in outrage. The bird tried to stop and reverse but managed to slice a claw right across Amanda's shoulder as Danny knocked the thing back with his fist.

Feathers flew, blond hair whipped around, and blood beaded on Amanda's bronze skin as the hawk retreated.

Danny made sure the hawk wasn't coming in for a second dive before he turned and dropped to his knees next to Amanda and touched her back. "Alright, you're okay, he's gone."

She was shaking and sucking in her breath with long raspy gasps, but she managed to say, "Nobody messes with my dog."

Danny's heart was thumping about a thousand beats a minute, and he shook his head. "Jesus. I guess not, Princess." He laughed in relief. "That is one lucky poodle."

Amanda sat up and shook her hair back. Baby was clutched in her trembling hands, and the damn dog looked oblivious. Her tongue lolled on her chin, and she gave a yip of excitement when she saw Danny. The only sign of her near-death experience was her orange hair bow, which was drooping to one side, and some grass clinging to her striped doggy T-shirt.

He lifted Baby out of Amanda's hold with one hand and wrapped the leash firmly around his wrist. He dropped the dog to the ground and reached back for Amanda. "Come on, sugar, let's get you cleaned up."

"Everything stings," she said, as she took his hand. "Ow. Ow. Ow."

Danny saw her knees when she straightened up, and he whistled. "Took a top layer of your skin clean off."

She looked down at the bloody, dusty, gravel-pocked mess her knees and shins were. "Eewww. No wonder it hurts like hell. And my shoulder feels like my finger did when I cut it with the nail scissors then accidentally spilled half a bottle of nail polish remover on it."

"The hawk clipped you." Danny tried to sound calm, but he was feeling a little sick. He wouldn't have been able to forgive himself if Amanda or her dog had been seriously hurt. As it was, she looked like she had taken a dirt bath. "Can you walk, or do you want me to carry you?"

That drew a snort of amusement from her as she gingerly took a step. "I'm five foot ten. Carrying me is not an easy feat."

"I've carried bales of hay that weigh more than you." He wasn't lying. Meringue was probably heavier than she was.

"Is that supposed to impress me?" She took another step while he wrapped his arm around her waist in case she went down.

"It's just a fact, that all." Their hips bumped and Danny jerked left, trying to adjust so he wouldn't bruise her up any worse. Only he was still holding her and she was taking small steps, so they wound up knocking into each other even harder.

"We're doing the bump," she said, with a forced laugh. "Are we having a seventies moment?"

No, he was having a serious moment. Looking over at her, a feather sticking out of her hair, her eyes wide and glassy, her lips cracked and dusty, her chest dangerously close to popping out of her dress like twin water balloons, Danny saw an amazing woman.

"That was brave, you know, diving onto the dog like that." It had done things to his insides—was still doing things—to see her risk herself for someone else. Amanda was a caring person, though somehow he had the feeling that she had never been cared for.

He wanted to find out about her, understand, hear what her life had been like. He was starting to suspect that all that money hadn't bought a whole lot of attention or affection for Amanda from her parents. There was a look she sometimes had, beneath that sneer, that just ached with want.

He could see it in her when she looked at Piper.

And he didn't think she even knew it.

"*Stupid* is probably more accurate than *brave*." Amanda limped alongside of him, wincing. "But truthfully, if I had to do it again, I would. I mean, I couldn't let that thing hurt Baby. She's just the sweetest little pumpkin . . . and I would do anything to keep her from getting hurt."

She looked at him then, thoughtful, a slight smile playing around the edge of her lips. "You would have done it too. I know you would have. You were trying to get around me to save her."

Danny shrugged. "I wouldn't want to see an innocent dog get killed either."

"You're just a big marshmallow, aren't you?"

That wasn't any big secret. He had always been something of a sucker. "Maybe that's why I could never get the girls. They don't want nice guys. Too boring."

"You're lying. You were probably homecoming king, all-star football player, everyone's friend. I bet the girls were throwing themselves at you."

"Nope. Just Shelby. And that took some convincing. I'm telling you, women are the same as girls—they don't want Mr. Unexciting." Hadn't Shelby told him that in so many words when he'd suggested they get back together at the beginning of the summer? Right about the time Boston and then Amanda had strolled into town?

Danny didn't begrudge Shelby her happiness with Boston—he cared about her and wanted her to have whatever she wanted. But the truth was, Danny was dull, and he knew it.

Amanda stopped walking and shrugged her shoulder, wincing at the pain. She stared him straight in the eye. "Mr. Exciting isn't all he's cracked up to be. Some women would prefer to find Mr. Dependable, Mr. Honest, or Mr. Unselfish."

All three of those described him, or at least he liked to think they did.

But he didn't have a chance to respond, because his

mother had come out of his house and was standing with her hand over her eyes.

"What the hell was all that ruckus about? You scared Piper half to death."

"Where is she?" Danny picked up the pace, wanting to reassure his daughter.

"In the house, showing your father her Barbies." Willie shook her head. "Never thought I'd see Daniel down on the floor playing with a doll, but he's taken with that little girl."

Then she took in Amanda's appearance. "You fall in the yard wearing those high heels of yours?"

"No," Amanda said in a tight voice. "I was attacked by a hawk."

"What? You're joking." His mother looked Amanda up and down with a raised eyebrow.

"No, she's not. Her dog was in the drive and a hawk swooped down looking for a little lunch."

To his mother's credit, she didn't laugh, though he suspected she wanted to. "Dog okay?"

"Yes." And Baby gave a bark of excitement to prove the point, rushing toward the door when she saw Piper emerge.

"What happened to you?" Piper looked horrified.

"It's a long story," Amanda said, leaning on his arm. "One I'll tell you later after I've recovered with a full-day spa package including Swedish massage and a soothing facial, all while sipping a giant mocha latte."

Willie and Piper just stared at her. Amanda sighed. "Or not. Maybe I'll just wash my knees and get on with it."

"Don't be a fool," his mother said. "Your shoulder is sliced clean open. Get in the house, and I'll clean you up."

Amanda hesitated. Looked to Danny for guidance. He nodded. Though she had a gruff approach, his mother was a good nurse in situations like these. Better than him—his hands were too big and clumsy, and blood didn't always sit right with him. He could slaughter a chicken and never blink, but give him a little human bleeding, and it was iffy.

His mother shouted, "Get! Now! In the house."

Amanda jumped. "All right. Sheesh. Hold your horses. Or cows or chickens or whatever. I'm not my usual speedy self today."

When she limped to the door, she put her hand on Piper's back and rubbed it. "I'm pretty tough, aren't I, kid? I tried to tell your dad, but he wouldn't listen. So I showed him instead."

And Danny couldn't help but grin. She had grit, Amanda Delmar.

♡

Willie sized up the blonde as she perched on the toilet lid.

She was a mess. Dirt and twigs in her hair, dust covering her from head to toe, and grass blades clinging to the terrycloth of her dress. Her feet were dusty and brown, her knees had gravel imbedded in them, and her shoulder was smeared with a sluggish stream of blood from a two-inch scratch.

No tears. No complaining. Just impatience and a haughty look like she wanted to be done with the whole thing.

Willie had to reassess her opinion of the girl just a little. She wasn't a whiner, and she was loyal to her dog. That said something about a woman.

She got out a washcloth, lathered it up, and set it on the counter next to bandages and antibacterial gel. "I guess we forgot to mention the hawks."

"I guess so," she said dryly.

"We didn't used to have any around here, but in the last few years we've seen their numbers go up. They keep the mice and moles down, so they're helpful. But they have been known to make off with a small dog or two."

Amanda shuddered.

Willie adjusted her reading glasses—wasn't fifty too damn young to wear reading glasses?—and started in with the tweezers.

"Ow! Shit, that stings."

Now the whining started. "You want me to leave the gravel in? Let skin form around it, so it gets infected and you have white knots of pus on your knee that the doctor eventually has to lance open and suck out?"

That shut her up. The blonde tucked her palms under her legs and pursed her lips closed.

Willie quickly picked out gravel with the tweezers, dropping the bits into the wastebasket she'd moved next to her feet. "Funny thing about the hawks . . . my nephew Owen got married two years ago to a real piece of work. Thought she was something. But we saw through her—she couldn't look any of us in the eye, if you know what I mean."

"Oh, I know what you mean."

And given the tone of Amanda's voice, Willie was certain she did.

"But Owen, he was determined. He thought we were a bunch of nosy old women and what did we know? So she plans this whole big ridiculous wedding, with limos and tuxedos and doves. Can you imagine? She said the pair of doves represented their love and should be released on the steps of the church after the ceremony. So they hired this handler to let those rented doves loose."

It still made her chuckle just thinking about it. "And off this perfect pair of white doves goes up into the summer sky . . . and one of them gets picked off by a hawk not sixty seconds after their release."

"Are you serious?" Amanda snickered.

Willie moved to her other knee. "It was a sight . . . the whole crowd gasping. And not six months later Owen finds the slut with an eighteen-year-old bag boy from the grocery."

"They got divorced?"

"Yep. He kicked that trash out to the curb where she belonged." Good riddance, the whole family had thought. "He's dating a nice girl now."

"That's an absolutely horrible story," Amanda said, tucking her hair behind her ear. "But really freaking funny." She started to laugh. "I shouldn't laugh, it's terrible."

Willie chuckled. "I always thought it was funny myself. That's why I told you the story in the first place."

The blonde was okay, Willie had to admit. When she didn't have anything to do with her son.

"You know, Amanda, I don't have anything against you." She started dabbing her knees with the washcloth. "You've been good to my granddaughter. But my son seems to have developed a crush on you, and I'm hoping that you'll discourage his interest."

There, that sounded damn polite.

"Why?" Amanda asked through gritted teeth.

Willie eased up with the washcloth, wondering if she was being too rough. She stood up and went for the shoulder wound. "Why? Because you're not the kind of woman Danny needs in his life. He's looking for a farmer's wife, someone not afraid to work hard and be around for the long haul."

The bleeding had stopped, so Willie made quick work of Amanda's shoulder. She'd use butterfly tape to keep the wound closed, and they could skip the stitches. It wasn't that deep or long.

"Danny hasn't met a lot of women like you—any, for that matter. He's attracted to you, and that's understandable. But he's got a child now, and he really can't be fooling around with a rich girl."

"Are you finished?"

"Hmm?" Willie pulled the backing off the bandage. "Not quite, I have to tape this dressing down and then you'll be all set."

"No, I mean are you done warning me not to get involved with your very-much-grown son?"

That was a belligerent tone. Willie shifted her eyes to

Amanda's. The blonde was holding her head high, haughty, looking cool and unimpressed. It was a good trick, that confidence and self-important presence. It reminded Willie that in her own way, Amanda was formidable. She was used to walking into a room and commanding attention.

"Yes, I believe my point is clear."

"Then let me give you my opinion on the matter. If I were interested in pursuing the attraction between Danny and I—which I'm not—it would be none of your damn business. He is an adult who can date whoever he wants, and he does not need his mother telling him who to marry any more than I need my father telling me to find a real job. It is possible that we'll both make mistakes, but those mistakes are ours to make, and perhaps you should focus on your own sex life more than your son's. Your husband looks a little neglected."

Willie stared at Amanda Delmar for a long minute before she burst out laughing. "You know, I really do kind of like you. You've got guts for a skinny girl."

She taped the bandage down over the shoulder wound. "Too bad you're rich. That's one flaw I'm not sure I can get past."

Amanda gave her a rueful grin. "I've been disinherited, remember?"

Willie had thought about it and come to her own conclusions. "Your father is just trying to get you to bend to his will. He has no intention of cutting you off for good."

"Maybe." Amanda pushed off on the counter and stood up, giving her knees a tentative bend. "But I wouldn't bet the farm on it."

And Willie had to laugh.

Chapter 15

$\mathcal{D}$anny Tucker didn't think he could handle any more worrying. He'd done enough of it in the last two weeks to set him up for life, and Piper wasn't even half grown yet.

Between always watching his daughter, always wondering if he was doing the right thing, worrying over every last word that came out of his mouth, he was just about worn out.

There had been no resolution on the custody issue, since the lawyer said no one seemed to actually have legal guardianship of her. Her stepfather did by default, but anyone could contest that. Danny needed a DNA test, and he needed it before he filed his claim and riled up any relatives who might change their mind and want Piper.

Then there was his fear that Piper wouldn't adjust to the farm, to going off to school, that she still didn't completely trust him.

Now on top of all of that, he found himself worrying about Amanda.

She'd proven she was tough this afternoon, but underneath the outer layer she rivaled him for softness. And he was worried about her, about what she was going to do if her father never forgave her.

He was worried that she had her pressure point, and once she reached it, she was going to hare off and return back to her old life.

Before he'd had a chance . . . a chance to do something. Tell her something. Touch her and . . . something.

Or something.

His brain hurt from trying to make sense out of things.

"I've got it." Amanda juggled her dog's leash, her purse that couldn't hang over her injured shoulder, and her house keys all in one hand.

"You don't have it. Stop being stubborn." Danny took the keys away from her, passed the dog leash to Piper, and gave Amanda an exasperated look.

He was feeling strung-out and dangerous, a feeling so foreign he wasn't sure what to make of it. But all the worrying, and the wondering, all the thousands of little details that needed to be tended to had him a bit edgier than normal.

Then when you added into the equation that he wanted Amanda six ways to Sunday, and she had said no, quite firmly, in the chicken coop, he definitely wasn't at his best. Now she was walking around trying to act like her legs weren't torn to hell and back and had to sting, and as if she didn't have a care in the world.

"I'm not stubborn. I'm independent." Then she frowned. "Well, not financially. Until now anyway. I guess I am now. But I'm definitely *emotionally* independent."

That sounded horrible. He didn't think she meant it that way, but it sounded so lonely—like she cared about no one and in return there wasn't a soul who cared about her.

"Do you want me to call your father and let him know what happened?" Danny felt responsible for her accident, and he thought he should let her father know she was alright.

Amanda stepped through the door he pushed open. "There is absolutely no reason to tell my dad I was attacked by a hawk. He'd either suggest I deserved a good clawing, or he would say, 'That's nice, sweetie,' which means he's not listening to a word I say."

Piper had wandered into Amanda's parlor, which was filled with knickknacks the owners of the house had accumulated over the years and left in place. His daughter was down on her knees staring thoughtfully at a porcelain figurine. Danny couldn't tell what the figure was from where he was standing, but Piper sucked in her breath and tilted her head.

There were another six figures on that table alone. He figured she'd be good for a solid fifteen minutes.

He needed to talk to Amanda.

"Amanda."

But she had different ideas.

"I'm going upstairs to change. This dress is trashed. And I'm starving."

Danny clung to hope. "How about I order a pizza? We can eat dinner with you, then we'll get out of your hair. A pizza's the least I can do."

She paused with her foot on the first step. But she just said "Sure" without looking back, in that casual voice she had. The one that he had decided was her fake voice, the one she used when she wanted people to think she was an empty, shopaholic, party girl, with a sharp tongue and credit cards to burn.

That wasn't her.

And she proved it by turning and calling, "Piper, why don't you come up with me? I could use some help."

"Okay." Piper abandoned the figurines and ran toward the stairs. Baby barked and ran alongside her, the leash still trailing.

"Do you mind waiting?" Amanda asked him, her chin over her injured shoulder as she looked back at him, her green eyes mysterious and closed.

"I don't mind." He was Mr. Dependable, after all.

Waiting.

♡

Amanda wondered if hawks carried rabies.

Maybe that could explain why she had suddenly wanted Danny Tucker to sweep her off her feet and up the stairs.

Which was ludicrous. Nobody had ever carried her any-where, not even before she'd grown giraffe-long legs. Their longtime housekeeper used to nudge her with her knees and hands, like Amanda was a sheep that needed herding, but that wasn't the same thing.

No, she had actually wanted him to carry her in his arms, settle her on the bed, and touch her banged up knees with the tenderness he showed his daughter.

God, that sounded kind of sick. Like she'd developed a daddy complex or something. Next she'd be foaming at the mouth and dating her father's friends.

"Why are these pennies laying in the hall?" Piper asked.

Because her friendly household spirit didn't want to see her penniless. Amanda had started to feel kind of touched each time she came into the hall and found another pile of twenty, thirty, sometimes a hundred pennies.

"I keep meaning to pick those up," she said vaguely, not wanting to go into the nuances of humans who refuse to stay dead with Piper.

"It's from her, isn't it?"

"Her who?" Amanda started rifling through the dresser in her bedroom. She didn't have enough drawer space in this house, and her father hadn't even shipped her fall and winter clothes to her. If he actually respected her request and shipped her things, she was going to burst out of these closets. She had a dozen coats alone.

"The ghost. I can hear her, she's crying. But she wants you to be happy."

Right. Piper could communicate with ghosts. While a good party trick, Amanda thought it was a little unnerving. "Well, I want me to be happy too. And I do appreciate the pennies."

"She knows." Piper sat on the bed and gave it a good bounce. "Can I meet her?"

"The Crying Lady? Are you sure you want to?" Amanda hadn't heard her crying since the night she'd had the argument with her father. She wasn't sure she wanted to renew their friendship—or the nightly moaning.

"Yes." Piper nodded.

Struggling not to sigh, Amanda pushed her dress to the floor and stepped out of it. The strapless bra was annoying, but she wasn't going to shed it in front of Piper. Instead, she just pulled on a tight T-shirt over it, taking care with her shoulder, and a pair of terrycloth shorts. A peek in the mirror showed the country was killing her. Chopped-off hair, a tan that was fading, and all her makeup disappeared. Without money to maintain her nails, she had finally succumbed to the horror of having them soaked off by the nail tech at Cut Above, Hair by Harriet's competition. She now had stubby little discolored natural fingernails.

Good thing she'd brought her self-tanner lotion, though. She could use it tonight to stave off fading. Running a brush through her hair, she went for the bronzer, brushing some over her cheeks and nose with a flourish.

"Need some?" She turned and waved the poufy brush at Piper.

Piper shook her head. "It smells bad."

Amanda laughed as she switched shoes, from heels to rubber flip-flops, taking in her bruised and scraped knees ruefully. That was sexy. Not.

A touch of lip gloss, a smoothing of her shorter hair, and

she was ready. Not necessarily in top form, but good enough for pizza in Cuttersville.

"I like your hair like this better. And you don't have any of those lines on your stomach that my mom did. The ones she always said were my fault for being a porky baby." Piper sat on the edge of the bed, her expression thoughtful, as her skinny legs dangled toward the floor like thick twigs.

"You were porky? I find that hard to believe."

"Ten and a half pounds."

"Wow. I'm impressed. You ought to go into the Baby Hall of Fame with a number like that."

"You going to have babies, Amanda?"

Amanda sat on the bed next to Piper, her knees groaning. Time for acetaminophen. "Someday. When I meet a man who's not a jerk."

"My dad isn't a jerk. Anita keeps saying he is, but I think she's wrong. I think he . . . likes me. And you. He likes you too."

Those big, chocolate-brown eyes stared into hers and Amanda's heart expanded, filled, swelled to capacity, and burst into a million pieces.

"He more than likes you, sweetie, he loves you. And I love you too." It didn't make sense, since Piper was just a scrappy little kid who had been mistreated, and Amanda was a jaded, selfish, rich girl, but she loved Piper. With everything in her.

And it was going to hurt like hell when she had to leave her.

"You do?"

Piper sounded so unsure, so disbelieving, that Amanda wrapped her arms around her and gave her a side-splitting hug. "Yep. Sure do. And I haven't loved a lot of people in my life, so you're sort of like in an exclusive club. Membership privileges include hugs whenever you want and the use of my makeup and jewelry."

She released Piper. "Now let's go meet that woman in the mirror."

It was a ploy to distract Piper and prevent herself from bursting into tears in front of the kid.

But Amanda didn't expect Piper to gasp when she looked into the mirror.

"She's beautiful . . . even with the tears running down her face." Piper's voice was soft, her finger reaching out for the mirror.

Then Piper stopped, even as a chill ran through Amanda. She hadn't really expected Piper to see anything in the mirror. Even though she'd heard the crying, seen the pennies, it hadn't felt real. She hadn't been able to connect it with a person. She didn't have to look into someone else's eyes, see their pain.

Piper was. She tipped back her baseball hat. Then she finally just lifted it off as she studied the mirror and then turned to Amanda. Then to the mirror, then back again, eyes wide, hand trembling, mouth open.

"She looks just like you."

"What do you mean?" Amanda's heart was pounding and she was a little freaked out, if anyone cared.

"Her hair is twisted up . . ." Piper's hands spun around the crown of her own head. "And her face is rounder, but she looks like you, Amanda."

Amanda didn't see anything but that same cloudy film that always covered the mirror. Piper was too short to reflect into the mirror, and Amanda was standing to the left. Even if Piper did see her reflection, obviously she would look identical to the way she did standing there.

"Is she saying anything?" Not that Amanda believed there was really a woman in that mirror. Not much, anyway.

"She's asking if we've seen him. If he's back yet."

A shiver crawled up Amanda's spine at the same time impatience slammed into her. Was she still whining about that man? They'd talked about this before. Surely if she just thought about it, she'd see no man was worth an entire one hundred years of tears. Her skin must be an itchy mess.

"You ladies coming down?" Danny called from the hallway. "Pizza will be here in five minutes."

"Pizza!" Piper turned and streaked past Amanda to Danny, like she hadn't just stood as interpreter to the dead.

Danny stood in the doorway, looking big and solid and sturdy. Like a marble statue. No, not marble, because there was never anything cold about Danny. He was like a tree, a nice towering oak.

"You okay?" he asked.

Was she okay? She was broke, only two weeks from eviction from this house, estranged from her father, and she had given up her apartment in Chicago. She had no life skills, no financial acumen, no job experience, and a temporary position that was ending in three weeks.

Then there was the hawk attack, the carnal temptation she had just barely managed to resist in a chicken coop, of all places, and a dead woman with a broken heart—who looked like her—wailing in the spare bedroom.

"I'm fine." And she was. She felt *real*. Honest. And even if it was temporary, she felt like she mattered to Piper and Danny.

Like she was important. To someone. To herself.

Even if her nails looked like hell.

♡

"Why did you and Shelby get divorced?" Amanda asked.

Danny shifted a little in the wicker chair clustered around a table on Amanda's front porch. He hated wicker. It stuck to his ass and his back and made creaking sounds whenever he moved.

Amanda didn't seem to mind wicker. She was curled up in her chair, knees under her chin. She'd eaten three pieces

of pizza to his six, and they had been sitting silently together, watching Piper play in the front yard with the dog.

"I know it's none of my business, but I'm sorry. I'm
nosy. I want to know."

There were no easy answers to hard questions. It couldn't
all be boiled down tidily into something like infidelity or
money troubles or alcoholism. "We got married young.
Sometimes these things don't work out."

He took a swallow of his ice tea, catching an ice cube
and crunching it with his teeth.

"That's it? That's all you're going to tell me?"

"It's complicated. I love Shelby and I always will.
We've got a history. But that doesn't mean we ever should
have been married."

Though he'd been happy enough. It wasn't any wild
love affair or anything, but they hadn't argued. They'd respected each other. But after Shelby's miscarriage and a
few years of growing up, they had looked at each other and
seen that they were friends, not lovers. Nothing more than
that.

But that hadn't stopped him from asking her back. He
wanted a family that bad.

"She was pregnant, wasn't she?"

He just nodded, staring at Piper as she rolled in the
grass, giggling when Baby jumped on her chest. It was on
the tip of his tongue to ask Amanda why she cared when
she spoke again.

"Does it bother you that she's with Boston now? That
she might someday have his child?"

"Nope. I'd be happy for her." And he would. He wanted
Shelby to have the joy he felt when he looked at Piper. He
wanted the wrong he'd done to be righted.

"You're something else, you know that?" Amanda shook
her head, looking confused. "I don't understand how she
could have left you . . . she did leave you, didn't she? You
wouldn't have left her."

"True enough."

"And you won't say anything bad about her—you won't tell me what happened between you."

He looked over at her. She looked upset, her narrow chin digging into the flesh on the back of her hand. "There are some things, between a man and his wife, that are sacred, whether we're still married or not. I respect Shelby too much to gossip about her."

Her head tilted toward him, her full pouty lips being pushed out by her hand. "You're a good man, Danny Tucker. Why couldn't I have met you someplace without chickens?"

He shrugged. "Because then I wouldn't be the same man. I'd be someone else." And if she had grown up in Cuttersville, she wouldn't be the same woman.

She laughed. "God, you're so reasonable. I love that. You make so much sense all the time and always look like you're puzzled that it's not so obvious to everyone else."

"Is that a good thing or a bad thing?" It sounded kind of dull to him. Not that dull was anything new when it came to him.

But she sighed. "You have no idea what a good thing it is."

He didn't understand the look she wore now, the one that stole over her narrow features when she thought no one was looking. "Tell me about your father, Amanda, your childhood. What was it like?"

"I could tell you the standard version, but I'm not up for it tonight." She pulled her plump lip into her mouth, let her teeth slide over and back away from it, streaking the tender flesh with angry red splotches. "The truth is, it was lonely. It's almost a cliché, but it's true. Boston and I have a lot in common that way. Workaholic parents, a big empty house filled with furniture you can't touch. No playmates. One very distracted housekeeper and a series of nannies who never stayed long. Just long enough for me to get used to them, then they got married, or pregnant, or found a better-paying job, or discovered they really hated being stuck with a child. It was always something different, but always the same result. I think I saw my dad once a week for a couple of hours."

"That doesn't sound like any sort of life for a kid." Danny had always known, at the end of the day, he was more important to Willie and Daniel than anything, even the farm. They had made time for him, dragged him along if they needed to get things done.

"When I did see my parents, it was because they wanted to show me off, or make sure I was improving correctly, becoming a perfect little girl who would grow into a perfect little Stepford wife. So I became exactly what my father wanted—an empty, vain woman—and yet now he seems to think I should know how to take care of myself independently. Well, I don't know how. No one ever taught me."

"I think you're doing just fine on your own."

"He doesn't respect me. He doesn't love me." Her voice was a painful whisper punctuated by a sob at the end. "I can't believe I even care. I shouldn't. I don't. But I do."

It made him angry that her own father didn't see all the wonderful things he did in Amanda. "Which only goes to show you you're not empty at all, Amanda. You have a bigger and a better heart than he ever could, and I feel privileged that you're helping me care for my daughter."

She gave him a watery smile. "You're just saying that so I won't cry like a baby and embarrass you."

"I may not be exciting, but I'm honest. I mean it." And he was starting to think that he was falling in love with her.

"You're making it really, really hard to keep saying no." A finger brushed under her eye to capture a rolling tear.

He knew what she was talking about. His request for one time, just one time to experience each other's bodies, just one time to pretend that there could be something between them that resembled a future.

After seeing Piper healthy and happy, there was nothing he wanted more than that one time. The wicker strained as he leaned toward her. "Then don't say no."

"I'm tough, but I'm not that tough." She dropped her feet to the porch boards, stood up, and called to Piper. "There's a ball in the garage. I'll go get it and you can toss it to Baby."

Danny knew exactly what Amanda meant. He wasn't sure he could handle a night with her that couldn't lead to another night. But then again, he wasn't sure he could live without ever having seen her naked.

Nor was he certain he could sexually satisfy her if he did get her naked.

Then again, shouldn't he give it the old college try?

Except he'd never gone to college.

With good reason. He was obviously an idiot.

Chapter 16

*P*ainting a room was a lot harder than it looked.

The project that the week before she had so confidently embarked upon now seemed like a dissertation on Amanda Delmar's ignorance.

Pour, roll, paint. What could be so hard about that?

Everything, apparently. The problem with paint was that it got goddamn everywhere. The floor, the woodwork, the ceiling, her arms, and her Betty and Veronica T-shirt. Oh, yeah, and the wall when she got lucky.

But then it didn't coat evenly. The walls were so dull and dingy that the white went over it in streaky little uneven patches, and she could see the roller marks. And hello, a roller loaded with paint was really freaking heavy. Her shoulder was killing her, which meant she now had two bum shoulders, since the left one was still healing from her close brush with Bird of Prey three days earlier.

Piper had gotten bored with the whole thing about six hours earlier and had been playing in Danny's room. Then

Willie had come by with lunch for them and had taken Piper into the yard to play on her swing set. Amanda realized that she probably should give up the fight, fling the roller out the window, and watch Piper like she was being paid to do. But Danny wanted her to housekeep, too, and he had agreed to her redecorating plans.

Besides, she could not fail. Painting this room was some kind of a metaphor for her life, and she was going to succeed, damn it. Even if it killed her or ruined her clothes.

Setting the roller back in the pan, she stood back and surveyed the room. Two walls down, two to go. For the first coat. Clearly after it dried, she was going to have to do it again.

Whoopee.

"This is for the happiness of a small child," she reminded herself as she scratched her nose with the back of her arm.

Her cell phone rang, and she went to the dresser and picked it up, grateful for the distraction.

"Hello?"

"This is me, who are you?"

Amanda rolled her eyes. "Stuart, this is Amanda. You called me."

"Oh, shit, I did, didn't I?" Stuart took a sip of something, the liquid slurping sound right next to her ear. "I got the kid's sketch you sent, and he's raw, but the talent is there. Get him in art school, and in about five years we'll talk."

"Cool. I'll see what I can do." Amanda actually thought Brady would fit better in art school than roaming around Cuttersville.

"But listen, that's not why I'm calling. I have a job for you. Can you be here in two days?"

Amanda stared blankly at the streaky bedroom wall. "No, I can't be there in two days. I have to stay here until Piper starts school."

There was a long silence. "You're fucking kidding me. You're going to pass up a chance to spend six weeks in Europe on a buying trip with me so you can babysit? Cherie, you have lost your mind."

The idea of a trip like that should have her hopping around the room with excitement. But the thought of traveling with Stuart, martini lunches, late nights . . . felt a little flat. And she had made a commitment. She had to keep it. That little girl was counting on her.

"I can't, Stuart, okay? Piper is emotionally vulnerable. I said I'd stay, and I'm going to."

"The father has a big dick, doesn't he?"

The comment was so unexpected she started laughing. "Stop it! I have no idea." Though that wasn't entirely true. It had bumped up against her in the chicken coop, and Danny was no *petit garçon*. "It's always about dicks with you, isn't it?"

"You know it, sweetie. Alright, well, never say Stuart didn't try and make you happy."

"Thank you, Stuart, I do appreciate it, I just can't this time." And she wasn't sorry, either. She didn't want to go to New York yet. She just wasn't ready to leave.

"Au revoir."

"Bye, handsome." Amanda set down her phone and reached for the roller.

Then she spotted her shorts.

"Shit! Damn!" She had a big paint blob on her denim shorts. With a rag that was already speckled with white, she scrubbed the spot off and threw the towel down on some newspaper. "That's it."

The shorts had to go. She could not afford to be replacing her clothes every other day. First her Juicy dress done in by dirt, now her shorts almost ruined. She stripped them off and threw them into the hallway. Her bra and panties were white as was her T-shirt, so even if she did slather paint all over them, you wouldn't be able to see it.

Not that anyone saw her panties anyway.

The T-shirt followed the shorts. Mrs. Tucker would think she was nuts, but they were all women here, and what she was wearing wasn't any different from a bathing suit.

She'd just be sure to put her clothes back on before Danny got home. No problemo. Neither one of them needed any further temptations. He had avoided her since the other night when she had blurted out all her pathetic feelings about her father, and she was glad he'd been scarce. Danny was dangerous. He made her feel things she couldn't afford to feel if she wanted to retain some kind of dignity.

He made her want things she couldn't have.

He made her daydream that she could be a wife and a mother, and actually be good at it.

He made her think she could have a career if she wanted, be respected.

He made her think she could have it all, and that was oh, so dangerous.

It was better this way, to avoid each other and stay reserved.

Amanda bent over to pick up the roller.

"Holy shit . . ." Danny's strangled oath filled the room. "What the hell are you doing?"

She jerked upright, splattering paint from the roller on the newspaper she'd spread out. And on her leg. "Ummm, I'm painting." Damn, her panties had nudged up into her rear, she could feel them. Trying for nonchalance, she turned around and gave Danny a brilliant smile.

"In your underwear?" he asked in outrage, his voice unnaturally high.

His cheeks were ruddy, and his fists clenched tight. And he had an erection. Not that she'd looked for it or anything. But it kind of jumped out at her.

"Well, I didn't want to ruin my clothes with paint splatters."

"But you're willing to sacrifice your underwear?"

"They're white." And cotton. Plain Jane practical underwear, so it wasn't a big deal. Too bad she suddenly felt naked. "If I drop paint on them, it won't matter because it's white, too."

He rubbed his jaw, his eyes locked on her face like he was afraid to look down. "Princess. Paint doesn't wash off. It just dries on your clothes."

"Duh. That's the whole point." And her arm was getting tired, so she turned toward the wall and started going up and down.

"But sweetie, when it dries, it gets hard. Little, hard, unbendable patches of paint are not going to be comfortable on your bra."

"Oh." Cool white droplets rained over her arm as she rolled and contemplated a crusty bra. "Well, it seemed like a good idea in theory."

He didn't say anything, and she was hoping he wouldn't. *Just keep it closed, Tucker.* She already felt like an idiot, and she was also feeling a little flushed. Not from the heat of the small room, but from that bulge in his jeans.

A big masculine hand clamped around her wrist. She was so startled she almost dropped the roller. "Why are you on top of me? You keep doing that, and I have to tell you, it's getting old."

Danny didn't move away. Oh, no. That's not what he did. He yanked the roller out of her hand and let it hit the newspaper with a crisp thwack. Then he took her arms and very gently turned her around.

Problem. He was a hairbreadth away from her. Conjoined twins had more space between them.

"This isn't on top of you," he said, his voice husky and tight. "But tonight I can show you on top of you."

Well.

"I'm going to give you a quick Painting 101 lesson. Then I'm going to finish my work for the day. Then tonight after dinner I'm going to encourage Piper to eat dessert at my parents' house unless you tell me no."

Before she could think, answer, swear, beg, he moved his hands to the small of her back, leaned forward, and kissed her.

Disco music exploded in her head. Boogie nights, baby. Danny was both gentle and urgent, considerate and aggressive. He was taking her mouth, working it over, licking and sliding and sucking his way deeper and deeper inside her while she gripped the belt loops of his jeans and clung.

He pulled back, leaving her lips wet and lonely. "Tell me no, Amanda. Tell me we can't do this tonight."

She sucked in a breath, trying to reassure herself that her lungs knew what they were doing and she wasn't suffocating, no matter that it felt like she was.

How could he ask her to do that? How could he expect her to be the rational one? She was in her freaking underwear, and his erection was jammed right between her thighs.

There was no remembering her own name right now, let alone why they weren't supposed to have incredible sex and live happily ever after until the next morning.

When she didn't answer, he did it again. Kissed her. With lots of tongue.

That wet collision had her panting and burning and extremely aware that the crotch of her panties was being compromised. She was damp with arousal and shocked at how easily that had happened. It wasn't like she normally needed a tube of KY Jelly or anything, but it took more than a kiss.

Usually.

Not the case today.

But he felt so good, so hard, so real, so caring, and his calloused hands had left her bare back and were playing with the waistband of her panties. Flip down, roll up, flip down, roll up, until she wanted to scream.

"Tell me no, Amanda. Tell me we can't." Danny knew he wasn't being fair to Amanda. She kept telling him no, over and over, and he kept asking. He knew she was attracted to him sexually, knew that eventually she would say yes if he kept harassing her about it, and that he should let it go. Do the right thing.

But fucking-damn, it was hard. Too hard. He couldn't do it.

She was in her *underwear*.

Looking hotter than hell. Looking long and lean and firm, bronzed and beautiful. Looking like all she needed was a spritz of oil all over her and she could be on the cover of *Maxim*. Her panties couldn't be serving any other purpose than ensuring her shorts could zip, because they only covered the absolute essentials. She had small, firm breasts, and her bra was shoving them up and out of the half-moon cotton cup.

He was helpless. He was hopeless. He was a quivering blob of ball-busting lust.

Lips on hers, kissing, biting, hands sinking inside the back of her panties, stroking, stroking. His throbbing cock pressing, pressing, while he tried to think rational thoughts.

"Yes," she said in a whoosh of hot air. "Yes, yes, damn it all to hell and back, yes."

He swore his knees went weak with gratitude. "Are you sure?" he asked like a dumb ass.

"Oh, yeah. I'm as sure as sure can get. But if you want, I'll put it in writing." And she nipped his bottom lip.

"Not necessary," he panted, giving her another quick kiss. That turned into another. And another.

While the kisses grew hotter and longer, his fingers somehow managed to stroll to the front of her panties. He cupped her, felt her heat against his hand, while she jerked an inch back and looked at him with glazed eyes.

For a split second he thought they could finish this right

then and there. He could just undo his jeans, pull her panties aside, lean against the unpainted wall and be there together in about sixty seconds.

Then sanity returned. He had learned something in nine years.

Lust was empty and selfish.

He didn't want that with Amanda. Those were not the feelings he had for her. He wanted to show her how special she was, how he cared, how he wanted to see her happy.

"Sorry. Damn, sorry, Princess." Pulling his hand out of her panties, he took a step away. Grabbed a deep breath. Put his hands behind his back and into his pockets so he wouldn't lose control and reach for her.

She gave him a suspicious look. "Sorry for what?" she growled.

They'd had this conversation before. And she hadn't liked his answer that time. Crap, he couldn't remember what he'd said and how he'd done it wrong. But she hadn't liked the whole apology thing.

"I just mean that I'm sorry that . . . it's not tonight. Because then I would . . ." He was really having a hard time with this. He was not a seductive kind of guy, and if he tried to be sexy, he was going to sound like Romeo, the porn version.

She didn't look impressed either. Her hand had snuck up to her bare hip and her lips pursed.

Maybe if he wasn't looking her in the eye he could do this. But when he did, right after noticing the little blue horse stitched on her panties, he thought about how many suave and sophisticated men she must have encountered in her life, and he froze up solid.

So he pulled her toward him, tempted himself by fitting her right along the length of him. Nuzzling his mouth into her hair, he grasped for some courage and the right words.

He whispered in her ear, "I would make love to you. I

really, really want to right now, but I'm going to wait because I want to take my time. I want to satisfy you."

"Nice save," she said.

Damn. She wasn't buying it.

But it was true. So he said exactly what he'd been thinking, in his own words. "I mean it. Sure, it entered my mind to just unzip, scoot your panties over, and go at it right now, but I figured that would be cheating both of us. So I pulled back and said I was sorry. Sorry. I want you to get everything out of it, that, ah, you need."

Amanda gave a husky laugh and ran her lips over his chin. "Mr. Unselfish."

"I try." Danny stripped off his T-shirt and tossed it on Piper's bed.

"What are you doing?" Amanda shot him a nervous look, at the same time she dropped her eyes and ogled his chest.

He was grateful for all the hours of manual labor he put in. He never needed to work out—pitching hay and other chores kept him in shape. But now wasn't the time for her to be exploring his chest. Later on that night he planned to carve out plenty of time for that. "I'm going to help you paint."

"Oh. Right. Of course."

Danny pulled a drawer open on the dresser and removed one of his large T-shirts that had two tears near the hem. Gathering the shirt up toward the neck hole, he yanked it over Amanda's head. Her hair spread across her face, and she blew at it.

"What the hell?"

"A paint shirt. Whole dresser full of them. Feel free to use them whenever you want to paint, or clean, or whatever."

She stuck her arms through the sleeves and tugged it down. "Paint shirt. Wow. What a concept."

He surveyed the room so far. "It looks like you're doing pretty good." If he ignored the paint droplets from one end of the room to the other, the streaky wall, and the various big blobs of dried paint on Amanda's body. She looked like she'd been in a paintball war and lost.

It was time to raise the flag and surrender.

"Flattery will get you everywhere." Amanda reached for the roller. "The problem here is that the wall just like sucks the paint up."

Danny liked that Amanda didn't pout or give up. She just fought her way through, but when help was offered, she wasn't too stubborn to take it either. "You actually have too much paint on the roller. You need to roll until there isn't any more coming off."

He put his hand over hers and pushed hard on the roller, up and down with her until they had covered a three-foot-wide area. "Start at the bottom and work your way up, using a pattern so there won't be streaks."

Hip bumping into her backside, their arms aligned, her hair falling over her shoulder, Danny found himself leaning forward. And she was leaning back.

She looked cute in his shirt. Felt good in his arms. Had a way with his daughter.

"I never thought that manual labor could be sexy, but I'm thinking that it is."

"Tell me about it." He was glad he'd taken his shirt off. He was sweating.

"So . . . do you have any sort of like, explanation for what is going on between us?"

"Nope."

"Oh."

He brought the roller to a stop, out of paint. Out of patience. He wanted her.

"Then I can take it from here, because we're about to end up in the same place we were before."

Danny froze with his free hand two inches from her ass, which he had been about to grab and grind against. "I don't know what you're talking about."

"Uh-huh." She nudged him with her hip. "Move it, Tucker. I'll see you after dinner."

Damn. "You have amazing self-control." He backed up and grabbed his shirt off the bed.

"Tell me about it." She looked at him over her shoulder. "Except when it comes to handbags. I can never resist a good handbag."

And she winked, which made him want to groan.

Danny beat a retreat before he tested her self-control any further.

His was already shot to hell.

Chapter 17

*P*iper's scrawny legs reached for the sky, her head tilted back, an expression of abandon on her rosy cheeks, as she clung to the chains of the swing. Danny was pushing her—he didn't need to, she was eight, after all—but he liked to do it.

He liked the pressure of his hand on her small, sweaty back, liked sending her soaring high up into the air so that she smiled and gasped with delight. Piper didn't squeal or laugh loudly or demand *higher*, but nonetheless she looked and acted and felt like a child when she was swinging.

That pleased him. As did the way she moved around the house now, without hesitation, and the way she no longer scooted away from his touch. Her shoulders were straighter when she stood, and she didn't cower. Her skin had a healthy glow that had been missing when she'd arrived, and despite Amanda's obsession with slathering sunscreen on her, Piper was slow-roasting her way to a tan in the August heat.

It had only been a bit shy of three weeks, but he liked to think they were both settling in, and that there was good to show for it in Piper already. Eventually, he hoped she would trust him. Love him. That he could be a real father despite having missed the first eight years of her life.

He wouldn't ever forgive himself for that, would always ache for what he hadn't seen, hadn't been able to do for her, but he was grateful for what he did have. He had the rest of her life, and that was a pleasant future to look forward to.

"That's high enough," she told him, lifting her hand off the chain to point to the swing next to her. "But can you push Anita?"

"Okay." He was trying to roll with this whole made-up friend business, but truthfully, Amanda was better at it than he was. He always felt like a first-class fool talking to the air. But for Piper's sake, he pulled the empty swing back and let it go. "Hang on, Anita."

Piper dropped her bare feet to the ground and swiped them back and forth until she slowed down. "Let me push you."

He figured she was talking to Anita, so he stepped to the side. But Piper jumped off the swing and pointed to it. "Sit down."

"Me?" he asked in surprise, slapping his thumb onto his chest. He eyed the slingshot seat with suspicion. "I don't think that will hold me, baby girl. I'm a big guy."

"Hairy too," she said with a perfectly straight face. "Like a gorilla. That's what Anita thinks."

"Hey!" Danny burst out laughing. "I am not hairy. And the hair I have is blond, so I'm nothing like a gorilla."

"Let me push you." Piper patted the seat encouragingly and gave him a smile.

Like he could resist that. "Alright, but I'm telling you, my butt is not going to fit in there."

But it did. Just barely. The swing set creaked a little under the strain of his weight. "By the way, tonight you'll have to sleep in my room, because Amanda has stunk yours up with paint. I'll sleep on the couch."

"Okay. Can I bring my butterfly comforter?"

"Sure thing." Her new bedding had arrived, and she had been using it already. The rapturous look on her face when she had opened the bag had given him naked joy.

Piper's hands pressed against his back, but he didn't move an inch. He tried to lean forward and make it easier for her, but he was stuck in the sling seat and couldn't get any leverage.

He tilted his head back so he could see her. She was biting her lip and straining against his back to make him move, her feet slipping in the dirt. Her eyes locked with his, upside down.

"Do you love me?"

He almost fell off the swing.

"Anita says you can't, because you never knew me before, and because Mark says only a mother could love me."

"I love you, Piper." Danny sat up, chest tight, and voice trembling a little. "Come on around here." He pulled her onto his lap in the swing. "I love you more than anything."

She studied him sideways, her dark, wide eyes searching. For honesty, for someone she could trust, he guessed. "Amanda says she loves me too."

And Danny had one more reason to like Amanda Delmar. "Yes, she does, baby. And so do Grandma and Grandpa. We're your family, and we'll always love you."

Her bony backside shifted on his lap, and her voice trembled. "Promise?"

Little hands dug into his jeans above his knees. Danny nodded firmly with all the assurance he could thrust into the gesture, knowing he would probably have to repeat the words many times over the years.

"I promise. I'll always love you."

♡

Amanda didn't know why she was feeling nervous. This was no different than any other date she'd had in her adult life. She was acutely aware a man wanted to have sex with her.

But this time, she wanted to have sex with him right back.

And frankly, that hadn't happened that often. When it did, it was after she had made the rational decision to sleep with a man.

There was nothing rational about her feelings for Danny Tucker, as was evidenced by the fact that she was wearing denim shorts and a paint-spattered T-shirt nine sizes too big for her and still feeling rather sexy. She sipped her coffee at the table and ran her finger over the lace tablecloth. It was good coffee, the real thing. Danny had bought it for her, she knew, though he didn't say that. It was just in the pantry all of a sudden, a nice bag of freshly ground beans, French roast blend.

He was such a nice guy, and she was going to have sex with him in about five minutes.

Piper had run off to Willie and Daniel's house for the much-coveted blackberry pie or cobbler or torte Willie always seemed to be producing. Bless her.

"Let me just get these dishes in the dishwasher," Danny said as he got up from the table.

And then rip your clothes off was implied.

Amanda felt ridiculous just standing there watching him while she pictured him with no pants on. So she started clearing the rest of the dishes from the table. "Here." She handed the plates over to him so he could rinse them.

Having another meal with his family was starting to become a habit. One that probably wasn't wise. Because in spite of the overabundance of carbs and starch, she actually enjoyed herself. They were so unpretentious, so honest. So unimpressed by money, status, names.

It made her life feel like a Rubic's cube. Unsolvable.

There didn't seem to be a place for her in either the world she'd been born into, or this one here on the Tucker farm.

But tonight, she had decided none of that mattered, and that she was going to enjoy her time with Piper. Her time with Danny.

"Do you think I'll be able to paint the second coat tomorrow?"

"Yep. Then Brady can get started on the butterflies the day after."

"Cool." Amanda put the butter back in the fridge. "When is your appointment with the school counselor?"

"Tuesday of next week. She'll assess Piper. It's too bad we don't have the records from her previous school, but they wouldn't release them for me until I have custody."

"How long will that take?"

"We're going straight to the clinic after the appointment at the school to have the blood drawn. I wasn't going to tell Piper what the blood was for. I didn't want her to worry that maybe I'm not her biological father." Danny dropped silverware in the basket and shook his head. "I know the tests will tell the truth—I'm her father. But if she knows, she'll just worry until the results come back, which won't be for a week or so. Do you think it's wrong to lie to her?"

Amanda thought Danny had the most amazing natural instincts for being a parent. He thought things through, from every angle, and he always, always put Piper first. "I think that it's not lying. It's simply not telling the whole truth, and you're right. There is no reason to give her something to worry about."

It should have felt odd, to walk over to Danny and stroke his cheek, but it didn't when Amanda did. "Trust yourself, Danny. You know what you're doing."

His arms came around her. He sighed. "Thank you. For everything. All of this has been a lot easier because of you."

Standing in his small kitchen, surrounded by cheap flat-ware and Danny's big farmer arms should have felt weird. Like she'd fallen into someone else's life, or done a reality show switcheroo. But it felt more real than anything she'd ever done in her life.

Nothing artificial, nothing stylish. Nothing artfully arranged, nothing designer.

Just a sense of contentment with a man she trusted more than any she'd ever known before.

Dangerous, scary, bad thoughts that could get her into serious trouble. But she didn't care. She just wanted to ab-sorb the moment, revel in it, roll the feelings over her so later on, she could pull them back out of her memory and remember that there were good men in the universe, though few and far between. So when she was dating men who thought manual labor was slicing the gouda cheese, she would remember that there were men who sweated for the food on their table.

So she could remember Danny when it was impossible for her to see him again.

He patted her butt in that friendly, affectionate way he had. "You've been a big help, Amanda."

"Since we're passing out certificates of appreciation, thank you for trusting me with Piper. Giving me a job." Then because she was in danger of feeling a little sappy, emotions a bit too close to the surface, she added, "And for trusting me in your home with a paint roller, even though you knew I had no clue what I was doing."

He gave a soft chuckle. Kissed her lightly. Reached into a drawer.

A drawer? Amanda pulled back. She happened to know the oven mitts were kept in there. O-kay. Somehow she'd never pictured Danny having a Betty Crocker fetish.

Until she saw he had a box of condoms in his hand.

"You keep condoms in the oven mitt drawer? I would have thought your dresser would make more sense."

He cleared his throat, avoiding her eyes, which was just adorable. He was embarrassed. "Well, uh, I threw them in there and forgot to move them."

"Whatever. Yay you for even remembering them. I don't have any." She'd dumped the remaining few she had in the pile of Logan's belongings that she had tossed out of her apartment into the hallway. When he had run swearing after his wallet, she had closed the door and locked it.

It had been satisfying, but not nearly as funny as it would have been if he'd been naked. But he had pulled his shorts on after sex, so he could call his girlfriend on his cell phone while Amanda had been in the shower. Fortunately, she had forgotten her new apricot body scrub and had stepped out of the bathroom and caught his duplicitous conversation.

Not that she wanted to remember her humiliation with Logan when she was with Danny.

"So let's go use one or two."

Danny didn't say anything. He just took her hand, turned around, and pulled her out of the kitchen, across the living room, down the short hall. She wanted to say something, to crack a joke, to laugh seductively, to tug her hand out of his. But her heart was thumping hard and her mouth was dry.

Nothing witty was rattling around in her nervous brain so she just followed him, the only sound her flip-flops slapping on the carpet.

Her dusting duties didn't include Danny's bedroom. She had walked by a hundred times when the door was open and had never given it much more than a cursory glance. It was like the rest of the house—functional, but lacking in décor. There was a bed, unmade, plaid sheets glaring at her. A dresser with two drawers half open. A fan blowing on high. Lots of dirty shoes lying around, and several crumpled-up pairs of jeans. The closet was open, revealing— surprise!—more denim and enough T-shirts to suggest he needed a support group for cotton addicts.

"It's not much," he said, kicking two pairs of shoes under the bed.

"It's fine. But if you ever want to get in touch with your inner-decorator, let me know. I'll guide you." Amanda kicked her flip-flops off by the door.

"I don't have an inner-decorator. That wouldn't leave any room for beer."

She would not laugh. That would only encourage him. But even as she covered her mouth with her hand, she couldn't stop a wheezy sort of chuckle from slipping out. That petered out when Danny stripped off his shirt and let it drop to the floor.

"Take that shirt off, Amanda. I just want to feel you." He wasn't waiting for her, but was tugging at her shirt, lifting it over her breasts.

Which reminded her of her shortcomings. "There isn't a lot of me to feel. I'm optimistically an A cup. I would buy training bras for the fit if they didn't have those goofy little pink bows on them."

And why was she doing that? Warning him, turning her chest into a joke. Being defensive, revealing herself to be needy. Now he would feel obligated to give her a compliment. Or worse, tell her it was okay, he couldn't ask for everything.

He did neither. He just ripped off her shirt. Then popped open her bra and stuck his mouth right on her nipple and gave it a suck.

No talking. Good plan. Amanda dug her fingers into his back. Then promptly dropped them. Logan had said she was a back scratcher and that it was annoying.

Danny pulled her closer and made little murmurs of approval as he moved from one breast to the other.

Amanda moaned. Then clamped her lips shut. She muttered, "Don't you think we should close the door? And lock it? What if Piper comes back? Or your mom?" God, there was a scary thought. Willie Tucker walking in on Danny licking her nipple. Her desire disappeared.

Hot, cold, hot, cold. She was a regular thermostat.

Danny lifted his head and scrutinized Amanda. She looked tense. She sounded a bit on the edge of hysteria.

He was nervous enough himself, as it was, afraid he wouldn't measure up to her previous lovers. Her obvious uncertainty wasn't going to help one bit.

Reaching behind her, he shut the door and pushed the button in to lock it. "We'll hear them come in the kitchen door."

"We will?"

Maybe. "Sure." Danny pushed her bra off her shoulders so it would fall to the floor. Amanda stood there in her denim shorts and nothing else, looking a bit like she'd just decided to sell her soul to Satan and was regretting it.

And he had the most horrible, uncomfortable thought that here he was planning on having sex with Amanda on this bed and he had just told his daughter she would be sleeping there that night.

Danny just stood staring at Amanda, in doubt.

Something wasn't working here.

But Amanda seemed to give herself a mental shake, because she went over to the bed and lay down on her side. The move should have looked sexy as sin, but instead looked practiced to him. Like she was posing, not being spontaneous.

He popped the button on his jeans, aroused in spite of all his random, colliding, doubting thoughts. Amanda was laid out on his bed. It was impossible not to react, even if it was halfhearted. Which meant he was an idiot. He shouldn't be thinking at all. He should just be diving on her. No wonder he sucked at making love to a woman. He was slow.

Feeling like an ox climbing into bed with a gazelle, he managed to climb up beside her without tipping her onto the floor. Her pouty smile was looking a little strained.

He gave her a kiss, a soft one, that didn't lead to anything. It was just a nice, what-the-fuck-are-we-doing? kind of kiss.

Amanda's hand started roaming over the front of his jeans. Around and around and Danny wanted to crawl under the bed and bludgeon himself to death with her flip-flop. She wasn't finding anything.

She sighed. "This isn't going to happen, is it?"

Or maybe he could smother himself in the pillow. "I don't think so." He tried to will himself to rise to the occasion, but there was no cooperation.

"I'm sorry. It's my fault." She flopped on her back and rested her hands on her stomach above her shorts. "I'm giving off weird vibes, aren't I?"

He was pretty damn sure they both were. "I think we're both thinking, worrying."

"My last boyfriend . . ." She pulled the bed pillow over her chest and hugged it. "God, I can't believe I'm going to tell you this. But I overheard him telling someone that he wished I'd get a boob job. And that I had a nonexistent ass. And that, uh, my skills in bed were lacking."

"You're kidding." Danny forgot all about his own discomfort and brushed Amanda's hair back from her cheek. He propped himself on one elbow. "That's crazy. And rude, the asshole. You have a fabulous body. Sometimes I think I need a bib when I'm looking at you."

She gave a tight laugh. "You're very sweet, but I know I don't have any breasts. I got implants a few years ago, but I had them taken out nine months ago, right before I met Logan, ironically. I wanted to be me, just me, and thought that would be enough. Guess I was wrong."

"No, you weren't wrong. You don't need bags of saline shoved in your chest to make you attractive and desirable." The very thought made him angry, nauseous. "What a jackass. And he called himself your boyfriend? How could he say things like that about you?"

Amanda turned a little, and he could see luminous tears

hovering in her eyes. "Because he didn't give a shit about me. I thought he did, but it turned out he had a girlfriend on the side, the woman he actually cared about. A woman he actually enjoyed having sex with. I was just his meal ticket."

When a tear rolled down her cheek, he wiped it with his thumb, distraught at the pain splashed all over her face. "Oh, Princess, that's just so wrong . . . I'm so sorry."

"I've never been so humiliated in my whole life. And apparently it's stuck some doubts in my head, because I was standing here and all I could think was that what if I am lousy in bed and no one had the guts to tell me? I didn't want to disappoint you and embarrass myself." She rolled on her side, toward him, and gave a laugh. "Of course, I've already embarrassed myself by dumping all this on you. *Here are all my flaws and insecurities*—how unsexy is that?"

But it was actually very sexy. It leveled the playing field.

"I'm so damn glad you said something." Danny stroked her breast, held his hand over the warm flesh. "To tell you the truth, I was getting a little performance anxiety. I figured you've been with all these charming rich guys, and I'm just a hick. I've only had sex twice since my divorce from Shel three years ago, and trust me, neither time was anything to write home about. I was starting to think it was me."

Her eyebrows shot up. "Well, aren't we a pair? It's almost funny."

Danny lay down beside her and pondered the ceiling. He was so relieved, he did feel like laughing. Amanda didn't expect perfection from him. "Do you ever think things happen for a reason, Amanda? Like maybe you're here in Cuttersville because we both needed each other right now?"

She was quiet, and he started to think it had been a mistake to blather out his thoughts. But then she whispered, "I'd like to say that the reason I'm here in Cuttersville is boredom and a father with a warped sense of justice. But I don't know, Danny . . . when I'm here with you, like this, it seems too right to be an accident. I think maybe you're onto something."

He put his arm around her shoulder and pulled her in toward his chest. "No pressure. I just want to hold you."

"We're just going to cuddle? Sure, that's what all the boys say." But she nuzzled in along him, her cheek resting on his chest.

Danny thought her skin felt like butter, soft and creamy. They should probably get their shirts back on, but he was reluctant to let Amanda go.

"Danny? Do you think about the future? Do you ever wonder where you'll be in five years?"

That was easy enough. "Right here, Princess. On this farm, with Piper. I always figured I'd get married, but I don't imagine that will happen now. Piper will be my focus, not dating."

Though a foolish voice in his head suggested that maybe Amanda could be talked into staying on the farm. She loved Piper, after all. Then sanity returned, and he pictured an ugly breakup when Amanda got tired of life down on the farm and took off for the city. He imagined his heartbreak, and Piper's. Not a good road to travel.

He had nothing to offer Amanda except his heart, and he didn't think that would be worth much at auction.

"What about you? Where will you be in five years?" He could guess. She'd be married to some pretty boy, giving dinner parties and taking European vacations. Maybe she'd have a child of her own, though the thought made him kind of sick. He hoped whatever it was, she'd be happy.

"I don't know. I honestly have no idea." Her nails ran across his stomach idly. "If you had asked me that two months ago, I would have guessed I'd be doing the same thing at thirty that I was at twenty-five. Shopping, partying, traveling, being bored out of my mind. But I can't do that. I just can't go back to that. And I can't do the opposite of that either."

He wasn't sure what the opposite was, but it didn't matter if she couldn't do it.

"I have to find something in the middle, I guess. I have to find a career that I can enjoy. My cousin Stuart in New York has connections. He can get me a job. Maybe as an art buyer."

Something that was far away from Cuttersville, he guessed. He knew that. Had always known it. But he wanted to hold Amanda, keep her, love her. And ultimately that would stifle her.

"You'd be great at that." Whatever it was, exactly. But it sounded Amanda-like.

"I really don't know if that's what I want though. I don't know . . . I just don't know." Amanda sat up, putting her arm on the opposite side of his chest, so she hovered over him, her breasts touching his chest. "But I do know I'm so glad I met you."

"So am I." More than he could express with just words. He put his hand on the back of her head and guided her down to him.

When her mouth met his, she had already opened it for him, and Danny was grateful all over again.

Chapter 18

*D*anny Tucker had a way of making Amanda forget who she was. Or maybe he let her forget that she had to be anything but herself.

With Danny, it didn't matter what she was wearing or how her hair looked, or if her makeup was au courant for the season. She didn't have to name-drop and technology-flash and have the hottest ideas for entertainment.

She just had to be herself, and that after-school-special-sounding cliché was liberating.

He kissed with a kind of tender recklessness. It was hot and eager and filled with an intensity she had never felt, and didn't understand. The way he held on to her back, moved across her mouth, was like he wanted to absorb her into him, hold on, make it last.

The effect on her inner thighs was exhilarating. Danny wanted her, and help her, she wanted him. She coveted him; she had to have him. A desperate part of her brain knew she would never meet another man quite as sweet as

Danny, and she wanted to feel him inside her before he changed his mind.

She tangled her tongue with his, encouraging, grinding her hips onto his after she climbed up onto him. Her bare chest pressed into his hot, hard flesh as she wiggled her mound against his erection. Oh, yes, right there, it was nice and perfectly positioned, and she moaned, ripping her mouth off his.

"Take off your jeans." And to prove she was serious, she grappled with the zipper on them, finally getting it down. She dusted a kiss on his navel, running her nose over the soft blond hair there.

Danny was breathing heavy, eyes half closed, and he didn't hesitate. He set her aside, undid his pants, and stripped them down his legs, giving hard little kicks until they fell off his feet. He sat up and reached for her, and she almost passed out.

Damn, he was so hot. He was like a sculpture with hair. Everything was hard and muscular and big. Everything. Yowsa, that fabric was stretched tight across his pelvis.

"Take off your boxers too," she said in a breathy voice straight out of the sorority house.

That freaked her out a little. She was tempted to glance around the room and see who in the hell had said that. She didn't demand men take off their underwear. She didn't use a wispy, sex-kitten voice. And she didn't lay on beds in her shorts topless with no sign of her hair extensions, and six weeks out from her last pedicure and bikini wax.

But she had never been with a man like Danny—brawny and earthy and unselfish.

Danny liked the bossy little slut voice. He gave her an arrogant grin. "If you insist."

His boxers went bye-bye and then he was lying next to her, moving in for the kill. He couldn't do it fast enough to suit her. She was aroused in a painful, achy, desperate kind of way that was as baffling as it was exciting. She was squirming in her shorts, and he hadn't even touched her yet.

When he did, it was only to strip her of her shorts, yanking them down until they were inside out. She gasped when the air hit her bare skin. He had taken the panties too.

"Thought I'd kill two birds with one stone."

"Good plan." And she would not be embarrassed. There was nothing wrong with her body. She wouldn't lock her legs together. Danny desired her, wanted her, would never use her.

"Amanda . . ." He sucked in his breath.

She forced her eyes open, heart pounding and shoulders tight with tension, even as she knew she trusted him not to hurt her. "Yes?"

He dropped his finger onto her breast, traced the outline of her curve while goose bumps rose on her flesh. His eyes roamed over her. "God, you're beautiful. I don't have any better words for it than that . . . but it's true. I've never wanted a woman the way I want you right now."

Something inside her swelled and burned, with hope, with tenderness, with desire.

She had laid herself out to Danny both literally and figuratively, and he took that and made it seem natural. He made her feel real.

"I want you too. And I don't want to wait anymore." With hot, trembling fingers, she reached out and stroked him, squeezing a little up and down the length of him.

He shuddered. "Were we waiting? I didn't think we were."

Reaching behind to the nightstand, he grabbed the box of condoms and shook one loose. Amanda reluctantly let go of his erection so he could sheath it. When he had it in place, he drew her leg over his hip, opening her up while they both stayed on their sides.

She liked facing him like this, both relaxed, their mouths close, shoulders even. It was comfortable and intimate, feelings she wasn't sure she'd ever really shared with another man.

Amanda swallowed hard as he settled her leg higher, forcing her to come apart for him. The position had her spread wide, vulnerable, and he pressed against her wet heat with a finger. Gliding up and down over her clitoris and dipping inside her, his finger was teasing and torturous. Danny stared at her, the left side of his head resting on the pillow.

"You feel amazing. Tight and slick. I want to push inside you," he murmured, nuzzling his nose across her cheek.

Amanda closed her eyes, arching her body toward his touch. He was doing the most delicious subtle things inside her, stroking here, pressure there. "I'm good with that."

He removed his finger right as his mouth took hers with passion. The man could kiss. One lip lock and he had her feeling like the sexiest woman this side of Vegas. And it was more than that. It was that when he kissed, she could feel emotion in it. She could feel that when she was with him, she mattered to Danny.

It was just as arousing as any stroke of his fingers.

The room was hot, the sun still streaming in through the windows, and the bed was creaking beneath them. But Amanda was only vaguely aware that a world existed outside of Danny Tucker's naked body. She took a quick glance down at him as he knocked on her door, so to speak, with his penis.

The whole leg thrown over his hip thing seemed a little innovative, though visually damn sexy. "Is this going to work?"

"I have no idea, but I'm willing to try."

Okay, then, she could be spontaneous too. "Try away."

He didn't just try. He made it work. Danny put his hand on her ass to keep her immobile, and he entered her with a big push that knocked the air right out of her overworked lungs.

"Holy shit . . ." was his opinion.

"Aaahhh" was hers. Her tongue tied in knots. Her fingers went numb. Her gut shivered, and her legs locked.

"You okay?" He hovered in her, throbbing and deep, his grip on her backside relaxing a little.

Amanda nodded, not sure she could speak. She dug her stubby fingernails into his shoulders and didn't care if he liked scratching or not. If she didn't hold on, she was going to end up on the floor.

Danny pulled back, then pushed in, and her head snapped back on a moan.

Then again, harder. Deeper.

She found her voice again. "Oh, God, that feels incredible."

Closing her eyes, she relaxed, let him build a rhythm, dropped her fingers down to his waist. His muscles flexed as he thrust into her, and his breath came in short staccato pants.

Then she was falling, without even a push. She was just sliding off into ecstasy, her orgasm a slow, undulating river of pleasure, unexpected and easy.

He pumped faster, and she dragged her eyes open, smiling in exhilaration at him. "I said it before, but that . . . feels . . . so . . . good."

"Tell me about it," he said through gritted teeth, his upper lip moist.

Feeling playful and satisfied and yet like she could lie there and let him sink into her for the rest of her life, Amanda bit at his mouth. "Mmmm."

Danny paused for a split second, long enough for her to realize he was about to come, so she squeezed her inner muscles tightly around him.

"Amanda," he whispered in a ragged voice. Then he exploded in her with a deep moan, hand convulsing on her thigh.

His eyes were locked on hers and as he pounded himself into her, Amanda knew that he was with her, he was one hundred percent focused on her and not anyone or anything else.

As he slowed down, she gave a soft laugh. "No wonder there's so much sex on a farm. It's really great sex."

He drew in a shuddery breath and brushed her hair off her cheek. "Never that great before."

Excuse her while she went and purred. She felt relaxed, sluggish, exhilarated. Wiggling a little, she scooted closer to him.

"I'm sweaty," he warned.

"I don't care." She wanted to feel him up against all of her, shoulder to toes, while he was still imbedded inside her.

"Good. And you know, I think the thing about great sex is that, it's even better when you do it with the right person."

His arms closed around her back, making her feel feminine and cherished. "That's true."

When he kissed the top of her head, she tried to remember why she wasn't going to trust another man with her heart. Why she wasn't going to let a man control her future ever again. She couldn't even seem to remember why it was important to leave Cuttersville behind at the end of the summer and return to her regularly scheduled life.

All she could seem to think about was that it would be really simple to fall in love with Danny Tucker. One green light from her brain to her heart, and she'd be there.

The only thing that stopped her was the knowledge that she was more liability than asset to a man like Danny. She came with a heap of insecurities and a host of selfish issues, and had little or no practical skills.

But that didn't mean she couldn't enjoy this with him while she was here. He was willing, they both understood there was no future, and he was giving her back something she had forgotten to give herself—respect.

Danny liked her for who she was, and so did she.

"You know you have a farmer's tan." She ran her hands

over his hip. He was golden bronze from the waist up. Below that, he was like bleached cotton.

"Well, what an amazing coincidence, since I'm a farmer." He gave her a wry grin as he shifted a little and pulled out of her.

She sighed a little at the loss. "I could fix that for you."

"I don't want it fixed." Danny rolled over, reaching for his boxer shorts. "I don't really care."

"You don't care that your butt is white?" she teased, as he flashed same said butt when he stood.

"No. I really don't. It's not like I have to look at it." He stepped into his boxers and gave the waistband a snap to get it in place.

Amanda laughed. "You're so practical. I love that about you."

Then she almost choked, realizing she had said the "L" word without thinking. His eyes widened, and she was sure hers did too. They could probably pass for a couple of bull-frogs staring at each other.

She really didn't want him to get the wrong idea. To think that she was dangling after him. That she was going to expect something from him beyond friendship and some incredible sex.

Sitting up, she let her hair fall over her face to hide any telltale redness that might be clashing with her tan. His T-shirt was the only piece of clothing within range, so she swiped it and pulled it on. "We should get dressed. Piper could be back any minute."

Danny picked his jeans up and stuck a foot in one leg. "You know what I love about you, Amanda?"

"Oh, God, I can't even imagine." Still a little embarrassed, she swung her legs toward him and scooted off the edge of the bed.

"Everything."

His calloused hand fell on her cheek, and Amanda gave a little involuntary gasp, touched to the point of near tears.

Her brain tripped the stoplight from red to green, and her heart sped ahead right straight into love.

Then he grinned, his hand falling away. "Except for your dusting. You can't dust for shit."

She gave a watery laugh. "Watch it, White Butt."

But it was too late. She had fallen in love with Danny. She couldn't go backward now, and she wasn't sure how to go forward. So for now, she'd just stand still and see what happened.

Chapter 19

*D*anny licked his ice-cream cone and relaxed as much as he could in a plastic chair too small for him. Piper had chocolate from her nose to her waist, specks and dribbles and smears. He wasn't sure if she was actually eating her ice cream or just throwing it all over herself.

He would have thought a kid at eight could be a little neater, but he had soon learned he didn't remember a whole lot about being eight. In all fairness to Piper, it was near ninety degrees and her cone was melting faster than she could lick. Amanda was in line getting another ice cream since she had dropped hers leaning over to wipe off the bench with a napkin before she sat down.

They were in town to collect Brady, the maestro who supposedly was going to turn the splotchy walls of Piper's bedroom into a butterfly garden. Danny had his doubts as he took a gander at Brady, sitting with his broken leg out in front of him, sucking industriously on a shake.

He'd done something different with his hair. It was short

all over, except for the front, where it cascaded straight down in individual spokes of hair. It looked like an art experiment gone wrong. A red waterfall. Weird. It was weird. And he wasn't sure how the hell Brady could see around that hair enough not to walk into walls, let alone paint them.

The urge to just reach out with the scissors and snip was overwhelming.

The kid had always been a little rebellious, slamming Cuttersville every chance he got and counting the days until he could leave, but walking around with hair in your eyes didn't seem rebellious, just stupid. And if Danny wasn't mistaken, Brady was wearing black eyeliner.

Yet Piper adored him. She giggled at everything he said, handed him his crutches every time he stood up, and generally flirted with him without knowing that's what she was doing.

It gave Danny indigestion. Having a girl was complicated. The thought of facing the teenage years struck terror in his heart, and he hoped like hell promiscuity was taught, not inherited. If some boy touched Piper at sixteen like he'd been touching her mother, Danny wasn't sure he could be held accountable for his actions.

It also made him wish Piper would have a stepmother to talk to. A blond one. With long legs.

"Butterflies like this?" Brady asked, showing Piper a sketch of a cartoony, smiling butterfly on a napkin.

She shook her head. "No . . . that looks babyish. But I don't want one like in magazines. I want a butterfly who looks like she's going to fly over the rainbow." And she capped this thought off with a shy smile.

Brady lifted an eyebrow. "Over the rainbow, huh?" He looked at Danny. "The kid's a tough sell."

Danny shrugged. "Just do something in between cartoons and *National Geographic*." He caught a drip from his cone before it landed on his hand. "And Piper, sweetie, maybe we should just let Brady do what he thinks is best. He'll make it look pretty, won't you, Brady?"

The sound of that almost made him laugh. Here he was, a twenty-six-year-old farmer with muddy boots, and Brady looking for a spot in the punk kid hall of fame, and they were supposed to know something about pretty?

Piper bit her lip, so Danny added, "I think it will be a fun surprise for you if he just goes in and paints a butterfly garden. Whattya think, baby girl? We'll let him do the worrying, and we'll just enjoy the picture when it's done."

"Good advice." Shelby strolled up to their table, a big smile on her face.

"Hey, Shel. What are you up to?"

"I've been to the doctor."

Danny took a long look at Shelby. Her cheeks were flushed, and she was grinning ear to ear. Couldn't be too serious then.

"Everything okay?"

"Come here," Shelby said, crooking her finger at him.

"What?" Danny stood up, his back wet with sweat from the plastic chair. "You're going to steal my ice cream, aren't you?"

She had a devilish look on her face, and he shifted his cone away from her. "I'll get you one of your own if you want, Shel."

But instead of grabbing his cone and licking it, she reached up on her tiptoes and whispered in his ear. "I'm pregnant."

Danny snapped his head back and looked at her eyes shining with happy tears. "That was awful fast—you've only been married a month."

"Birth control isn't always foolproof." She squeezed his arms. "Are you happy for me?"

"Yeah. Of course I am." He felt his own lips splitting in a grin. This was good. This was right. Maybe now that he had Piper and Shelby was having her own baby, they could both heal a little from the loss of their child, the loss of their family. "Congratulations, darlin', that's fantastic news."

He picked her up off the ground, ice-cream cone and all, and gave her a big smacking kiss on the lips. "You'll be the best mom around. Just make sure you take care of yourself, alright?"

"I will." She hugged him back, holding on tightly for a second before releasing him.

Amanda sat down in Danny's abandoned chair. "When you're done making out, here's your change." She threw a dollar and loose coins on the table in front of Piper.

Danny knew that tone of voice. It was Amanda being hurt and trying to act like she wasn't. It was her fake, sarcastic voice, and it told him clear as water that she was none too pleased with his attention to Shelby.

He didn't feel the least bit guilty for hugging his ex-wife when she was sharing such happy news with him. But what he wanted to do was snuggle right up to Amanda and reassure her. He wanted to pull her into his arms, plant his hands firmly on her butt, his lips right on hers, and show everyone that he cared about her. That he had seen her naked, been inside her body, and that she was his.

But she wasn't his. And they had agreed that in front of Piper there would be no butt-grabbing, kissing, or any other male-female relations that would only confuse her when Amanda left.

It was the right thing to do. He wouldn't hurt his daughter for anything in the world. Nor would he parade casual sex in front of her. Not that he felt casual about Amanda, but there was no other label for a couple who were having sex with no intention of creating a future together. He couldn't explain mutual consent and living in the moment and enjoying what they had now to Piper. Bad enough some day he was going to be pinned to the mat by her for his relationship with her mother. He didn't need to open that discussion when she was eight years old.

Nor could he describe the complexity of what he felt for Amanda to anyone without it seeming idiotic. Yes, he cared about her. Yes, he was falling in love with her. Yes, he could see settling in and loving her for a good long time. But no, they couldn't be together.

It seemed stupid even to him.

"Shelby has some good news, Amanda." Danny settled for putting his hand on the back of Amanda's shoulder and squeezing. No one would think anything of that. He touched people all the time.

Except Shelby was grinning at him, her eyebrows up under her hair, and Brady had a knowing little smirk on his face.

Amanda didn't toss his hand off, but she stiffened when he touched her. "That's wonderful, Shelby. Did your tour become part of a reality show or something?"

Shelby laughed. "No, I can't imagine the Haunted Cuttersville Tour hitting the airwaves. My news is more personal. I'm having a baby."

"Dude." Brady clapped Shelby on the back. "That's so cool."

"Congratulations."

Danny watched Amanda's reaction. She looked pleased for Shelby, but something else . . . wistful, maybe. Or maybe that was just him wishing it were wistful.

"Does Boston know?"

"I called him on his cell and told him." Shelby looked sheepish as she reached for Danny's ice-cream cone.

He let her have it without a fight. Eating for two and all that.

"I know it was kind of tacky to tell him over the phone, but I didn't want to wait until tonight. Of course, first thing, he said he was leaving work, which I didn't think about."

Tires squealed as a car flew into the parking lot. "There he is now." Danny recognized that fancy car.

"Oh, Lord." Shelby winced as Boston pulled into the spot at full speed and hit the parking barrier. "Maybe I should have waited to tell him."

Danny had to agree, given the look of complete and utter shock on Boston's face as he fast-walked across the parking lot.

"Are you sure you're pregnant?" he demanded, taking his wife by the arms.

"Yes," Shelby said.

"How did this happen?" Boston asked.

Amanda snorted, and Danny knew they shouldn't be listening to this conversation. He was about to herd Piper off to the truck, when his daughter stopped licking her ice cream long enough to say, "You make babies by having sex."

Every face swung in her direction with varying degrees of disbelief and shock displayed. Danny felt a pain in his chest. So much for thinking he was keeping her innocent. That hurt—pricking little needles of guilt jabbing into his heart. He didn't even want to know how she had knowledge of sex and conception.

Amanda slung her arm around Piper. "Wow, you're pretty smart, kid. So tell me how it works."

Piper shrugged, obviously not giving this conversation the same importance he was. She sucked on her drippy chocolate cone. "The man and woman take their clothes off and go to bed. Then the sperm goes from the man into the woman's egg and it makes a baby. I read all about in a book my mom got me from the library when Marcus was born."

Danny relaxed his hold on Amanda's shoulder. He'd just about poked his thumb through her flesh in horror. But thanks to Amanda's rational question, it turned out Piper just had standard birds-and-bees knowledge. It struck him that Amanda's manner with Piper wasn't always what one would think of as maternal, but her instincts were dead-on. She had a way with her, no question about that.

She had a way with him too. Listening to her, watching her, feeling her jealousy made him question why they couldn't just be together. For real. Like a family.

He loved her, quiet and steadfast. But with a passion that was hot enough to start a barn fire. He liked her. He respected her, admired her. Couldn't get enough of her. And she was going to leave him unless he convinced her not to.

"Didn't you know that about making babies?" Piper asked Amanda.

"Sure," Amanda said. "But I was just checking to see what you knew. Boston obviously had no idea. Maybe we should get him that book."

Boston was the only one not to laugh. Danny actually felt kind of sorry for the guy. Here he was finding his whole life was about to change standing in front of the Dippy Whip.

"Alright, Brady. Ladies. Let's head back to the farm and give the Macnamaras some privacy."

Everyone ignored him since Shelby was giving Boston an earnest look and asking, "Aren't you even the tiniest bit happy? I know it's sudden, but . . ."

Boston covered her mouth with his hand and collected himself. "Shhh. Of course I'm happy. I'm sorry, babe, I know I'm acting like an idiot. But I was just shocked, that's all. I'm very, very happy."

"Having a baby is a big responsibility," Piper said.

Danny wanted to laugh. When Piper ripped off comments like that and the whole baby-making information, Danny thought that he saw her mother's parenting at work. That maybe the reason Piper was such a great kid, and adjusting so well, was because Nina had been a good mother. Maybe she'd just had bad taste in husbands.

Fortunately, Boston smiled at Piper's comment as he pulled Shelby into his arms. "So you think I can handle it, Piper?"

Piper nodded, tossing the last bite of her cone in her mouth. "Just remember to feed it, and you'll be okay."

Amanda held Piper's hand as they crossed the parking lot to Danny's truck.

She was still embarrassed over the way she had sniped at Danny for hugging Shelby. His ex-wife was having a baby, and he had been congratulating her. Danny was an affectionate guy.

Yet she had thrown down his money like a child. Like a bratty heiress.

God, she couldn't think about it without wincing.

This was why she couldn't stay in Cuttersville. She obviously wasn't finished growing up, and no matter if she had realized she was in love with Danny or not. He and Piper deserved better than her.

The minute school started, she needed to get the hell out. Less than two weeks. Then she would leave, having honored her commitment to Piper and hopefully not damaging either one of them in the process.

She wasn't sure she was going to be able to walk away without some serious pain, but it was the right thing to do. Piper and Danny deserved a woman in their lives who already knew who she was. Who belonged.

Which meant she wasn't going to be able to have sex with Danny again. If she did, she wasn't sure she'd have the strength to leave him.

"I think that man is trying to get your attention," Piper said, pointing to her left.

Amanda jerked herself out of her thoughts of surviving twenty-four-hour horniness without allowing herself to touch Danny and glanced over. And sighed. "That's my father."

She gave Brett Delmar a wave to let him know she saw

him and moved Piper back to the sidewalk in front of the ice-cream store. Her father was driving a rental car, his eyes hidden behind sunglasses, but he still looked angry. She could see it in the tilt of his head, the tension in his shoulders.

This wasn't how she wanted to spend her afternoon, but she knew this was a good thing. She needed to resolve a few issues between the two of them, and she needed to do it in a calm, mature manner. No sarcasm, no biting remarks, no threats. At least on her part. She couldn't prevent him from behaving that way.

That was the crux of it. She couldn't change her father or his opinions. She had to be responsible for herself, first and foremost, and stop tossing the blame ball in his lap when she was intimidated or afraid or hurt.

Danny was still talking to Shelby and Boston, and Brady was making his way toward them with small swings of his crutches, his shorts in danger of dropping right off his hips.

Piper glanced back at him. "Maybe I should help Brady."

"With what?" He wasn't carrying anything. Amanda knew the signs of a crush when she saw them. Piper had the eight-year-old hots for Brady Stritmeyer. "You like Brady, huh?"

Piper nodded. "He's nice to me and he doesn't make fun of my hair. And he's sexy."

"Sexy?" Amanda burst out with a laugh. The kid was a riot today.

"That's what my mom always called boys she liked."

Keeping an eye on her father, Amanda swung Piper's hand back and forth. "Well, I can see that. But I don't think you should call Brady sexy in front of your dad. It might freak him out, you know what I mean?"

Piper nodded and her free hand came out, palm flat, fingers slightly spread. "I know what you mean. There's one way to talk to girls, and another way to talk to boys."

Amanda was spared a discussion of male-female dynamics by her father striding toward her. "Amanda."

"Hi, Dad. This is a surprise."

Her father was wearing his golf uniform—khakis and a navy three-button shirt. She wondered if he'd been yanked right off the course mid-hole and brought to the Cuttersville plant.

"Are you on your way to Samson?"

"I'm going to stop over there tomorrow, but I've really carved a chunk out of my schedule to see you."

That was kind of sweet. She smiled at him. "Well, I'm not exactly free at the moment, but we could have dinner together. I'll ask Danny if I can leave a little early."

Her father frowned. Amanda cleared her throat and put her hand on Piper's back. "This is Piper Schwartz, the little girl I babysit for. Her father is . . ." *My lover.* Amanda felt herself flushing as she turned to look for Danny.

"There he is. The guy in the jeans. That's Danny, Piper's father." Oh, God, she was starting to babble. Amanda pulled her teeth off her lip and ordered herself to be mature. Or at least pretend to be.

"Which guy? They're all wearing jeans." Her father lifted his sunglasses. "Is that Boston? Climbing all over that woman?"

"His wife. Yes. That's Boston. He just got some good news and they're celebrating." Amanda's tried to relax her locked-down jaw, but her teeth were clenched too tightly. "Piper, this is my father, Brett Delmar."

"Hi," Piper said, leaning against Amanda's hip. "Nice to meet you."

Piper had better manners than her father. Brett just glanced down at her and nodded. "Sweetie, go run along to your father. I need to speak with Amanda."

Annoyed at his presumptuousness, Amanda opened her mouth to tell Piper to stay, but she was already running toward Danny, clearly intimidated. "Dad, you can't do that. I'm getting paid to watch her."

"Then maybe you can tell her to wash her face. She was filthy."

Determination to be mature was collapsing, but she just squeezed her fists together and tried to stay calm. "We just ate ice cream. Now if you'd like to meet me for dinner, that would be wonderful, but right now I am working." She wanted to add *you should understand that* but restrained herself.

This was a time to mend their relationship, not bring up old resentments. He was who he was, and she either had to accept that or spend her life resentful.

He stuck his hands in his pockets and rocked back on the balls of his feet impatiently. "Oh, come on, Amanda. Can we just give up this charade? Your mother is worried about you. Just come home, and we'll find you a real job."

If he patted her on the head, she was going to scream. "What happened to tough love? You're the one who started this whole thing."

"I just wanted to get you home and humble you a little. I never expected you would resort to looking after some hick's dirty kid."

Amanda swallowed hard and chose her words very, very carefully. "Dad, please don't insult Danny or Piper. They're wonderful people, and it's been a privilege spending time with them. I know you mean well. I know you want me to come home and you probably didn't intend to cut me off for good. But truthfully, while it's hard and uncomfortable and inconvenient, I'm doing okay without your money, and it's been a positive, growing experience for me. I want to learn to take care of myself."

Brett stared at her. "You're serious. You'd rather stay here in Podunk than come home?"

"Yes."

He shook his head. "I don't understand you."

"And I don't understand you. But we can learn to work around it." She tried to give him a smile, but she couldn't quite manage it.

"No matter what I give you, you don't want it. You sneer and spit at it." His voice was bitter, his gray eyes hard and opaque.

That caught her so far off guard, she reached for his hand, vision blurring. "All I ever wanted was for you to love me."

His jaw worked. "Don't be childish. You always had that."

Amanda felt her head shaking back and forth before she was even aware she was doing it. He was standing there, and he believed everything he said was the truth—and she supposed it was from his perspective.

They could never see eye to eye on this. And neither one of them could change who they were or the past.

Amanda couldn't forget that he had wanted a son, that he had been harsh and judgmental. But she could forgive. She could move on, with her own life.

"Daddy, go home. I'm not coming back to Chicago. Not to punish you or to throw a temper tantrum, but because I need to see if I know how to be a real person instead of Barbie with a college degree."

"What are you talking about?" He rubbed his chest like he had heartburn.

Amanda reached out and kissed his cheek. "Trust me. I'll be fine. If you text message me Mom's phone number at the spa, I'll call her and let her know she doesn't have to worry."

"What are you going to do here?" He waved his hand around wildly.

"Exactly what I've been doing. Taking care of Piper and learning to live on a budget." When it was time to leave in September, she would make her way to New York and stay with Stuart for a while. She would find herself a job—hopefully in the art industry—and get herself on her feet.

"I can give you an allowance."

Her dad was starting to look panicked now. But Amanda didn't want the money between them for a change. She wanted to try and have a relationship with him that didn't rely on cold hard cash. "I'm fine for right now. But I'll let you know if I need some."

Danny and Piper were hovering by the truck, obviously waiting for her, and Amanda waved them over.

She introduced Danny, and her father had the sense to stick out his hand and shake, though he looked too bewildered to make conversation.

"You have a wonderful daughter, sir," Danny said, tossing her a smile. "She's been taking care of *my* daughter like she's her own, and I'm very grateful to her."

While Amanda contemplated kissing him for being so damn sweet, her father just nodded. "Good, good."

"Amanda, you can have the rest of the day off if you want to spend time with your dad. Piper and I can find something to do on our own."

"Actually, my father is leaving, aren't you, Daddy?" Amanda squeezed his hand. "I'll call you soon." Impulsively, she gave him a hug. "I . . . I love you."

He didn't say anything, but his arms came up in what could be called a loose embrace. Amanda figured that was progress.

She turned and started toward the truck. "Let's go. Brady's probably fallen asleep waiting for us."

Danny put his hand on the small of her back as they walked. He said in a low voice, "You okay?"

Nodding, she stopped and waited for him to unclick the door locks. She didn't trust herself to talk, feeling a little raw and a lot like crying.

"Piper, come on, baby girl."

Amanda turned and watched Piper scramble to catch up with them. She shoved something at Danny.

"Amanda's dad told me to give this to her. He said it's all he had right now."

Danny took the wad of money from Piper. "What the . . . ?" He started shifting through it. "Jesus Christ, this is over four thousand dollars. I'm holding a freaking fortune in my hand in the middle of the street." He blanched. "Where the hell is your purse?"

"I didn't bring it."

Danny shoved the money in his pocket, patting and smashing to make sure it was all in there. "Let's get home before a strong wind comes along."

Amanda looked across the street to where her father was pulling away in his Lexus rental car. "Bye, Daddy." She waved to him.

He didn't look back, but she suspected he was looking in his rearview mirror.

Money couldn't buy love, but maybe her father didn't know that.

Maybe she hadn't given hers any more freely than he had.

Chapter 20

*D*anny was going to ask Amanda to stay.

It was probably a huge mistake. She would laugh at him. Recoil in horror. Tell him no.

He knew the chances that Amanda would be willing to stay in Cuttersville on his farm as his wife were about as big as a dust mite. Sometimes even love couldn't make up for things like chickenshit. And he didn't even know if Amanda loved him or not. He was sure she cared about him, but love was another something altogether.

Plus seeing Piper shove that big wad of cash in his hand—a little afterthought from Amanda's father, and money he just happened to be carrying around—reminded Danny that Amanda was wealthy. He knew it, but sometimes he could convince himself it didn't matter. But he couldn't casually give Amanda four thousand dollars, not even if he saved half his life for it.

So while he would like to make Amanda his wife, he wasn't going to mention that to her just yet. First he had to get her to agree to stay on for a while, and he didn't want to wait until the day she was leaving to talk about it.

As it was, they had yet to discuss the fact that they had had sex four days ago. At the time, they had agreed not to reveal their relationship to Piper, but in the days since it was becoming apparent to Danny there was no relationship to show.

Amanda treated him like a friend, and an extremely platonic one at that.

Call him stupid, but he had just kind of assumed there would be more sex coming his way. That since they'd started, there wasn't any reason to stop having sex, until she had to leave.

If she had to leave. Which he didn't think she did.

So the plan was to tell her how he felt, convince her to stay, then get to enjoy her company and her body forever. He'd let her on to the getting married thing later when she was good and used to him and the farm.

Simple.

Not really, but he was hoping. Or fooling himself.

Brady had finished in Piper's room, and Amanda was hanging the blinds and drapes. Danny had asked her that morning if she needed help, but she had refused. Now he could hear her muttering and complaining and reading the directions out loud. Piper was plugged in to *Nick Jr.* on the TV, the poodle asleep on her lap.

"Hey, baby girl." Danny paused to just look at her. He could stare at Piper for hours, amazed at the reflection of him in her features, yet at the complete uniqueness of her. Their appointment for DNA testing was the next day, as well as Piper's school screening, and he was anxious about it. Just wanted to get it done and over with it.

But when he watched Piper like this, the sun streaming across her cheeks, her fingers buried in the dog's fur, he didn't care about any of that red tape. He had a daughter, and he was blessed.

"Hi, Dad," she said, without even looking away from the TV.

His heart dropped down to his boots. That was the first time she had called him Dad. And that she did it without thinking just turned him into mush. Damn, he was a sap. She could ask him for anything, and he'd try and give it to her. Yet he knew he'd have to learn something from Amanda and her father.

Money and things didn't matter. Just being there did. Like his own parents had with him.

He tickled across the back of her neck as he walked past her, pulling a giggle from her. Then he tickled the air next to her. "Does Anita like it when I tickle her too?"

Piper nodded. "She's laughing." Then her attention went back to the TV, and he kept walking.

At least he'd picked the right side to locate Anita this time. Usually he found himself talking to nothing, only Piper would insist it was the wrong nothing.

Complicated business, imaginary friends.

Amanda was standing on a chair, hammer raised in her hand and aimed straight at the window. It made for a scary picture.

"What are you doing, gorgeous?" Danny leaned on the door frame.

"What does it look like? I'm hanging this curtain rod." She gave a monstrous whack with the hammer and sent a nail straight into the wall, a bracket clanking, but holding in place. "There. I just have to do the other silver thingy, and I think I can click the rod into it. The directions were crap in English. I read the French version, and it made so much more sense."

"Well, good." Danny looked around the room. He had to admit it looked pretty damn cute. Brady's butterflies flittered across two walls and disappeared behind the window. Grass was painted around the perimeter of the whole room, and the comforter was cheerful and bright. It was a totally different room, one that Piper could call her own.

All for a couple of hundred bucks. He was impressed. "It looks great in here."

"It damn well better. I've slaved away in here for over a week."

"I appreciate it." Danny came up behind her, drawn to that spot on her back where her shirt was pulling up. It had been so long since he'd been able to touch her, and then it had just been such a quick burst of passion. There had been no time to taste and explore her nooks and crannies.

Lifting her shirt, he kissed her back.

"Danny!"

"Yeah?" He moved his lips across her warm skin.

"I'm going to fall off this chair." She tried to move away from him. "And we're not supposed to be carrying on in front of Piper."

He held her so she didn't get away from him or fall off the chair. "Carrying on? That doesn't seem like an Amanda expression. And Piper is in the other room glued to the TV."

Danny dipped his tongue into her belly button. He loved these shirts she wore, tight and always shifting up and up.

"I'm in the middle of something here. Big hammer right above your head. Woman not used to using tools potentially dropping it. Does that sound more like me?"

It did. Plus, she had a good point. Danny stepped back and assessed her progress. He saw the rod with the curtain already on it sitting on the bed. As Amanda drove another nail into the wall, he picked up the rod. Then he handed it to her so she could click it in place.

"This looks so awesome." Amanda hopped off the chair and looked around the room with a grin. "I rock."

"Yes, you do." But Danny wasn't looking at the room. He couldn't take his eyes off Amanda. She had pulled her hair back into a funny little ponytail. There was blue eyeshadow dusted across her lids and bubblegum-pink shiny stuff on her lips. Her shorts were white, her shirt sky blue.

She looked like blue cotton candy from the county fair.

He wanted to eat her. He wanted to keep her here with him.

"Don't leave, Amanda." He spoke before he could get further distracted by her body. He wanted to make love to her, but he wanted to tell her how he felt first. "Stay with me, here."

The grin fell off her face. "What do you mean?"

"I mean, stay in Cuttersville. Past the first day of school. Stop being Piper's babysitter and start being my girlfriend. You'd have to live in your house still, so we wouldn't be setting a bad example for Piper, but we would . . . date." Danny stuck his hands in his pockets and trailed off in embarrassment.

What the hell had he been thinking? Why would Amanda Delmar, who could do whatever she wanted, wherever she wanted, choose to stay in a pissant town just for him? But since he'd already made a fool out of himself, might as well go whole-hog.

He took a deep breath and went for it. "I think you're really amazing, and I don't want to see you walk out of my life. I love you."

Amanda thought she could count on one hand the number of people who had spoken those words to her. And only half of them had meant it. If even. The only person Amanda was completely positive about was her grandmother. Her parents had never told her they loved her.

Danny Tucker was telling her he loved her, and she believed him.

Which was why she said so very eloquently, "Oh, my God."

Emotions threatened to overwhelm her. He had no idea what that meant to her, to know that he, a guy with such integrity and honesty, could see enough of value in her to love her.

She had come to Cuttersville bored, aimless, and searching for the answers when she didn't even know the questions.

Instead of easy solutions, she had found a man who loved her, with no strings attached. And she didn't deserve it.

"Is that all you're going to say?" Danny stuck his fingernail between his teeth and bit it. His cheeks started to turn the color of a tomato.

"No." She closed the distance between them and cupped his cheek, tears threatening. "I love you too, Danny." It was easy to say, because it was the truth. She hadn't thought it could be that simple, and she knew in her head that it wasn't, but her heart didn't give a crap right at the moment. "And just to drive the point home, I have never said that to a man. Ever."

The last word was barely out of her mouth when Danny covered her lips with his. With a kiss so sweet, so tender, she swore she could hear violins. Pachelbel's "Canon," the wedding song. Oh, yikes. That was bad.

Struggling for composure, she pulled back, desperate for space. If she didn't stay strong, rational, she was going to find herself on the way to Chapel of Love for a Vegas wedding.

"Danny, we have to talk."

"Okay." He reached for her and kissed her forehead, her temple, her eyelid. "I love you. I love you. I love you. You're beautiful, you're wonderful, I want to marry you." Those strong arms of his pulled her back easily. "See? We're talking."

Tears sprang into her eyes. He wasn't going to make this easy. Her vision blurred, her heart ached, her body betrayed her by bending toward Danny.

But she had to get this out before she let her emotions rush her downstream, and ultimately to a crash that would hurt Danny. And Piper. And her. She didn't care what happened to her in the end, but she couldn't live with the idea of hurting Danny or his daughter.

"Don't say that. We can't be together."

He stiffened. "Why not? And I'm talking about marriage,

you know, not anything casual. I know it's soon now, but maybe in a year or two . . ."

Damn it, she wasn't doing this right. Amanda rubbed her forehead and tried to extract herself from his arms. He wouldn't let her leave. Not that she was trying all that hard. That was the whole flipping problem. She wanted to marry Danny. She wanted to think that love could conquer all and all that happy bullshit.

But she knew better.

She knew in real life the spoiled rich girl would drive the good farmer out of his freaking mind in about twelve months.

"I'm not the right woman for you."

"Don't tell me what's right for me."

Whoa. That was a tone she had never heard from good, old, reliable Danny Tucker. He sounded pissed off with a capital P.

"Or do you mean I'm not right for you?" He dropped his arms and made as if to back up.

Amanda took a page from his book and clung to his T-shirt, preventing him from getting anywhere. "No! If anything, you are too perfect for me. You're honest and loyal, hardworking and kind."

"You make me sound like a minister."

Irritated that she couldn't seem to convey herself, Amanda made a sound of frustration. "I mean that I am a spoiled, immature bitch who needs to grow up, and you deserve better than that."

There. That would learn him. It was a very valid and well-articulated point.

"That is complete bullshit."

Or bullshit. "Hey! Excuse me, I think I know my own shortcomings." She dropped his shirt and turned away. She was trying to save him from her. The very least he could do was show some gratitude.

"No. Obviously you don't. As far as I can tell, your only shortcoming is low self-esteem."

"Low self-esteem? Excuse me?" That made her sound so pathetic. She liked spoiled bitch better.

"Yes. You can't see the things about you that make you wonderful. And you exaggerate your flaws."

"You know, Farmer Philosophy, this conversation is going nowhere."

"I want you to stay." He crossed his arms, stubborn, like a little boy who wanted to extend his bedtime.

Amanda sighed. She really did love him, in a way that she had never really thought herself capable of. In a complete, unselfish way. She only wanted Danny to be happy.

"Don't tempt me."

Bad thing to say, since he was walking toward her. "We can get a prenuptial agreement, you know."

That stung a bit. "I would never try and take the farm from you!"

Danny stopped dead and started laughing. "No. I meant to protect you, not me. Why the hell would you want a piece of land in the middle of nowhere and some chickens?"

Now that he mentioned it, she wasn't really sure. But there was something so powerful about a place to call home, a piece of the earth that belonged to you and yours. She could see why the Tuckers stayed generation after generation.

"You're the one with money, Amanda, not me, and I just wanted you to know I'm not after any of it. Though I hope you put that money from your dad in the bank. Jesus, I can't believe he was carrying four grand in his wallet."

"He doesn't like credit cards. He wants to feel his money in his hand."

"Well, regardless of how much you have, I don't want it."

"I don't have that much." It certainly couldn't touch Hollywood stars, and Bill Gates's kids would never be calling her for a loan. "When I turn thirty-five or when my dad dies, whichever comes first, I get twenty million."

Danny just stared at her. "What?"

"I get twenty million dollars. My mom gets the rest—the cash, the businesses, and all the real estate."

He was giving her a really strange look. Amanda licked her lips and was sorry she did. She got a tongue full of lip gloss.

"Million dollars? Twenty. *Million*. Dollars." His hands went into his hair. "Jesus. Jesus."

She was starting to catch on. "Is that more than you expected? It's not that big a deal, honestly. Twenty mill doesn't go as far as it used to, and I don't even get it for nine more years."

But Danny looked green. Like he might turn and pitch his lunch all over Piper's new comforter. "What?" Maybe it was a little bit of a shock, but she didn't think it should make him sick. "Are you okay?"

He shook his head. "No. No, I'm not okay." He squeezed his fists together then dropped them. "You were right. We can't get married. It was stupid of me to think we could."

She didn't understand what had changed. "Danny . . ."

He moved past her to the door. "I'm sorry. I shouldn't have brought it up in the first place."

While she stood there feeling run over by a train, Danny paused and looked back at her. "I hope we can still be friends. I do love you."

And he left, leaving her standing there like a total geek. Wishing that he hadn't actually agreed with her. She didn't want to have to continue resisting a determined Danny, who insisted he loved her and they could be married and live happily ever together. Resisting would be really freaking hard.

But having him walk away sucked even worse.

Chapter 21

*D*anny mowed down harvested corn stalks with his Kubota tractor, and it felt good. Every crush and crunch and snap made him feel just a little bit better. Every row he plowed reminded him of who he was and who he would never be and why he was just fine with that.

Twenty million goddamn dollars. Jesus.

He had asked a woman who had all that money to marry him and take care of his daughter down on the farm. He wanted an heiress who shopped Michigan Avenue and dropped thousands of dollars without blinking to hunker down on Green Acres with him.

And he had said chickens were stupid.

This was what happened when he didn't take things slow. When he didn't think his actions all the way through or gather all the facts first. He made a fool out of himself and got his heart squashed like a pumpkin dropped on concrete.

He should have kept his dreams and his dick to himself.

Another row hit the dirt with satisfying swiftness.

When he turned the corner, he saw his father leaning against his pickup, staring at Danny. He was wearing dirty, dusty jeans, boots, and a T-shirt—a farmer's uniform.

Danny shifted the tractor to neutral and called, "You need something?"

"Turn that off and get down here."

For a second his heart about stopped. The DNA tests. They were negative. But then he rationalized it had been only three days since the blood had been drawn. There was no way they could have results that fast.

The school assessment had gone well. Piper had scored well enough to be placed in the third grade where she should be. The counselor had suggested therapy, though, to smooth the transition, and given that the pediatrician had recommended it as well, Danny had gone ahead and made an appointment with a family psychologist.

They would probably both need it when Amanda left in a week.

"What's wrong? Piper okay?"

His father spat in the dirt. "She's fine. Your mother and I are taking her into town to get her school supplies. You see that list? It's got about a hundred things on it. What happened to just pencil and paper and get on with it?"

Danny reached for his wallet. "Let me give you some money then."

"No, we got it." His father held up his hand. "You know, your mother and I are really happy to have Piper in our lives. She's a joy."

Feeling that now familiar feeling of pride, Danny shifted. "Yeah, she is."

"And your mother asked her to spend the night at our house tonight—like a sleepover—and she said she wanted to. Hope that's alright. You know how your mother gets."

Danny was a little surprised Piper had agreed, but he nodded. "Sure, that's fine."

"So, while we're all over at the farmhouse, maybe it would be a good time to mend fences with Amanda."

Danny stilled. "What do you mean?"

"I mean you need to patch things up with her if you don't want to spend the rest of your life feeling sorry for yourself."

Leaning over, Danny swiped a milkweed and worked it between his fingers. "I have no idea what you're talking about."

"I'm talking about you being in love with Amanda and Amanda being in love with you, but both of you walking around with long faces pretending the other doesn't exist."

They had been avoiding each other pretty industriously, but hell, he was embarrassed. And angry. And disappointed. "Dad, don't go there. Seriously."

"Maybe it's not my business, but when I see my son as unhappy as you are, I'm going to make it my business. Have you told Amanda how you feel about her? Willie and me, we talked, and we think Amanda would make a darn good wife for you."

God, he had a headache, and it wasn't from the sun. "Amanda is rich. She's going to inherit millions of dollars. She does not want to marry me."

"How do you know?"

"She told me!" It still hurt to remember her saying that. "Now I've got to get this straw taken care of. You think we're due any rain? It's been a dry summer."

"You've been sniffing silage, boy, if you think you can turn the subject like that with me."

Though throwing himself into the silo—and letting the toxic gases knock him out—held a certain appeal, it wasn't a good long-term solution.

"What do you want me to say, Dad? I asked Amanda to marry me, and she said no."

"Because of the money?"

Danny frowned. "Well, no, she said no before that all

came up. She said she can't marry me because she needs to grow up still."

His father looked thoughtful. "Huh. The girl is smarter than I even gave her credit for. She does have some things she needs to work out, with her dad and all, but there's no reason she can't do some growing right here, with you. Nobody is ever really done growing."

For a split second Danny felt hope but then growled in frustration. "This is stupid. If she doesn't want to, she doesn't want to. What am I supposed to do?"

"Convince her. She wants to, Danny. She's just got herself mixed up trying to do the right thing." His dad adjusted the bill on his ball cap. "You know, you let Shelby walk away from you. I'd hate to see you do the same thing a second time around."

Danny felt his jaw drop. "Excuse me? And what was I supposed to do to keep Shelby with me? Tie her to the bed?"

"That might have worked."

A snort flew out of his mouth. He couldn't believe he was having this conversation. And he couldn't believe his mild-mannered father was standing there and suggesting that he fight for a woman who didn't want him. "So what do you think I should do about Amanda?"

God only knew what his father would say next.

"Seduce her. Willie and I have Piper tonight. Make her dinner, and let nature take its course."

"We're not horses that need to be bred." He was done with this bizarre detour into his father's philosophies on getting the girl.

"You got condoms, don't you?"

"Jesus." Danny turned and headed back for the tractor. Senility had struck early.

Both his parents had lost their minds.

The thought was only confirmed when his mother greeted him at the back door an hour later wearing a T-shirt that said HAVE A WILLIE NICE DAY. It was outlined by the shape of the state of Ohio.

Despite his black mood, he couldn't help but laugh. "What are you wearing?"

His mother preened, pulling the hem out. "Like it? Amanda got it for me. Ordered it special a couple of weeks ago. Wasn't that sweet?"

"Yes." It was. Damn.

He was hot, tired, sweaty, and he had spent the past hour going back and forth with himself about Amanda until he was dizzy. Maybe his father was right and he should really go for it with Amanda. Convince her that what was important was that they be together because they loved each other.

Then he did a one-eighty and decided that would be about as smart as strolling into the chicken coop naked with corn kernels stuck all over him. Another rejection would hurt just as much.

But when Amanda walked into the room, Piper on her back, Danny knew he had to give it one last try. One last-ditch effort to see if there could be anything between them, despite her money and his lack of romance.

If not—which he was ninety-nine point nine percent sure would be the case—at least he would have one last night with her. One last chance to make love to her, with the whole night to enjoy it.

"Piper and your father and I are about to head out for the store. Can you take Amanda home early?"

Danny tried to catch Amanda's eye, but she was ignoring him, making fake choking sounds as Piper wrapped her arms around her neck to hold on.

"I'd be happy to take Amanda home." And take her clothes off her.

Look out Romeo. Danny Tucker wasn't going down without a fight.

♡

Amanda hid a wince behind her hand. Great. Just what she wanted. Danny driving her home, alone, without Piper as a buffer between them.

Every minute of every day was torture, time to be suffered through until she could take the pieces of her broken heart and limp to New York. Maybe there she could find a masseuse to release the kinks of tension locked all over her neck and shoulders from walking around squeezing her muscles tight. Men on Viagra couldn't be stiffer than this.

She spent all her time trying to absorb the sight and smell of Piper and the house, the yard, and the view of the corn stalks waving under the blue sky. The kid was probably starting to wonder why she was sniffing her all the time. While next week couldn't get there soon enough to suit her sanity, at the same time she couldn't imagine that she would never see Piper or Danny again.

Basically, she was a freaking mess. And in no mood to be alone with Danny.

So after Piper left with her grandparents, Amanda just wanted to get it over with. It was a ten-minute drive. Danny and she would ignore each other, she'd hop out of the truck, and that would be it. The next day was Saturday, so she'd spend the weekend packing and then Tuesday Piper started school. She'd hang around to see how the first day went, then she was leaving for New York. With her paychecks from Danny, she had purchased a one-way ticket for seventy-nine dollars, after thoroughly searching for the lowest fare.

Another positive result of her time in Cuttersville—she now knew how to make a budget and how to search out lower prices. She'd gotten rather fond of popping in to Wal-Mart and buying ninety-nine-cent nail polish.

Which reminded her of exactly how much crap she had to pack. She needed to get home to the gray house and start shifting through it.

Too bad she couldn't seem to find Danny to let him know she was ready to go home.

The door to his bedroom was closed. She knocked. Nothing.

Then she heard the shower. Damn it. He was taking a shower. He was naked. And wet. Not a good place for her thoughts to go.

They went to an even naughtier place when the water shut off. She could just step into the bathroom. She doubted he had locked the door. That wasn't Danny Trusting Tucker's style.

Then again, barging in on a man she had turned down for marriage wasn't her style. A man who was horrified by the thought of her money. Or at least, it had never been her style in the past. She had usually let the men do the chasing. They chased, she sort of ran, eventually they caught her, then the sex was so-so.

With Danny, the sex had been phenomenal. Both physically and emotionally satisfying. And that had only been a quickie.

Just think what they could do if they had some time to really work on it.

Not that they did. Because she was leaving. Both today and on Tuesday.

The bathroom door opened.

Danny was wearing nothing but a white towel around his waist. Nothing else, but a few water droplets running down his chest. His wet hair was sticking up, and his finger smoothed over it as he came to a sudden stop.

"Oh, sorry. I forgot my clean clothes in my room."

"Uh-huh." Danny was a really bad liar. She had the sudden feeling that his little stroll across the hall looking like a woman's wet dream was no accident. She crossed her arms over her chest. Stupid traitorous nipples. She was going to tape the damn things down if they didn't behave themselves. "You did this on purpose, didn't you?"

"Did what?" He widened his eyes. "I'm sorry if I'm keeping you waiting, but I really needed a shower. Been working, you know," he added, like she had no idea he had spent the day in the sun on the tractor.

Of course, he wouldn't know that she'd spent half the day sneaking peeks out the window at him.

"I'll just get dressed while you grab the dog. We can leave in a minute." Danny's arm reached right past hers, and his damp skin brushed hers. "Excuse me."

"What?" He was invading her space again, and he smelled clean and sexy, like soap and straw.

"I'm just trying to get into my room to get my clothes. I can't open the door with you standing there."

"Right." Amanda meant to move, but somehow her feet didn't do anything. They were like Quebec, determined to be independent.

"Unless you don't want to go home." Danny leaned closer to her. A drop from his hair landed on her arm and rolled. He picked up her hand and sucked the water droplet off her wrist. "Do you want to go home?"

There were so many ways to answer that. Most would be lies.

She didn't want to go back to the dwarf cottage and count the pennies that would be lying in her hallway. She didn't want to listen to the woman in the mirror crying when she felt like doing the same thing herself. She didn't want to lie alone in an empty bed, staring at the ceiling, wondering if she were doing the right thing.

Wondering if it were too late for her and Danny. Wondering if there was a her and Danny, or if she had somehow imagined the whole thing. Nothing about this summer quite seemed real, and neither did a future in New York seem real.

Her father had given her four thousand dollars, and she could make that last now that she understood some basic means of cutting costs. But she had no real desire to spend money, his or hers or anyone's.

And she didn't want to walk away from a naked Danny. "I . . ." She cleared her throat.

Danny's hands stroked across her waist, played with the fabric of her floral skirt. His lips brushed across the top of her head. "Stay tonight. Forget about everything else . . . just let me hold you. Let me love you. Just for here, now."

"What about the money . . . leaving . . . Piper?" It was a token resistance. She was already curling her fingers into the fabric of his towel.

"Don't think, sweetheart. Just feel."

He kissed her, and she couldn't resist. Didn't try. His hands were gentle, his mouth firm but reserved, waiting for permission. So she gave it to him by throwing her arms around his neck and opening her mouth for him.

She could feel it when she was with Danny. The difference between him and all the other men she had kissed. He loved her. It was there, in the way he held her. It was there, in the way he sighed, and in the dark brown of his eyes.

"I don't want to go home." Not now, not ever. But she would start with now.

Danny paused for a second, his lips on Amanda's neck. She was willing to spend the night with him. He wouldn't read any more into that than the obvious. She wanted to have sex with him, and it would be enough for him. He would take what she could give while she was still here, and he would make tonight last as long as was humanly possible.

"Good." He breathed in the scent of her, a soft, fruity smell that reminded him of bubble gum. Amanda always had lotions and glosses and powders on her, and while the scents were enticing, he wondered what she would smell like with nothing on her, just bare flesh.

Pushing the straps of her pink shirt off her shoulders, he traced the line of her clavicle bone with his lips, going lower and lower until he reached her breasts. The shirt was stretchy, and he skimmed it down over her, happy to see she wasn't wearing a bra.

Danny loved Amanda's breasts, the way they were perfect round globes with tight cherry nipples on top. He had never gone for chesty women, always feeling a little startled by them. They were distracting in their disproportion, and he wound up studying them in fascination instead of actually doing anything with them.

Generally speaking, a woman wanted a man to do something with her breasts besides gawk at them.

With Amanda, that was easy to do. She was so long and lean, with no soft edges for a man to grab onto. Except for her breasts. They begged to be touched.

He pulled one taut nipple into his mouth and rolled his tongue over it. She gave a soft little cry that went straight to his groin. Using his thumb, he stroked one nipple while he sucked the other, feeling desire heating up every inch of his body from the inside out.

Flicking his damp hair out of his eyes, he pulled back. Her skin was dewy from his tongue and his hair, and she had pink splotches where his beard had chafed. He wanted to look at her, to savor her, to prolong the night that he knew was really good-bye.

Amanda reached out and tugged at his towel. "You don't need this, do you?"

"Nope." He was surprised steam didn't come out of there when she opened the towel. He was feeling pretty damn hot and humid.

With a flick of her wrist, she tossed it to the floor. "There. Now you should probably take my clothes off too." She gave him a saucy smile. "I don't want to wrinkle this skirt."

"I wouldn't dream of wrinkling your skirt." Danny reached for her, but she turned around. "Where you going? Let me unzip it for you."

"The zipper's in the back." Hands braced on the wall, she tipped her head over her shoulder. "See?"

The position brought to mind all kinds of interesting

thoughts, and Danny went for the zipper with trembling hands and a dry mouth. He wasn't sure if it was the quality of the skirt, or the force of his jerk, but the zipper went down smoothly in one clean motion. The sides of the skirt slid apart and dropped lower on her hips.

Danny ran his hands over her waist, behind the fabric, and gave the skirt a push. It fell down, and he almost went blind. "Holy shit."

It wasn't the back of panties staring at him. It was the string of a thong, surrounded on both sides by her creamy, tight ass. "Oh, honey, that's a beautiful thing."

Amanda gave a throaty laugh and stepped out of her skirt. But she stayed facing the wall, which gave him the opportunity to stick a hand on either side of that thong and squeeze. "You did that on purpose," he whispered, skimming his thumbs over the curve of her cheeks.

"Who, me?" Her breath caught when he moved his hands around to the front of her panties and cupped her.

His erection pressed against her backside, and he gave a little thrust, her warm skin giving a little under the pressure. "Yes, you. Now let's get that shirt off of you."

Pulling her hands farther up, until they were over her head but still pressed to the wall, Danny took the bottom of her shirt and tugged up. It caught a little on her breasts, then gave with a little bounce. In the blink of an eye, he had Amanda naked expect for that scrap of white lace and her sandals. The rest of her was gloriously bare, and pinned against the wall, ass pointed enticingly toward him.

"Turn around," he said, determined to go slow, no matter what his body thought about pushing that lace string aside and sinking inside her.

She didn't turn or pirouette, but sort of rolled herself across the wall until she was facing him, her arms still over her head. One knee bent a little and her chest rose and fell as she gave hard, urgent breathes. Then she licked her lips, slowly, wetting from one side to the other.

Danny forgot slow. He closed the space between them and sucked that pouty bottom lip into his mouth, his body colliding with hers and shoving them both back against the wall. He kissed her hard, his hands grinding her against him. A rational part of him thought maybe he was being too rough, but Amanda gave a low moan.

"You're so hard, it feels so good," she whispered.

Her eyes were glazed, her cheeks flushed, her lips shiny, the stickiness of her lip gloss smeared over both their mouths.

"Come here," Danny said, wanting to get her in the bedroom before he took her against the wall.

Not that there was anything wrong with that.

But he wanted more. He wanted slow. He wanted to taste her, right between her thighs, sinking his tongue inside her while she squirmed.

To speed things up, he reached around her waist and thighs and picked her up.

She squawked. "Oh, my God. You are not picking me up. You can't carry me, I'm too tall."

The hell he couldn't. Danny adjusted her in his arms and tilted her so she tumbled against his chest with her perky breasts. He gave her a soft kiss and turned to his bedroom door, gripping the knob with a sweaty palm and pushing it open.

"You are actually carrying me to bed. I can*not* believe this is happening. I think I'm going to orgasm just from this."

Though he felt a little bewildered at her reaction, he also found the look on her face damn sexy. "You can come if you want, but it might be more fun to wait until my tongue is on you."

Danny walked toward the bed as Amanda sucked in her breath. "Tongue on me where?"

With a little maneuvering, he managed to get a finger between her thighs and press right against the front of her thong panties. "Right here."

"I can wait then."

He laughed and plunked her down on her butt on the bed. Amanda didn't hesitate, but lay back and let her knees fall apart. Danny crawled up between her legs and played with the strings on either side of the V of the thong. He could see her dark blond curls behind the white lace, and his mouth flooded with moisture in anticipation of tasting her.

Her ankles moved restlessly against the bed. "Just rip the panties. Get them off, please."

It was tempting, but he hesitated. "How much did they cost?"

"I don't know! Maybe a hundred bucks."

No ripping today. "For something the size of a corn husk? No, we'll just slide them down, nice and easy." Danny worked the panties down inch by inch, leaning over her as he spoke, his mouth so close to her flesh he could see the goose bumps rising, smell the sweet scent of her desire.

It was pretty obvious to Danny that up to this point, neither of them had even known what sex could be like. It was like watching black-and-white TV and suddenly being plunged into color. When Amanda squirmed and wiggled, reaching for him with trembling fingers, soft desperate moans falling out with each breath, Danny's body tensed with excited arousal. He had never felt this sort of passion, this power, this heady delight in pleasing another person.

Then he ditched her panties, grabbed her ankles, and spread her nice and wide. Amanda jerked on the bed, but she didn't say anything. Her eyes were half-closed, and her fingers dug into his plaid bedsheet. He'd forgotten to make his bed again, and she was a beautiful blond contrast to the navy darkness.

Swallowing hard, Danny leaned over the apex of her thighs and ran his palm over the dusky curls. She sucked in her breath, a raspy, harsh sound that collapsed into a sigh when his finger slid along the center of her mound and slipped between the curls. He sank into wet heat.

Danny paused, his erection throbbing against the bed, and counted to three. He was in control. Sort of. "You like that?" He pulled back, swirling his finger over her clitoris before sinking in again.

"Yes." She bit her lip.

"How about this?" He replaced his finger with his tongue, closing his eyes as the taste of her exploded in his mouth. She was slick, sweet, her body quivering around him, thighs drifting closed to clamp around his head.

"Danny . . ." she groaned.

He'd never liked his name, tried to switch everyone to calling him Dan at least a hundred times to no effect, but hearing it ripped from Amanda in complete ecstasy gave him a whole new appreciation for it. He wanted to hear it again. He stroked in and out of her with his tongue, over and over, faster and deeper. Then he pulled back quickly and gave a quick lick and suck at her clitoris.

"Danny!" She dug her fingers in his hair and came, half rising off the bed.

He hung on, even when she kneed him in the gut with her thrashing legs, and he ran his tongue over her until the last of her spasms quieted. She flopped onto her back and shuddered.

"Oh, yeah."

Hell, yeah.

But he wasn't about to give her time to think or relax or even catch her breath. Slowly, stealthily, he brought a finger to her again, tickling around her inner thighs, tugging gently at her curls, whisking around and around but never actually touching inside her.

"Stop that," she said, pushing at his hand. "You're teasing me." Her mound rose toward him, her thighs clamping together like she wanted to catch his hand and hold it there. "I want you inside me."

"No."

Her eyes popped open. "What do you mean, *no*?"

"Not yet," he said calmly, opening her folds with his thumbs and stroking once down the center of her before letting go.

"Okay, maybe this is a dumb question . . . but why the hell not yet?" Amanda looked a touch frustrated. If the clenched teeth and wild eyes were any indication.

But Danny didn't like to rush anything. He'd rushed through making love to Amanda the first time, and he was going to take this nice and slow. He was going to drag the pleasure out like chewing gum, long and taut.

"Because I want to do that again."

"*That* again?" she said, glancing at his mouth, her thighs trying to push closed as she yelped in surprise. "Nobody does that twice in a row . . . and there must be a good reason why. I don't think you should . . ."

Danny did a brief battle with her thighs, which he won. She wasn't really putting that much effort into it, and he was bigger. Once they were spread, he planted his elbows on them so she couldn't move, her protests spiraling into a heady moan.

"I want to do it again."

"Okay, okay, fine, do it, I don't want you to cry or anything . . ."

Her trembling sarcasm dwindled out when he did it again.

Put his mouth on her and tasted.

Chapter 22

*A*manda lasted a whole delicious five minutes before she came the second time.

And she was pretty sure she only begged and whimpered once or twice.

When her body stopped convulsing and her pupils returned to their normal position, she let go of the comforter and wiped the drool off the corner of her mouth. "Okay, so I don't know why people don't do that twice in a row . . . of course, maybe they do and I don't know . . . but that was amazing . . . waaah!"

Amanda yelped when Danny gripped her thighs and rolled her over onto him. Her moist inner thighs collided with his chest, and her breasts dangled over his forehead. "What the . . . ?"

But before she could even stabilize, he yanked her thighs toward the headboard, sending her chest flying back until she was . . . *oh.*

"Again," he said.

The man had baked his brains in the sun too long. She could not just sit there, on his mouth, not when she could barely feel her Jell-O legs and her lungs had collapsed somewhere on about the nine-hundredth moan.

"I . . . I . . ." She was trying to protest, but her lips were numb and her tongue was six sizes too big. And damn, damn, it felt good. It felt inside-out, hands-on, hot-damn kind of good, and she closed her eyes, arched her back, and rode his mouth.

When she came the third time—a sexual milestone marked with panting and incoherent religious babblings like "Help me, Jesus!"—Danny took pity on her.

In a move that would have her Ashtanga yoga instructor jealous, Danny had her dropped onto her back and was rolling on a condom before she could even swallow her spit. Nor did he expect her to untangle her trembling, useless legs, but just took it upon himself to spread them with his knees. And while Amanda tried to keep her eyes open and her heart from levitating out of her chest, Danny entered her with a hard thrust.

His groan was loud, agonized. Amanda had no ability left to moan, and no energy to even wrap her legs around him as he stroked in and out of her. Her body was so swollen, so excited, so overstimulated, that she was absolutely certain she'd never be able to walk again. She was just going to lie there for the rest of her life with Danny deep inside her and undulate like an inchworm.

Looking up at his face, seeing his excitement, hearing his wild, out-of-control bursts of pleasure, she figured it was a good use of her time. And what a plus that she was enjoying it too—so, so much.

Then he pulled completely out, and she yelped with surprise and horror. "What? What are you doing?" Oh, my God, she felt like a kid whose ice cream had fallen off the cone.

"I'm too close, too close," he panted.

"So?" She pried a hair off her lip and tried to uncross her eyes.

"I want you to be satisfied before I do." Sweat rolled down off his forehead toward his nose.

Amanda reached up and wiped it away, very much aware that she was staring at the best man she'd ever known. Her voice was a hoarse whisper. "In case you hadn't noticed, Mr. Unselfish, I already was satisfied three times. Now get back in there."

He kissed her. "Just remember that I love you. Truly love you."

She gripped his shoulders right as he joined them again, and she felt the tears prick, blurring her view of his strong, steady expression. He loved her, and she had done nothing to earn it. But maybe that was the gift of a pure love—no one had to justify or explain or perform tricks to deserve it. It just was.

"I love you, Danny." Amanda found the strength to wrap her legs around him, to lift herself toward him and meet his movements so they were joined as tightly as they could be. "I . . . I . . ."

Had lost the ability to speak. But she wanted to say that she didn't want to leave, that she wanted to stay right there, with him, for as long as he wanted her to. That she could learn to be the kind of wife he needed.

But nothing came out, and he covered her mouth with his, hot tongue pushing into her urgently. Then he lifted his head and stared straight into her eyes as he exploded with tight, raw moans.

No man had ever locked wide-open eyes like that with her while he had an orgasm, and the intimacy, the vulnerability of it, sent her body into shivering spasms, a mini-climax to match his.

They thrust, locked in pleasure with each other, until Danny relaxed all his muscles with a shudder and dropped down onto her. He was crushing the very life out of her, but she was so limp, so satiated, she didn't care if she suffocated. She'd die happy.

But he lifted his chest and dusted little kisses all over her mouth, her cheeks, her nose, her forehead in a way that made her giggle. Truly. Giggling. It was weird, but there it was, and Danny laughed with her.

"Why are we laughing?" he asked.

"I don't know. But I just feel so good, so alive, so exhausted."

Danny rolled onto his back and pulled her on top of him. Naked man was such a nice, warm, hard bed.

Amanda yawned. "You wore me out, and I didn't even do any of the work."

He gave a soft chuckle. "I'm used to manual labor."

"You're very good at it."

Danny patted her butt. "You're not so bad yourself. Now go to sleep."

"Okay." He didn't have to tell her twice. She was semiconscious already.

As Danny's hand stroked along the small of her back, she drifted off into sleep with a contentment she hadn't felt since she was five years old.

Willie pushed her rocker back and forth on the front porch and wished the damn thing creaked. If it did, maybe she wouldn't hear the soft moans punctuating the air, drifting over to her from Danny's house.

Sure, she'd known that by taking Piper for the night, Danny and Amanda were more likely than not to end up in bed together. It had been part of her and Daniel's strategy. But Lord, she hadn't wanted to *hear* it.

"I never realized quite how much the sound carries on a clear night," Willie said to Daniel, who was drinking a beer and reading the paper under the porch light.

"Me either." Daniel folded his paper. "You, ah, close Piper's window?"

"Yep. Got the fan running." On the other hand, obviously Danny's windows were wide open. "You think they realize their window's open?"

"Willie, I don't think they'd realize if the house was burning down around them." Daniel stuck his paper under his arm and lifted his beer. "Maybe we ought to head into the house. The 'squitos are biting anyway."

Fine by her. Willie stood up. "She's a nice girl, isn't she? Underneath all that money. I wouldn't have thought it, but it's true."

"Yep. He loves her, you know."

Willie knew that. She saw it every time her son looked at Amanda. It made her happy at the same time it scared the bejeezus out of her. Little Shelby had hurt Danny, more than he'd ever admit, and she didn't want to see him go through that kind of pain again.

She had to trust that if Amanda Delmar stayed, it would be for good. Part of her was certain Amanda would, which was why she'd agreed to Daniel's idea to take Piper for the night, but a small piece of her was scared for her son.

Daniel put his hand on her back as he moved around the wicker chair toward the front door. "Quit worrying. He's a grown man, Willie."

"Yeah, well, a mother never stops worrying about her child. It's written in the rule book."

"You know what else is written in the rule book?"

Willie stared across the yard at Danny's house, thinking, worrying. "What?" she asked in distraction.

"That a man never stops wanting his wife."

Daniel had octopus hands when he was in a mood, and clearly he was tonight, because suddenly he was everywhere. "Daniel James Tucker, your granddaughter is in the house."

But she was already turning toward him a little. She was

only fifty, after all, right in her prime. They had a good twenty-five years of passion ahead of them still.

"Exactly. She's in the house, and we're out here."

Well, he had a damn good point.

♡

Danny woke up just like he always did, when the sun started creeping through the blinds on his window and Rudy started his daily speech. Rudy bleated every morning, and Danny woke at dawn every day alone.

His life had a pattern, a familiar one, that he liked, but an empty bed wouldn't be something he would miss. But today might be the only chance he had to wake up next to Amanda, so he was going to enjoy it.

She was still sleeping, her hair falling in her eyes, mouth open a bit. No snoring, just soft, soundless breaths in and out, her eyelids twitching like she was dreaming. Sometime during the night, she had slid off of him, but she was still tucked up against his hip and chest.

Her fingers splayed over his stomach, and he liked that they fit together so well, that making love to Amanda was exciting and easy and intimate, with no awkwardness between them. They had both brought issues to the bedroom—doubts and insecurities—but with a little trust between them, those problems had been laid to rest. And then some.

"Good morning." He kissed the top of her head, hoping she'd wake up, but not willing to really shake her awake. That would be selfish, though he was sorely tempted.

Fortunately, she stirred and gave a little mewling sound. "Morning." Her eyes opened and she smiled up at him, nuzzling into his chest. "Did I really do what I think I did in the middle of the night, or was that just a really hot dream?"

Danny had woken her up at two A.M. and been pleasantly surprised that she wanted to work out some more issues and insecurities about performing oral sex. By performing it on him. He had been happy to comply and had nearly ripped the sheet in the process. "No dream, Princess. And after that, I think I'm going to have to promote you to queen. You were amazing."

It had him hard all over again just thinking about it.

Amanda grinned. "Glad you liked it." Her hand started roaming south. "And let's see . . . we already established you're Mr. Honest and Mr. Unselfish. Last night showed you're Mr. Exciting too."

She found him and squeezed the length of him in her hand. Danny bit back a moan. "Now you're clearly Mr. Dependable."

He was more like Mr. Full of Regret. "I hate to say this, but I have to go to work. I'm supposed to be at the construction job site at 6:45, and it's 6:15 now. It's a twenty-minute drive."

It burned in him, the urge to blow off his responsibilities and stay wrapped up in Amanda for the rest of the morning. But that wasn't him. He had made a commitment. He had a job to do. He needed the health insurance for his daughter, and he couldn't change who he was in the core of him.

There was a lot he needed to say to Amanda, but there was no time right now and he didn't want to rush through what he wanted to lay before her. Which was his heart and his hope and a plan to spend their future together. He wanted one chance to tell her how he felt and let her decide once and for all before she left in a few days.

If she left.

But now wasn't the time to discuss it.

"Alright," she said, pulling her hand away. "But I expect compensation tonight."

Danny sat up and studied her. She didn't look like a woman who was planning to ditch him in a day or two. She looked . . . happy. Carefree. Sexy.

It was reassuring enough that he was able to get out of

bed, throw on some clothes, and give her a kiss good-bye. Avoiding the dog, who was sleeping on the circle rug at the foot of the bed, he padded to the kitchen in his socks. He was starving, having skipped dinner the night before for more pressing physical needs. Scrounging in the pantry, he found a breakfast bar.

He had half of it in his mouth and was reaching for his boots when Amanda stumbled into the kitchen. Swallowing the dry mess in his mouth, he said, "You can go back to sleep, gorgeous. Piper won't be back for hours."

"I need coffee. And I'm starving. What are you eating?" She ran her fingers through her hair and put a hand on her hip. She had pulled on one of his T-shirts and looked sexy and rumpled.

He held up the wrapper for her to see. "Help yourself to anything in the pantry or the fridge. You know where the coffee is."

"Yes, I do." She already had the can out and was dumping what looked like a hell of a lot of grounds into the machine. Filling the pot with water from the sink, she asked, "What time are you going to be home?"

"Around two. We're framing a barn, and we should get a good start on it, but I need to get back and put the corn in the silo. We're supposed to get rain tomorrow, and it needs to get put up before then." Danny sat down at the kitchen table and jammed his foot into a boot. Like Amanda really gave a crap about his crop.

She turned on the coffeemaker, twisting the pot a little to make sure it was lined up, and turned around. Leaning against the counter, she yawned. "Why don't we ever eat the corn for lunch? There's like three million ears of it right out in the yard, and we never eat it."

"It's not sweet corn. It's feed corn, grown specifically to feed livestock. It wouldn't taste any good to us."

"You really work hard, don't you?" She studied him, hands folded over her chest.

Danny shrugged. He did what needed to be done. Amanda turned and rooted in the cabinet for a coffee mug while he laced his boots and stuck the other half of the cereal bar in his mouth. Damn, he didn't want to leave and go sweat with a nail gun in his hand. He wanted to stay.

"You going to be around when I get home?"

Now it was her turn to shrug. "Sure, if that's okay."

"Yep." It was more than okay. It was exactly what he wanted. Danny stamped his feet in his boots to get a better fit. Then he stood up, reached for the keys to his truck lying next to the phone. Shoved his wallet into his pocket.

Amanda poured herself a cup of coffee and took a deep, fortifying sip. "Aahh. That's better."

Danny meant to leave. He meant to just turn and leave, maybe giving her a little kiss good-bye. Instead, he found himself pausing in front of her.

"I wasn't going to say anything, Amanda, and I don't want you to answer. But I just want you to think about this while I'm gone today." He cupped her cheek with his hand, drew his thumb over her lip. "I want you to stay here with me, forever. As my wife."

She opened her mouth, eyes wide, and he spoke again before she could. "I know it's asking the world of you, and there are a million details and complications that we should discuss, but I just want you to think about it today. Think about how you feel."

Again her lips parted, like she was going to say something. He quickly covered her lips with his hand, his heart pounding. God, he couldn't take her rejection right this second, when they still had the scent of each other on their skin, and he felt so much love for her, he could just about burst from it. "Shhh. Don't answer. Not yet. Think about it."

"I don't . . ." she said behind his fingers.

He cut her off with a kiss, one that he hoped poured all of his emotions into her.

One that he hoped wasn't good-bye.

"I'll see you tonight."

"Okay. Tonight," she said, her green eyes bright and glassy.

If this were the end, he would never forget the look of her standing in his kitchen, looking beautiful and sensual.

It was a perfect moment of hope and happiness, and God, he hoped it would last.

When he pulled out of the driveway, she was in the doorway, her mug in front of her lips, wearing his shirt and a sweet smile as she waved to him.

He almost wrecked the truck staring into his rearview mirror.

Chapter 23

"**R**eady, set . . . Go!"

Amanda ran across the hard dirt toward Willie and Daniel's house, her Skechers taking the jarring impact of her feet slamming down. Baby barked and ran alongside of her, little poodle legs straining to keep up.

When she reached the mailbox in front of the farmhouse, she touched the rooster on the side of the plastic box and headed back. Her lungs were burning, her legs straining, and a really disgusting line of sweat was trailing between her shoulder blades. As she crossed the finish line, a ribbon stretched between two Barbies, she ground to a halt and bent over.

"Thirty-eight seconds!" Piper shouted, holding up the watch in her hand.

"Geez, that's hard work." She sucked in her breath and stretched her legs. "And I think I'm actually getting slower, not faster. What's your record?"

"I did it in thirty-four seconds."

"That's because your legs are shorter," Amanda told her, smiling at Piper. God, she loved this kid. She was just such a sweet, happy child, despite everything that had happened in her life, and when she looked at Piper, Amanda felt pure, unselfish love.

"Nuh-uh! You should be faster because your legs are *longer*."

Amanda laughed. "Okay, you caught me. But I am wearing a skirt, you know." She hadn't brought a change of clothes with her the day before, except for her gym shoes, not expecting to spend the night. She was back in her floral skirt, though truthfully, she couldn't claim it was constricting. "Or maybe I'm just a pokey-Joe."

Speaking of pokey-Joes, Amanda wondered where Danny was. It was almost two, and she was restless for him to get home. She had tried to tell him this morning how she felt, tried to tell him that she wanted to stay here with him, on the farm. As his wife.

But the goofball wouldn't let her speak, and now she'd spent the whole day in anxious excitement. She hadn't ever felt this happy, this sure of herself in her entire life. When she ran across this yard, she felt free, she felt satisfied. This could be her home, her family.

Being a mother to Piper and a wife to Danny could be the most meaningful thing she'd ever done in her life. Nothing else mattered.

And she had learned, through Piper, that you needed to love first, then love will come back to you. You couldn't take love or buy it or demand it, but once you gave it freely, without thought to yourself, you received it in kind.

"Baby, eeww!" Piper stood up, her shorts covered in dust, and went over to the dog. "Stop eating grass." She scooped up the poodle and cradled her in her arms. Baby yipped, but lay there contentedly.

A poodle wasn't exactly a farm dog, but Baby seemed to

enjoy running around, sniffing out God only knew what. She would adjust. And so would Amanda.

Lifting her sunglasses to wipe her dewy nose and cheeks, Amanda wondered how Danny would feel about her installing a pool. Probably it wouldn't be practical, but it would really be nice. Her pores were clogging as she spoke. "Maybe we should go into the shade. Baby might be hot."

When she dropped her sunglasses back into place and blinked, she saw a black truck pulling up the driveway. It wasn't Danny's truck, and she didn't recognize it. The tires were too small for the truck, and it bounced and jerked on the pitted gravel.

Piper made a strangled gasp. "That's Mark," she whispered, clutching Baby closer to her chest.

"Your stepfather?" Amanda shielded her eyes and tried to see the driver. She couldn't see very well, but it was a man.

"Yes." Piper was rigid, fear on her face. Her baseball hat was lying in the dirt, where it had flown off when she was running her race. She reached for it, slapped it on her head.

That gesture made Amanda furious. This was the bastard who had said all those damaging slurs to Piper about her hair and her behavior.

"Sweetie, why don't you take Baby in the house? I'll see what Mark wants." Amanda was already herding Piper toward the house, instinct telling her this couldn't be good. But she kept her voice even.

Piper didn't need any encouragement. She ran, her thin legs flying as she went across the yard and up the stairs to the front door, the dog barking wildly. Amanda did a fast walk, not wanting to run, but wanting to grab her purse. She wanted her cell phone in easy reach.

She had her purse over her shoulder, Piper hunkered down in the living room, as she stepped back out onto the stoop. Mark was climbing out of his car.

"Where's Tucker?" he said, giving her a once-over that made her skin crawl.

"He'll be home in a few minutes. Can I help you?" *You worthless excuse for a human being.*

"Who are you?"

With his oversized clothes and gold chains, he looked like a fake white gangsta rapper. Like Aaron Carter in a Spike Lee movie. He looked ridiculous, but he also looked like he wouldn't hesitate to use violence. Amanda figured it was better to just stay polite and get him to leave.

"I'm Danny's girlfriend." She was hesitant to even mention Piper in front of this guy.

"No shit?" He gave her a smile. A cold, sexual smile. "Well, if you ever get tired of living with Farmer Ted, give me a call. I could enjoy a beautiful woman like you."

She fought the urge to gag. Pulling her purse open, she started digging in it so she wouldn't have to look at him. "I'll keep that in mind."

He must have heard the sarcasm in her voice because he was suddenly in front of her, still on the walkway, but only two feet from her. "Where's the kid?"

"What kid?" Her hand searched for her cell phone while she stared him down, her heart pounding, her mouth dry.

"Don't play dumb with me, bitch. Where's Piper? I'm here to take her back."

Even with the screen door closed, she heard Piper's gasp from the living room. Trying to stay calm, Amanda swallowed hard. "You can't take her back. She's Danny's daughter."

"I have custody of her. Now where is she? I don't have all fucking day."

Amanda tried not to shift herself in front of the door and give away with body language that Piper was in the house. But she was almost twitching with the need to protect Piper. There was no way she could let this man anywhere near her. "She's with Danny."

His eyes narrowed. "You'd better not be lying to me."

She was lying like a rug. But she'd do whatever she had to. Her hand had closed around her cell phone, but she realized there was no one to call. Danny didn't have a cell, and she didn't know the number to Willie and Daniel's. If she had to, she'd call 911, but there wouldn't be any way for them to know where she was calling from, and somehow she didn't think Mark would stand there and let her give directions to the farm. Directions that she wasn't all that sure about anyway.

"Why do you want Piper? You brought her here in the first place."

Mark moved his foot to the stoop and something jingled in his pocket. He cocked his head and gave an amused exhalation of air. "Not that it's any of your business, but in my grief for Nina I wasn't thinking straight. See, I just wanted to get rid of the kid. I never thought Tucker would actually want her. Now I understand he wants custody, and I'm thinking maybe I miss her. Maybe I want her back. Maybe Tucker needs to show me how much she means to him."

Amanda's face went hot, her blood cold. She felt fear, disgust, rage all rise up in her with a sickening swirl. "You want money, don't you?"

It was always money. Well, she'd die before she let this prick take Piper, and she would starve before she'd let him get any money on the back of an innocent child.

"Damn right I want money. Since I still have custody of her, I'm taking her back until I get it."

"I don't think so." Her hand searched in her purse for something, anything to defend herself with if she needed to. "If you want her, take Danny to court, but you won't get her without a court order."

He stepped up onto the stoop, knocking her back into the door when she moved to avoid his touch. "She's in the house, isn't she?" His face came close to hers, his hot tobacco breath blasting her cheek. "Move out of my way, or I'll knock you out of my way."

His eyes were mean little slits, his skin sallow, his chin full of stubble. She could smell his sweat, a sour stale combination of dirt, cigarette smoke, and greed.

"If you lay one finger on Piper, I'll ram your balls into your throat." Her voice was hoarse, and it trembled just a bit at the end, but she meant it. She would scratch, bite, kick if need be.

"Move."

"No."

Mark took a step back, turned a little like he was going to leave. Amanda felt relief surge up in her. Then before she could register the movement, he rotated back, and the flat of his hand connected with her face.

Sharp pain cracked through her cheek, nose, and skull. Her tongue caught between her teeth, and she tasted blood. Her ears rang, and she stumbled to the left, nearly falling off the stoop. The door opened and Piper came out.

"No! Leave Amanda alone. I'll go with you, just don't hurt her."

Blinking hard to clear her watery eyes, Amanda lunged toward Piper. "Get back in the house!" She jerked Piper behind her and faced Mark. "You cannot have her, do you understand me? Never."

Her cheek throbbed, her eyes teared, and her nose was running. She was heading toward hysterical, and this goddamn bastard stepfather from hell was *not* taking this child from her.

Mark lifted a hand toward her like he was going to grab her. Amanda whacked him with her handbag. His expression indicated that had only pissed him off further. But the clank of her handbag gave her a thought. When he reached for her the second time, she pulled out her hairspray, took aim, and shot him right in the eyes.

Even as he let out a roar and swiped at his face, she kept

spraying, walking forward as he stumbled backward. When he fell off the stoop and landed on his butt, she shook the can again, ready to give him another round of Garnier Fructis Style Full Control Hairspray.

Piper held onto the back of her shirt, and Amanda called over her shoulder, "Get back in the house, Piper!"

Her hand was trembling on the can as she backed them both up, planning on getting in the house and locking the door. Hopefully Mark would just leave when he realized he couldn't get Piper.

But Mark was already scrambling to his feet, wiping at his eyes and swearing violently.

"Don't you take another step."

Amanda gave a sigh of relief when she saw Daniel standing in the driveway a few feet away, a shotgun in his hand, raised in the air and aimed at Mark. The gun made that Dirty Harry sound, the one that meant the owner was now free to pump bullets into you.

"Get away from those girls, and get your sorry ass off my land before I shoot it."

Mark's eyes were red and swollen, his cheeks streaked with tears. He clenched his fists tight, while Amanda held her breath. She gave Piper a gentle nudge, hoping to get her in the house still. Piper stumbled, her arms tight around Amanda's waist. She reached for the screen door at the same time Mark turned around and went to his car.

He spat on the ground and wiped his face on the sleeve of his sweatshirt before climbing into the truck. His parting words were lost to Amanda because she was backing Piper into the house, keeping her eyes trained on Mark.

But he just drove away in a cloud of dust, and Daniel lowered his gun.

Amanda almost wet her floral skirt in relief. She turned and picked up Piper, straining a little under her weight, but wanting to reassure her she was okay. Wanting to reassure both of them that they were okay. Piper flung her arms around her neck and clung tight to her.

"It's okay, he's gone," Amanda whispered.

"You alright?" Daniel asked, coming up on the stoop and ushering them into the house.

"We're okay." Amanda sank to the couch with Piper in her lap.

"I'm calling the sheriff's office, let them know about this. Then I'm calling the lawyer."

"Okay." Amanda petted Piper's back and took deep breaths. Piper was fine, she was still there. He couldn't take her away. Ever. No one was ever taking Piper away from her.

She kissed the top of Piper's head on her grubby hat. She understood now. Even though she thought she had before, now there was no question about it. Piper was hers. Hers and Danny's.

♡

Danny drove too fast.

He couldn't stop himself. He wanted to get home to his daughter and Amanda. He wanted to hear the truth, awful or not, about Amanda's feelings for him.

So he turned into the driveway at forty-five miles an hour and did a number on the undercarriage of his truck when he hit a hole in the gravel and bounced hard. He decided to slow it down a bit when he spotted a sheriff's patrol car in front of his house.

Going slow was no longer an option. A patrol car could only mean trouble, and he didn't want to even think what that could mean. He wasn't even sure how he got from the end of the drive to the house, but suddenly he was on the front stoop, wrenching the door open, his heart in his throat.

"What's going on?"

His father was standing in the living room, talking to an officer. Piper and Amanda were on the couch, arms wrapped around each other. Amanda had a purple bruise across her cheek and a split lip. Danny skirted around the end table and went down on a knee, grateful they seemed okay if a little bruised, puzzled as to what was going on.

He put his hand on Piper's back and stroked her. "What happened?"

"You Daniel Tucker Junior?" the sheriff asked him.

"Yes." He took Piper against his chest when she turned and reached for him, her thin arms held out wide. She'd never really done that before—asked for a hug. It scared Danny at the same time it pleased him that she trusted him now. "What's the matter, baby girl? Something happen?"

"Mark was here," Amanda said in a low voice. "But we're okay."

Danny stood up, Piper in his arms, making low *shush*ing noises to her. Anger settled over him, cold and furious. "What did he want?"

"Apparently he wants to dispute your custody of the child," the sheriff said. "Only when he tried to take her, your girlfriend here wouldn't let him."

Kissing the top of Piper's head, Danny looked at the bruise on Amanda's cheek. "He hit you?" he asked in outrage.

She nodded, looking nervous.

"Are you okay?"

Amanda nodded again.

He wanted to say exactly what he thought of a motherfucker who would hit a woman, and in front of a child, no less, but he couldn't while holding Piper. Turning to the sheriff, he asked, "Did you arrest him for hitting her? Trespassing? Attempted kidnapping? Piper is my biological daughter, and he does not have legal custody. My lawyer can tell you that. I'm in the middle of petitioning for permanent full custody. Mark was just her stepfather, and a verbally abusive one at that. Now that her mother is dead, she belongs with me."

Piper's shoulders started to shake, and Danny realized with horror that she was crying. In all this time, in the four weeks he'd had her, she had never cried. Not once. Not even when talking about her mother.

She pulled back from him now, and she was sobbing, her cheeks streaming with tears, her anguished breathing ripping his heart out of his chest. "It's okay, baby, it's okay. He's gone now, and we would never let him hurt you."

"I don't want to go back with him . . . I want to stay with you. Anita was really scared." Her words were punctuated by sobs that scraped and scratched at his raw emotions.

"You're never leaving me, understand? Never. You're my daughter. Forever. No one can take you away from me. You belong here with me and Grandma and Grandpa."

"And me." Amanda stood up, her skirt rumpled and her hair tangled. "I'm staying, Danny."

He shifted Piper's weight, lifting her higher, and stared at Amanda. Piper was cutting off his windpipe a little with her tight hold, but he didn't think he had passed out. This was real. Amanda was saying she was going to stay. With him.

Or for Piper? But they needed to talk about that later. In private. Danny turned and locked eyes with the sheriff, a middle-age man with a thick middle, a man Danny recognized as a volunteer coach for one of the local ball teams. "Can we wrap this up? I want some time alone with my daughter. She's been through hell."

Piper's crying had slowed, and she was giving dry, shuddery sighs, wiping her face on his T-shirt. "Dad, can you finish with the sheriff in the kitchen? And where's Mom? Amanda could use some ice on that cheek."

"She's at the outlet mall for the day, of all things."

"I'm fine," Amanda said, touching her fingertips to the purple mottled bruise.

"Lucky for him." His voice came out like a snarl.

The sheriff held out his hand. "Now don't be thinking about going after him yourself or anything foolish like that. I know you're upset, and rightly so, but let us handle this. We'll go have a talk with him."

"I have no intention of going after him." But if Mark ever set foot on Danny's land, or came near his daughter or his girlfriend or his parents, he'd shoot him. No questions asked. But he couldn't exactly say that in front of Piper.

Danny Tucker wasn't a violent man, and he was as easygoing as the day was long, but no one threatened his family.

And no one was taking Piper away from him.

The phone rang, and his father answered it. "It's the lawyer," he said, handing it to Danny.

With Piper still wrapped around him, he took the handset and had a brief conversation with the lawyer, outlining what he knew had happened. The lawyer mentioned a restraining order and a few other legal lines to take, and Danny authorized him to do whatever he needed to.

"All this mess today aside, I've got some really good news," Bill said.

"What's that?" Danny's arm was going numb from the position he was standing in, Piper in his arms and the phone propped with his ear. He could use good news.

"I put a call into the lab on the off-chance they'd have your results back, given these new circumstances, and they do. They're ninety-nine point six percent certain Piper is your daughter. Which is definitely a match. She's yours, and I don't think we'll have any trouble getting a judge to give you full custody."

Danny closed his eyes. He'd known it was the truth. But it was such a relief to hear the facts proved it too. "Thank you. That is very good news."

When he hung up the phone he looked at Amanda. His father had taken the sheriff into the kitchen and was answering questions from the looks of it. Danny gave

Amanda a grin. "DNA results came back. They're positive. She's my daughter, without a doubt."

Amanda stood up and put one hand on Piper's back and one on his arm. Her eyes were shining with tears. "That's awesome, Danny. That really makes a lousy afternoon better."

"What are you talking about?" Piper asked, peeling herself off his chest and leaning back to look at him. "What's positive?"

Danny kissed her forehead. "Remember when they took blood out of your arm and out of my arm? Well, they looked at both our blood and compared them. The patterns in yours match the patterns in mine, and that means you are definitely my daughter. It also means Mark can't ever come near you again without getting in trouble. No one can take you away from me."

She didn't say anything, just rested her head back on his shoulder. Danny knew he'd probably have to repeat those words many times. For both of their benefit.

Chapter 24

An hour later, the sheriff was gone, Willie had returned home, and Piper was tucked up on the couch between both her grandparents watching *Scooby-Doo*. She had a blanket and Baby draped over her, and she was licking a Popsicle.

Amanda figured Piper was going to be scared and nervous again for a few days, but with love and patience, they could convince her that she was safe and that she was staying on the farm with Danny forever.

And hopefully with Amanda too.

Danny hadn't exactly turned a cartwheel when she'd said she wanted to stay. Granted, the timing had been lame, but she would have thought he could have at least mentioned it in the hour since. Which meant maybe he wasn't mentioning it because there wasn't anything to say besides *whoops, changed my mind*?

"I need a shower," he said to her in a low voice. "But I want to talk to you first. Can we go out on the deck?"

"Sure." She gave a shrug and tried to pretend her heart wasn't about to break like acrylic fingernails. One hit and snap! Right in half.

If Danny wanted to marry her, he didn't look the least bit romantic right now.

He looked dirty and sweaty. Tired and angry. Weary. Yet at peace when he looked at Piper.

The sun wasn't at an angle so the house could create shade. The deck was stifling hot, and Amanda remembered Danny saying it was supposed to rain. It would be welcome, in her opinion, trampling down some of the dust and taking the edge off the blistering heat. She kicked off her gym shoes and let her bare shoes spread on the warm wood.

"Weren't you going to put the corn in the silo this afternoon?" She didn't think he'd take a shower just to get all sweaty again.

"It can wait." He stood at the edge of the deck, leaning against the railing, looking out at the fields.

She moved next to him, gripping the wood and trying to see what he saw. "We need that rain, don't we?" Even she could tell the plants were starting to strain, brown around the edges, wilting under the crushing heat. It had been weeks since it had rained.

"Yep." He turned and moved in close. His hand took her chin, tilted it. He studied the bruise on her cheek, his lips tight and white. "Are you really okay? I'm so sorry he hurt you."

The feather-light touch of his finger across her swollen lip, up to the tender flesh under her cheekbone, made her shiver. "Yes, I'm fine. But did you hear me, Danny, when I said I wanted to stay?"

Maybe it was wrong to ask, needy and grasping, or shrewish and demanding, but the truth was, she just needed to know. She needed to hear what her future was going to be, and for all his enthusiasm that morning, he seemed reticent. Thoughtful.

"*How* do you want to stay?"

She didn't understand the question. It seemed like what she was saying should be obvious. He had told her he wanted her to stay, as his wife. She was telling him she would. "What do you mean?"

His eyes were opaque, shuttered. When she caressed the front of his shirt, she noticed that his shoulders slumped in fatigue.

"Amanda. Staying will be a big sacrifice for you. Do you want to because you love me, or is this because you love my daughter?"

That he would be the one doubting, feeling vulnerable, amazed her. "I love you, and I would even if there was no Piper. I love Piper, and I would even if you were a complete jerk. The two don't have anything to do with each other." She gripped his chest, shook him a little so he'd get the point.

Danny covered her hand with his. He shook his head. "I don't have any money and can't buy you fancy gifts or take you around the world."

That was irrelevant, because she had enough money for all of them. And even if she didn't, and Danny couldn't stomach the idea of a wealthy wife buying him things, she would give the damn money away. If she had learned anything in twenty-five years, it was that money wasn't worth much if you didn't have anyone to share it with.

Daddy Warbucks knew that, and now so did she. She liked expensive things, had been raised to always have access to them, but at the end of the day, you can't curl up with your Prada pumps. At least not without taking an eye out.

"Danny . . ." How did she explain what he had given her? That he had softened her jaded edges and coaxed a trust from her that she hadn't thought could ever exist again after Logan?

Before she could speak, he did the unthinkable. He dropped to one knee, her hand still in his. "I can't give you the world, Amanda Delmar, but I'm offering you my heart, my friendship, my land. And my daughter. Will you marry me?"

Oh, God, oh, God. He was on his *knee*. Amanda's hand shook, pure joy rising up in her, tears queuing up to drop.

"I'm not Veruca Salt, you know, the bratty heiress from *Charlie and the Chocolate Factory*. I don't want the whole world. I never did. I just want a little love and a family." And the fact that she could say that out loud in front of Danny without him criticizing her as trite and simplistic was further evidence that he was the man for her. He understood what she was asking for, what she had been missing.

Danny stood back up and cupped her uninjured cheek. "You've got a boatload of love and a family, if you want it. I love you, Piper adores you, and my parents think I'm stupid for not proposing sooner. Of course, technically this is the third time I've asked you to marry me, and I'm hoping the third time's the charm. I'm starting to get a complex."

She laughed, a teary, blubbery, happy laugh. "Yes, I'll marry you. Right this minute if you want."

Danny kissed her, a pure, passionate, promise-filled kiss that made her toes curls and her heart sigh.

A few delicious minutes later, Danny pulled back and studied her. "You sure you're not going to mind being stuck here in Cuttersville? Once Piper starts school, you'll be on your own all day. Maybe you can get a job or something."

The horror. She'd seen what working for minimum wage was like and she'd pass, thanks. "I'd rather stay here and dust, if you don't mind. And I might look into breeding poodles. That would be fun, having more dogs."

More yippy poodles was a small price to pay for having the pleasure of Amanda's company. Danny would say yes to just about anything within reason now that she'd agreed to marry him. Become his wife. The thought made him grin all over again. "Sure. And maybe one could be a Labrador while you're at it?"

"I'll think about it," she promised, with a sexy little smile.

"You can go back to Chicago and see your parents whenever you want, you know. We'll make it work." He would do whatever it took to make it work. There was still some worry rattling around in him, that she would miss all the conveniences she was used to, but he had to suppress those insecurities. He'd seen Amanda when she'd first come to Cuttersville. She had been running away from an unhappy life, discontent and hurt, and she had opened up, thrived here on the farm.

She kissed his chin. "Of course we will. I might make a couple trips back a year to see my parents and to do some shopping, but I won't really miss anything. Except for gingerbread lattes, and that's a small price to pay. And then someone's got to take care of those chickens, you know, so it might as well be me."

"You're going to feed the chickens every day?" The thought made him laugh.

"Sure. Not if it's raining or anything like that, but I was thinking someone needs to look out for their interests. I'm going to initiate a chicken coop revitalization project. No hen left behind. That sort of thing. Fair shelter for all farm animals."

After swallowing almost all of the obnoxious laughter that rose up in his chest, he shook his head and grinned at her. Danny hadn't been unhappy, but he had been lonely. Now he had everything he could ever ask for. He clasped his hands around her waist and lifted her a foot off the ground. "Damn, I love you. You're smart, sensitive, and sexy. How'd I get so lucky?"

"Want to get even luckier?" Her breasts pressed against his chest as she traced a line across his lip with her tongue.

Uh, yeah. His body reacted accordingly and he got a massive hard-on. "Everyone's right there in the house . . . but what'd you have in mind?"

"You've never shown me the barn."

While he was tempted, it was no place for Amanda.

"No, Princess, it's dirty and full of cobwebs in there. Just stay for dinner tonight, and after Piper's in bed, we can sneak off to my room." The thought sent his blood racing thick and hot to his groin.

She slid back down to the ground but kept her ankle wrapped around his calf. "We're going to do a lot of sneaking for the next ten years or so, aren't we?"

"Lots of sneaking. Tons of sneaking." Sneaking morning, noon, and night if he had his way. "You know, practice makes perfect."

Kissing the side of his mouth, Amanda sighed. "Well, I'm committed to being perfect."

"You already are." He held her tight, then let her go so they could head into the house. "And you're damn good with a can of hairspray."

"It's a gift," she told him. "And Garnier Fructis hairspray is only like four bucks a bottle yet gives great hold. Good stuff."

Danny fit her hand in his and tugged her toward the back door, grateful for her bravery, relieved neither she nor Piper had been hurt. "I'm proud of you for facing down that asshole."

"So am I, to tell you the truth."

Impulsively, he leaned over and jerked her up into his arms, tossing her a little to get a good grip.

She let out a shriek as her arms flung around his neck. "Not this again." Her lips parted. "You'll turn me on, you know, with all this knight-in-shining-armor crap."

"Good." And he kicked open the door and carried her over the threshold into his kitchen.

Chapter 25

"Brady drew this?" Amanda was going to have to have a talk with that kid. He'd sketched her . . . fat.

"Yeah. I told him how to draw it." Piper bounced on the bed, holding her legs straight out. One of Amanda's suitcases jumped on the bedspread with each bounce.

Giving up the packing, Amanda studied the piece of paper in her hand. It was her with a really freaking round face. And bad hair pulled back in some kind of bun thing. It was a good sketch from an artistic perspective. But from the model's point of view, it sucked. Is this how Piper saw her?

"Why is my mascara running? I always use waterproof."

Piper stopped bouncing and looked at her. "You're not in the picture. It's the Crying Lady. In the mirror. And she's crying."

"Ah, okay." That was a relief.

Amanda dropped the drawing and went back to packing Baby's sweaters in the suitcase. Danny was going to wonder what they were doing up here. He'd hauled about sixteen boxes of her clothes and shoes out to his truck already, and she wasn't even finished packing. Clothes were breeding in her dresser drawers. And when you took seventeen pairs of panties and moved them to a box, suddenly they inflated like water toys.

At this rate, they would have her stuff moved in time for Christmas, not the first of October, which was their goal. Danny wanted everything moved before they got married on Saturday. Which was—woo hoo—only three days away.

Fortunately for her, he had more patience in his left ear than she had in her whole body. He didn't complain, just grunted as he went down the narrow steps with two or three boxes at a time stacked in his arms.

So she didn't have time to worry about the chick in the mirror when she had to finish this packing, so her husband-to-be would see that she really was making an effort. She couldn't get distracted. Not even if the Crying Lady looked remarkably like a pasta-consuming version of herself.

"Hey, Piper, can you help me pack all these shorts and stuff? I can't believe how long this is taking."

"Sure." Piper reached over and started transferring shorts from the drawer to a big box.

"Thanks, cutie. I had no idea I had so much stuff." Nor was she certain exactly how all of it was going to fit into Danny's house. *Their* house now, as soon as they finished moving in her stuff. But then again, her apartment in Chicago hadn't been that big. Maybe the third bedroom at Danny's would have to be given over to her stuff temporarily until she got it all sorted.

Piper worked industriously, and Amanda paused for a second to watch her. She was thriving. In just the ten weeks since Piper had moved in with Danny, she had gained weight, color in her cheeks, and confidence. Anita only came around once a week or so these days, usually when Piper was worried or scared.

She needed a lot of reassurance, and about every other

day she asked what would happen to her if Amanda and Danny got divorced. But she was doing well in school, and she was happy. Even her hair was growing in. She looked like Demi Moore in the movie *Ghost*, but hell, it was hair, even if it looked a bit military right now.

"Got the kid doing all the work for you, huh?" Danny paused in the doorway, wiping his forehead with his shirt-sleeve.

He was so freaking cute, Amanda just wanted to suck him up with a straw. She could not wait until they were married and she could wake up with him every morning. Right now they were having stealth sex, and while it was titillating at times, most days she just wanted to stay the whole night with him.

"She's better at it than me. She gets her work ethic from you and her good looks from me." But she stuck her jewelry box in the suitcase to prove she was trying.

Danny kissed the back of her head as he walked by. "We need to move it along, Princess. We're supposed to be picking your parents up from the airport in three hours."

Her father had been so thrilled with her choice of a husband, strangely enough, that he had insisted on paying for their wedding as the father of the bride, and had even spent a weekend fishing with Danny. She figured if he couldn't bond with her, being friends with Danny was the next best thing. Her father was her father, and he would never change, and him liking Danny was a hell of a lot better than him not liking him. And who could have ever conceived that she would be close with Willie Tucker, yet she was.

While Amanda had decided against a big wedding that would take forever to plan and waste gobs of money, they had settled on getting married in Aruba with family and a few close friends present. Her parents were flying from Chicago, meeting Danny's family, and then they would all hop a plane to the Caribbean together.

If she ever got all her crap together, that is.

"Alright, alright, alright. Just unload that drawer there while I get the blankets out of the closet." Amanda bent down, her Seven jeans straining from the position.

Danny made a strangled sound. She grinned into the dark closet. That would teach him to hurry her along. She had assigned him one of her lingerie drawers. Right now he was probably pawing through sheer black panties.

"We can't leave without the mirror," Piper said.

"What mirror?" Amanda flung blankets out behind her and reached deep into the closet, making sure she wasn't missing anything. Why the heck had she brought a cashmere throw with her to Cuttersville in July? She tossed it toward the bed.

"The Crying Lady mirror. She wants us to take it down off the wall."

Danny had two pairs of her panties in his hands when she reemerged from the closet. He clung to them as he stared at Piper. "Why?"

"I don't know. She's just really upset. I think we should do what she says."

Sure, so they could be sucked into some kind of paranormal vortex when they lifted that mirror off the wall.

Better let Danny do it. He was strong enough to resist any suckage that might occur.

Apparently he had different ideas. "I don't know, baby girl, that mirror belongs to the house. We don't want to damage it."

"Show him the picture."

Piper plucked the drawing off the suitcase and held it out to her father. "This is what she looks like. That's the lady I keep seeing in the mirror."

"That's Amanda. A sort of . . . rounder version."

Another reason to love him. He could tell the difference between her and Fatty Face. Not that she needed any more reasons to love him. He was doing pretty damn good already.

"No, it's not." Piper's voice caught. She sounded really upset and her lip was trembling, her fists screwed up.

Danny caved. "Alright, shh, it's okay. We'll go take a look." He dropped Amanda's underwear in the box.

They went down the hall together, stepping over the pile of pennies. "I hope she stops dropping the pennies after I leave. That would be such a waste."

Danny didn't say anything, obviously thinking that he was just indulging the two nutty females in his life. She didn't know how he explained the pennies, but he seemed to be of a mind that if you ignored something, than eventually it would go away.

Maybe he was right. But in the meantime, Piper was stressing out.

"Just lift it," she told her father, running her fingers over the glass.

He did, and it came off easily enough. When he set it on the floor, Amanda gasped. There was a cubby in the wall behind the mirror. And it was filled with papers and a few sacks.

"What's all this?" Danny took the papers and started rifling through them. "Old letters."

"They say he didn't do it," Piper said, biting her bottom lip. "She wants everyone to know he didn't do it."

Suddenly Amanda knew who she meant. The Crying Lady's dishonest husband. The one everyone had thought had been a murderer and a thief. "Let me see, Danny."

"You can't read them. They're in German."

But she understood. The woman cried because no one had believed that she and her husband truly loved each other. That he wasn't a criminal.

"What's in the bag?"

Danny shook it open. "A ring. A wedding ring, I think."

"It's gorgeous," Amanda whispered, running her finger over the silver band, with encrusted diamonds running all around it. "She must not have been able to wear it, afraid people in town would turn against her if they knew she still loved her husband, was waiting for him."

Danny rolled his palm so the ring turned. "It could be anyone's ring, Amanda."

"It's mine." Amanda lifted it up, a feeling of rightness settling over her. It wasn't a coveting of the jewelry. There was no *Lord of the Rings* freaky obsession invading her, but still, she knew it was meant for her.

Lifting Piper up into his arms, Danny tossed her a little to get a good grip. "What do you think, baby girl? It's pretty, isn't it?"

She patted his shoulders. "I think everything is exactly the way it's supposed to be now."

Amanda looked at her almost husband and her soon-to-be daughter and nodded. "You said it, girlfriend."

"Can we go home now?" Danny asked.

"Absolutely. We have plenty of time, by the way, so don't have a cow." She kissed his cheek, slipping the ring on her middle finger. "That's farm humor, get it? Have a cow."

"I get it." He rolled his eyes, but he was smiling.

Amanda laughed.

Sharing her life with the people she loved? Priceless.

Turn the page for a preview of
the new book by

Erin McCarthy,

My Immortal

Coming in September 2007 from Jove.

River Road, Louisiana, 1790

Rosa Francis was a demon.

She was a spirit, a chaotic blending of French restlessness, Spanish mores, and the pride of the *gens de couleur*. She was the fortitude of a mixed people heedlessly building a city in a tropical swamp at the mouth of the Mississippi, as well as the foolishness.

The father had told her she was the spirit of greed, the result of a ludicrous lifestyle reminiscent of the French Court that had no business among the cypress and the mosquito. It lived inside her, this desire for more, for extravagance, for rich and delicious foods.

For the lusty, erotic company of human men.

Some believed in her, feared her, particularly the slaves who lived in their squat wood houses on the plantations that were cropping up along River Road with increasing regularity. They understood the need to placate her, to keep her ravenous appetite satisfied, and catered to her desires by leaving out their best food for her to steal and offering her bold men as a sacrifice to her complacency.

The Creole plantation owners believed in her as well, though with no fear. Their wealth, their breeding, the arrogance in their own worth, led them to view her as entertainment. Some had seen her when she'd felt the urge to show herself, had widened their eyes in amazement, then run off laughing to tell their friends. She had on occasion flooded a field, or burned a crop to let them know that, while she was amusing, she could still be dangerous.

Their joie de vivre aside, they understood, and faithfully followed the slaves' example of leaving out food and clothing, though they reserved this generosity for only one day per year. On the summer solstice, they created a feast for her and let her roam through their yards, taking all she wished.

Tonight was that night, so long awaited that she shivered in anticipation, her sister Marguerite padding softly along beside her. Rosa preferred to glide, hovering slightly above the wet swamp as they passed through the Bayou St. John. The swamp was never silent, particularly at night. It was alive with the voices of thousands of living creatures humming in harmony—insects, snakes, and gators, weaving in and out of the reeds and living under the protection of the mighty cypress that watched paternally from the shore.

"Slow down," Marguerite complained. "I can't keep up with you."

"Then fly." Rosa was too excited to let Marguerite sour her mood. She knew her sister resented Rosa's slim body and long limbs, having been given a round and stout figure. Father had said Marguerite was the spirit of gluttony, the embodiment of the Creole love of money and objects, food and wine. Marguerite said her body was nothing more than the love of cake.

"I won't." Her sister's feet slowed even more.

Rosa laughed. "Fine. I'll go without you. *Au revoir.*"

She couldn't slow down for Marguerite, or for anyone. She could practically smell the salmon, the roasted duck, the wild peas and rice, the café au lait penetrating through the moist, hot air, enveloping her and urging her on. The hunger burned inside her and had to be satisfied.

She was stopping first at Rosa de Montana, a thriving plantation that belonged to the equally thriving Du Bourg family, for the simple reason that she felt it brought her good luck to begin her feast in a place of the same name as herself.

Phillipe du Bourg had been a generous man, with his money, his food, and his favors, and as such had been wildly popular in the exclusive circle of planters in New Orleans. He threw lavish parties, had guests living with him for years at a time, and was known to have fathered a good dozen or so children on his slave women. He laughed, he danced, he gambled, he drank, and he lived a full and privileged life that had suddenly ended when he'd ridden off on his horse wildly drunk and hit his head on the low-hanging branch of a magnolia.

His son, Damien, was not nearly so admired. He had returned from France upon his father's death, a vicious, pampered man of twenty-four, with a pasty-faced smidge of a wife who stood four feet ten and weighed eighty-five pounds in her skirts. Damien had been quite the favorite of the princes at court and as such had been given Marie, with the blessing of her titled family, who thought nothing of her health in the disease-infested wilderness compared to the one million livre fortune the Du Bourg's possessed.

Rumor had it that Damien had been making enemies left and right, was penurious with his money, and thought no boudoir beyond his reach, including that of the mayor's wife.

Rosa left Marguerite completely behind, sailing furiously, the wind rushing through her black hair, her wispy red sheath neither gown nor shift, but more an extension of her long, narrow body. She could see the gas lamps illuminating the house, the doors of its upper galleries open to allow the breeze entrance. Its white pillars stood in the shadows, cast-iron balustrades on either side, an impressive structure in defiance of the soft ground on which it was built.

There was nothing in the yard. Fury ripped through her exuberant mood with the force of a cyclone. There were no lamps lit in the yard, no food, no clothes, no giggling party-goers watching from the front porch. There was nothing.

Hitting the ground with more force than was required, she sank three feet into the soft soil and stepped out in a haze of anger. The rumors were true. Damien du Bourg was not the man his father had been.

He was also standing in front of her.

Leaning on a pillar, he watched her as he smoked a cigar, pulling on it tightly before blowing out a wreath of pungent smoke. He was attractive in a way few men could claim. Rosa studied the strength of his jaw, the long cheekbones, and the haughty tilt of his head. His sandy blond hair was pulled back in a short ponytail, and his loose white shirt was open at the chest, revealing a breadth of shoulders that caused her to shiver in feminine excitement. He wore no jacket, but had black tight-fitting pants that showed his thighs were as muscular as his arms, and his black leather boots were expensive, though well worn.

He held a flask in his other hand, which he put to his lips and drank from deeply. His expression was arrogant, his rich green eyes drinking her in as his lips did the liquor.

"Do you know who I am?" Her anger returned tenfold at his bold sweeping assessment of her.

"Since you have just stepped out of a three-foot hole, I imagine I do."

His nonchalance was creating a maelstrom inside her that was pushing and bubbling and popping. "Where is my food then?"

"I don't have any for you."

Her anger boiled over and before she could stop herself her fingers had spasmed, causing a crack of lightning to flash above their heads and a torrential rain to pour down, flattening her hair to her head and soaking her dress.

"That wasn't very smart." He stood dry under his porch roof, the corner of his mouth twitching upward. "All you did was make yourself wet."

Rosa blinked to clear the water from her eyes and frowned at him. "I want some venison or duck before I'll leave."

His foot propped up the column and he took another swig. "You come here and eat my food, and what do I get in return?"

He was missing the point entirely. He'd been in France too long, where the mysteries of the bayou held no sway. She quickly sailed through the ten feet between them and stopped inches from his face. "I don't ruin your crops, your plantation, your life."

As she brought the rain to a slowing, misting stop, he didn't blink, nor try to move away from her. She could see there was no fear in his eyes. His gaze dropped to her lips. "No one told me you were so beautiful."

Her other vice, her womanly desires, surfaced with the rapidity of the storm she'd created. It was a painful throb deep inside her, this need to feel a man's body wrapped around her own, an all-encompassing and voracious appetite that she indulged in less than she did her need for food. The roasted duck was forgotten, as were his arrogance and overbearing manners. She decided that while Damien had set out no food, he was offering to feed her other ache.

Confident of her charms, she smiled slowly, floating above the porch step, while mosquitoes buzzed around the lamplight. The starkness of his statement caused a sheen of feminine pride to set her skin aglow. She was beautiful, with the exotic look of a Spaniard, and she could have whatever she wanted. She wanted him now.

Rosa laughed deep in her throat, a sensual promise. "Yes, I am."

His answer was to close the inch remaining between them and press his hard lips to hers, the taste of the whiskey droplets on his mouth sending her into a spiral of pleasure. The wetness of his tongue, pushing urgently into her mouth, filled her with the masculine tastes of cigar smoke and whiskey, hot passion and urgent need.

Her hands gripped his head as she tasted thoroughly, enjoying his hard grip on her arms, the quick mating of his tongue with hers, his lustful willingness to succumb to sexual attraction. Beyond them she sensed movement on the porch. A small, pale woman was clutching her hands to her chest in horror, her brown hair unbound, her white nightgown prim and demure.

She belonged to the delicate French-designed house, with its long louvered windows and sweeping galleries, its wide front steps leading from the swampy jungle to the civilization of the drawing room. But her delicateness, her fragile bloom, did not belong with this virile man, whose appetites were as urgent and questing as Rosa's own.

"Your wife is watching," Rosa whispered in his ear now, sucking gently on the lobe.

"Is she?" He turned, still clutching her, and smiled. "Good evening, Marie. Care to join us?"

When she turned with a gasp and ran into the house, he laughed an emotionless laugh. "Poor Marie, she doesn't know how to have fun."

"And you do?"

"I do." He turned back with a ferocity that stole Rosa's breath, pulling her into him and molding her body to the length of his, her wet dress clinging to her small, rounded breasts.

His kisses trailed down her neck to her shoulder, worshipful hot presses that caused her to moan, her body aching with want. As his thumb brushed across her breast, teasing her nipple, she urged him on. "Yes. More."

"More," he agreed, lifting her dress past her waist with demanding hands, stroking her thighs possessively. With sure and greedy movements he went to the bodice of her sheath dress, pushing it off her shoulders to expose her breasts. With a groan of his own, he took her into his mouth, sucking and pulling gently with his teeth, cupping her bare, eager flesh with his soft hands.

Working open his pants, she pulled the hot length of him into her hands as her desire swirled and churned inside her, pushing out everything but the need to be possessed by a strong, reckless, mortal man. The storm brewed inside her, hot and tight, her infrequently indulged desires sparking like kindling, and she felt rather than saw that her thoughts had actually ignited the shrubbery on either side of the front steps.

He barely glanced over, murmuring, "The bushes are on fire."

"Shh, I know." She turned the rain back on with a tilt of her head, keeping her greedy hands on him, laboring over the smooth feel of his hard shaft until his panting breath hitched and he forcibly pushed her away.

"No more."

His ragged groan was her triumph, her glory in bringing a man to the edge of his control.

The gentle drops of water spattered across her arms, rolling down to her fingertips, and a fine swirling mist rose around them as she delicately poised herself over him. His back was flush against the solid column for support and he urged her body downward with his hands, spreading her thighs and easing her toward him until she hovered in breathtaking anticipation.

"I would ask you for something." His muscular arms held her hips tightly, keeping her still, his hardness teasing her softness as he denied her.

"What's that?" She let her eyes flutter shut, not caring in the least what he wanted. There was only her need, her rolling, throbbing desires seeking to burst forth out of her in a cascade of gloriously delicious sin.

It wouldn't be difficult to take control, drop herself down onto him and force the hot joining they both wanted, but he was whispering in her ear, distracting her, asking . . .

Her eyes flew open in surprise. She'd had humans make requests of her, beg for mercy, for more, for release. But this human, this Damien du Bourg, was asking boldly what no one had requested of her before. He looked serious, his eyes filled with lust, yes, but also a cold, calculated determination. She shivered under the onslaught of raindrops. "How do you know I can give you what you ask for?"

"I know who you are. You can do this." His face shined from the rivulets running down his cheeks, the lamplight reflecting off of his empty, joyless face.

She tossed her sodden hair back over her shoulder, pressing her bare breasts against the softness of his damp linen shirt. It was a foolish request, one he would live to regret, but Rosa thought Damien was deserving of regret. He had a black heart, cold and arrogant.

This wasn't the normal way of things, but she was young and impulsive. She thought it would be satisfying to see this proud man forced to serve her and the father, as he would have to if she granted him the escape from death he requested.

She hesitated long enough to warn, "If I do this, I can't undo it. Do you understand?"

Though his eyes darkened, he nodded. "Yes, I understand. Do it for me."

With a shrug, she told him, "It's done."

And with a soft groan, he moved, slamming her onto him, pumping up and down, exploding her mind and body with a thousand little gunshots of pleasure as she threw back her head in utter abandonment.

"Thank you," he murmured into her mouth as he kissed her hotly, the porch steps creaking beneath his boots as they rocked. "You won't regret it."

Though regret was the furthest thing from her mind at the moment, she knew with the clarity of one who can sense without seeing, that there was going to be hell to pay for this one.